Laughter Class
and Other Stories

Laughter Class

and Other Stories

Wendy Perriam

ROBERT HALE · LONDON

© Wendy Perriam 2006
First published in Great Britain 2006

ISBN-10: 0-7090-8107-3
ISBN-13: 978-0-7090-8107-4

Robert Hale Limited
Clerkenwell House
Clerkenwell Green
London EC1R 0HT

The right of Wendy Perriam to be identified as
author of this work has been asserted by her
in accordance with the Copyright, Designs and
Patents Act 1988.

2 4 6 8 10 9 7 5 3 1

Typeset in 10/13pt New Century Schoolbook
by Derek Doyle & Associates, Shaw Heath
Printed in Great Britain by St Edmundsbury Press,
Bury St Edmunds, Suffolk
Bound by Woolnough Bookbinding Limited

For Susie Boyt
– a perfect friend

Contents

1

LAUGHTER CLASS

'Ha, ha, ha, ha, ha.
Ho, ho, ho, ho, ho, ho.
Hee, hee, hee, hee, hee.'

As the hullabaloo subsided, the tutor beamed her encouragement. 'That was great!' she exclaimed. 'You've really got the hang of
it. But this time open your mouths much wider, throw your heads
back and rock from side to side, so that you're using your whole body
as you laugh. Is everyone OK with that?'

'*No!*' Anthea muttered under her breath. 'The whole thing's quite
ridiculous.'

'We'll do some laughter solos next. I want you each to take one of
the sounds we've been doing as a group, and give it all you've got –
lots of pizzazz, lots of body movement. I'll start you off, with "ha, ha,
ha".'

Anthea watched, aghast, as Joy broke into a peal of exuberant
'ha, ha, ha's.' The woman's eyes were shining; her mouth agape; her
fluid, flexible body shaking with genuine mirth. How could she
laugh with such conviction when there was nothing to laugh about?

'Now, you take over, Caroline, with "ho, ho, ho, ho, ho".'

Despite her age and girth, Caroline seemed equally uninhibited,
ho-ho-ing with such natural ease and vigour, the class applauded
spontaneously. And Barry, too, obliged without the slightest hesita-
tion, turning his 'hee-hee's' into an elaborate aria, tears of authentic
laughter actually running down his face.

'Right, Anthea, your turn.'

She fought a desperate urge to flee – to run full-pelt from the room and keep on running, until she was safely back in her flat. Laughter was a skill she had never mastered. It was difficult enough when someone told a joke – impossible in *this* situation, when you were expected to laugh to order, and in front of virtual strangers.

'I'd like you to use a new sound – "oinck, oinck, oinck". OK?'

Oinck certainly *wasn't* OK – an uncouth farmyard noise, and more idiotic even than the rest. Besides, she felt she needed a screwdriver to open her mouth at all; its hinges were stiff with embarrassment, and rusty from disuse. 'Oinck, oinck, oinck,' she faltered, aware that the strangulated whine emerging from her lips sounded more akin to agony than joy. It was like trying to sing when you were tone-deaf, or dance with two left feet – humiliating and purposeless.

The tutor came to her rescue. 'Let's *all* join in with this one,' she suggested. 'Come on, everybody, raise the roof with "oinck, oinck, oinck, oinck, oinck".'

Every voice from soprano to bass-baritone took up the ludicrous cry – only Anthea self-conscious and on edge; in fact, feeling like a completely different species. While *they* were raucous chimpanzees, she was a shy and silent creature – a mole, perhaps, or water-vole, secretive and serious. She couldn't even take refuge in her burrow, because she and all the rest of the class were standing in one big circle in the centre of the room, which made it impossible to hide.

As the horrendous din continued, voices from the past rose up to condemn her for daring to take part in this frivolity at all. 'Anthea, wipe that smile off your face.' 'What have you got to laugh about, my girl?'

She couldn't remember her mother laughing, not once in her entire eighty years. And the teachers at her school had also mistrusted laughter, regarding it as a sort of insubordination, and an infectious one at that, which had to be punished harshly and put down. And, looking at this hapless crowd, she could sympathize with that viewpoint. Laughter *could* be dangerous, turning normal rational people into uncontrolled buffoons.

'Oink, oinck, oinck,' re-echoed through the shabby room. Would they never tire of making fools of themselves? Someone ought to remind them of all the suffering in the world – the millions dying in Africa of famine, drought and AIDS; the poverty in *this* country: children lacking decent clothes and food.

At last, Joy clapped her hands for silence, her face still wreathed in smiles. What could *she* know about suffering? – a young thing, barely out of her twenties, who had probably never had a low mood in her life. Even her clothes shouted jollity and confidence; the brilliant purple caftan a dramatic contrast to her frizzy, flame-red hair, and the glittering gold bangles on her wrists adding their jangling contribution to the class.

'I was christened Brenda,' she'd told them, when they had first assembled this morning. 'But I changed my name to Joy because I'm a Joy-Enabler and Joy-Expander.'

Anthea had grimaced in distaste. Joy seemed so *extreme*. Basic contentment was enough of an assignment, without going overboard. Personally, she'd settle for something more modest – fewer fits of black depression, for example, and a cure for her ME. In fact, it was her doctor who had suggested the course, as an alternative to drugs or psychotherapy. But probably, like many in the medical profession, he didn't even *believe* in ME, but simply wanted to get rid of her. She had a good mind to report him for wasting her time and money. This course had cost £100, which would have been better spent on a weekend in the country, rather than two pointless days in a dingy Adult Education College, in an insalubrious part of London.

Joy had turned her back to them and was scrabbling in a huge carrier bag. 'I want to introduce you to some friends,' she said, withdrawing half-a-dozen cuddly toys and setting them out on the table in a row. 'First up is Chuckles the Chicken.' She pointed to a large felt bird that looked positively psychedelic – its acid-yellow feathers speckled with emerald, blue and red. 'And this is Happy the Hippo and his good pal, Blissful the Bear. Next to them is Frolic the Frog, then Madcap the Monkey and, my favourite of all, Giggly-Piggly.' She stroked the plush pink snout of an inanely grinning pig, the colour of candyfloss. 'And why they're important is they all know how to laugh.' As she went along the row, pressing each one's belly, they erupted suddenly in great guffaws and gurgles of laughter.

Anthea watched in horror, her gaze moving from the rollicking bear to the hysterical green frog. The pig, in particular, filled her with revulsion – an undignified, obese creature, with flaring scarlet nostrils and a protuberant stomach that vibrated as it laughed. And the monkey seemed completely manic, obsessively banging a tin drum as it giggled and sniggered in time with the honking hippo. Where on earth did one *buy* such monstrosities? Talking dolls she had heard of, and even dolls that wet their nappies, but never a giggling, vibrating zoo. When *she* was a child, toys sat stiff and silent, as if aware of the perils of the War – shortages and bombing raids and fathers who disappeared. This lot was so vulgar in comparison, literally falling about as they hooted, chortled, cackled. And of course, spurred on by their antics, all the class began laughing, too, so that once again the room resounded with meretricious mirth.

'Remember to breathe!' Joy shouted above the noise. 'Breathe joy into your lungs. And if anyone's still holding on to sadness, I want you to release it in a great long shuddering sigh.'

Anthea gave a brief, half-hearted splutter. She doubted that her sadness could be expelled in a single breath. Too much of it had accumulated over the last few years – the loss of her job, and subsequent move to a small and poky flat; the death of her only real friend, Daphne, from a relentless form of cancer; the death of her beloved dog, and now the constant fatigue and joint pains of ME. ('*Imaginary* ME,' she corrected herself, in Dr Tobin's brusquely mocking voice.)

The toys had laughed themselves to a standstill, but unfortunately the respite was short-lived. Joy pressed all their furry stomachs again, setting off another round of trumpeting and braying, to the accompaniment of more laughter from the class. If laughter was infectious, how come she hadn't caught it, she reflected with some bitterness? She'd had no trouble as a child, catching mumps and measles and chicken pox, nor any problem catching gloom and panic from her mother.

Joy picked up the large shaggy bear and gave it a friendly hug. 'Laughter isn't just a frivolous thing; it's a very serious matter, and essential to our health, you know. It improves our lung capacity, massages our internal organs, tones our tummy muscles, oxygenates our blood, reduces stress hormones and increases the levels of antibodies, lymphocytes and endorphins. It can help a whole load of medical conditions from asthma and bronchitis to high blood pressure and strokes.'

As Joy reeled off this impressive list, Anthea longed to interrupt and demand scientific proof. Her mother had died of a stroke. Could she really have been saved by a few good belly-laughs?

'Young children laugh about three hundred times a day,' Joy continued, returning the bear to the table. 'But once we grow up, we laugh on average only fifteen times a day.'

Again Anthea mistrusted the statistics. How could laughter be assessed, unless you kept the adult population under twenty-four-hour surveillance? And as for her personally, she doubted if she'd laughed fifteen times in the whole of her *life*.

'But, you see, if we laugh so rarely, we're missing out on the chance of bonding with our fellow men and women. Laughter strengthens human connections, makes us feel more open and free, and thus more trusting of each other. In fact, you've proved that quite magnificently today. When you first arrived, some of you were wary, or even quite suspicious, but look at you now – you're one big happy family!'

And I'm the orphan, Anthea felt. Having never had a family, not even a single aunt or uncle, she didn't find it easy to bond with such a disparate group. And, anyway, the others probably saw her as a miserable old bat who should have enrolled for crochet classes or Discovering Antiques, not for this anarchic course.

'If anyone wants to play with these toys, please feel free to do so. Play is very healing. It releases the child inside us, and helps us to take life a bit less seriously.' Joy broke off to consult her watch. 'Time's getting rather short, I'm afraid, but there's one more important exercise I'd like us to do today. Then I'll set you some homework. . . .'

'Homework?' Stefan groaned. 'When on earth are we meant to *do* it, if we're due back here tomorrow morning?'

'You've got all evening,' Joy retorted.

'I'm going out.'

'Me, too,' Aziz piped up.

'Well, my loves, you have to make *time* for happiness, if you want to increase it in your life.'

Fair enough, Anthea thought. Homework for her was simply part of life, either doing it as a child, or setting it and marking it in her adult role as teacher. However, Happiness Homework was a completely unknown concept and, if it involved more laughter practice, there would undoubtedly be trouble from her surly next-door-neighbours. The walls in the new building were embarrassingly thin, and the Atkinsons were bound to complain if they heard a chorus of ha-ha-ha's erupting from her side.

'The homework centres on forgiveness,' Joy informed them, 'which is absolutely crucial if we want to find true happiness. Holding on to anger and resentment is like taking poison and hoping someone else will die. But I'll explain that a bit later on. What I want us to do now is stand in one long line – yes, that's right, spread yourselves out and use the whole of the room. You'll need some space to swing your arms. Suzy, you're too close to Luke – move over a bit, my love. And, Anthea, don't skulk there in the corner. Come forward into the line. Good! Great! Now, I want you to suggest some things you'd like to have in your life.'

'A nice cool beer,' shouted Barry, ever the joker.

'A million pounds!'

'More sex.'

Anthea flushed at the mention of sex, which, she suspected, would be harder even than laughing – though perhaps similar in certain ways. You would have to be able to let go, willing to make a fool of yourself, and not care how grotesque you might appear.

'Be serious, please,' Joy admonished, looking anything but serious herself. 'Let's start with joy, shall we, because the goal of this whole course is to bring more joy into our lives. Can you think of some symbols of joy?'

'A rainbow,' Suzy offered.

'Yes, good one.'

'A smiling Buddha.'

'Excellent!'

'Wine and roses.'

'Wine in moderation,' Joy laughed.

'Cloud nine.'

'Brilliant! Right, that's enough. Now imagine all those symbols of joy up there on the ceiling. Can everybody see them?'

Anthea craned her neck. All she could see was a dangerous-looking crack snaking its way across the grubby off-white paint.

'Really visualize them. Admire the different colours of the rainbow, and the deep crimson of the roses. And use your other senses too. Feel the softness of the cloud. Smell the flowers. Taste the wine.'

Anthea could taste nothing but the chicken curry she had inadvisably eaten for lunch in the squalid college canteen. And could smell only the sweaty armpits of the fellow standing next to her. And as for clouds and rainbows, they reminded her of downpours – getting drenched, catching cold.

'Now you've each got a big basket positioned just in front of you and, as the joy flows down from the sky, I want you to scoop it up and put it in your basket. Don't be shy. Take as much as you want – there's plenty to go round. Anthea, you need to actually reach out with your arms. That's it – *hold* the joy, feel it sparkling and shining in your fingers. And now bend down and put it in your basket. Bend lower, relax your spine. This isn't just a mind thing – make your body part of it. Better! Much better!'

Better for whom, Anthea wondered cynically? She felt a total idiot, reaching out for nothing, then placing nothing in a non-existent basket. But Joy still had her eye on her.

'Don't stop, my love. Why restrict the joy in your life? Grab all you can get – and then more! Fill your basket till it overflows.'

Anthea winced at the 'my love,' which Joy used indiscriminately. If they were *all* her loves, the phrase was basically meaningless. With ill-concealed reluctance, she stretched up again to the mythical cloud nine, the illusory rainbow, the fictitious smiling Buddha. Her arms were aching, her back hurt, and she was blushing with sheer embarrassment. Again she felt alien from the others, who were hauling down great bales of joy, and laughing as they did so, really entering into the spirit of the thing.

'Right, now that your baskets are full, I'd like you to reach out for even more joy and throw it into your future – like this.' Joy gave a demonstration, hurling invisible joy in front of her with enviable strength and vigour. 'We need to store up a huge supply of happiness, to last us through our twilight years. So don't stint yourselves. Be greedy! Toby, do it with more conviction. Imagine the treasure-store that lies ahead.'

Yes, Anthea reflected, a treasure-store of pain, old age, and death. With no family or friends, who would visit her in the old folks' home, or shed a tear at her funeral? Yet, aware of the tutor's scrutiny, she threw a few small scraps of joy into her lonely, ailing future. The man beside her was wielding an imaginary spade and shovelling for all he was worth, stocking up on love, fame, wealth – whatever. And, all around her, other people were laying up huge stores of bounty with the same energy and verve. Only *she* had left it too late. Love, fame, wealth, whatever, were hardly likely to materialize at the age of sixty-seven.

'Well *done!*' Joy cried. 'That's absolutely brilliant! I predict dazzling futures for you all. Now turn round and face the other way, so that you're looking into your past, instead of into the future.'

There was a general shuffling of feet as the participants changed position, some using the lull to exchange whispered comments or giggle with each other. No one spoke to *her*, Anthea noticed with a pang. She had hoped to make a new friend today, meet an empathetic female, who shared her outlook on life. But, apart from blowsy Caroline, there was no one else her age. And the younger women were rather a peculiar bunch – beatniks and Bohemians, a weird Polish girl with a crew-cut and a lisp, and a full-of-herself Australian miss, who laughed like a hyena on the slightest provocation. As for the men, well, she wasn't very comfortable with the opposite sex – probably due to lack of practice. Her father had never returned from the War; she'd had no brothers (no siblings at all), and had attended an all-girls school, then taught in one herself until her recent forced retirement. Besides, the men on this course looked worryingly unwholesome – several with scruffy beards, or even stubble, and most dressed in baggy T-shirts and old jeans.

'I want you to throw joy into your past, which will *change* your past, transform it, fill it with all the things you lacked. If you were poor as a child, throw in sacks of gold and jewels. If you craved love and affection, give it to your child-self now. It's not too late. Everything you needed then can actually be provided.'

What about my *father?* Anthea silently implored. I never knew him at all. He was just bits of a dismembered corpse, scattered miles away in Normandy.

'Throw joy into your past,' Joy urged, making exaggerated heaving motions to exemplify her words. 'Throw peace and plenty into your past. Whatever you wanted, it's there for you now.'

What she had wanted most was a happy, normal mother, not a grieving widow, constantly in tears. Long after the War, her mother had continued to live in metaphorical black, refusing to pull herself together, even for her daughter's sake.

Suddenly she was aware of tears pricking at her eyes. Panicking, she blinked them back. It would be unthinkable to cry in public, spoil the joyous mood. This was a Laughter Class, for heaven's sake, not a Weeping Class. Yet treacherous tears were overflowing and trickling down her face. Appalled, she dashed for the door, slammed it behind her and stood outside, trembling with mixed horror and relief. She should never have come on such a course. It was extremely unwise to stir up these emotions, when she had managed to control them the whole of her life to date. She must go straight home and distract herself with some practical task. An hour of vacuuming or window cleaning would drive this nonsense out of her mind.

'Anthea?'

She froze. Joy had come in search of her. 'I, er, just needed a bit of air,' she explained, forcing a casual smile.

'Don't worry. I understand. That exercise can stir up grief, or loss, or very painful memories. But it's best to face such emotions, in order to let them go.'

'No, honestly, I'm fine. I've, er, got to leave now anyway. And I'm afraid,' she rattled on, desperation lending her fluency, 'I won't be able to come tomorrow. I forgot to tell you. I'm busy – tied up at work.'

'Work on a Sunday?'

She flushed. Lies, she'd been taught, were sinful, and she still experienced the deepest shame when departing from the truth. 'It's not that I didn't enjoy it,' (another shocking lie) 'but my free time's rather limited at present,' (again, patently untrue) 'so I won't be here. I'm sorry.' She tried to make the 'sorry' sound forceful and emphatic, so she could make a hasty getaway, but Joy took her hand and clasped it in her own.

'We'll miss you if you don't come back.'

That she *didn't* believe. Who would even notice – let alone care a fig – if she was there or not tomorrow?

'You've contributed such a lot to the class. I love your sensitivity and your sense of dignity, and the gentleness you show to other people.'

Anthea stared at her open-mouthed. The woman must be joking.

'Is there any chance you could change your mind and complete the course?'

'No,' she said tersely. 'None whatsoever. And now I simply must go.'

'OK, my love, that's your choice. But hold on just one second. There's something I want to give you. Promise not to move?'

'I promise,' Anthea mumbled, praying she'd be quick.

Fortunately she was back in less than a minute, holding something behind her back. An imaginary rainbow, no doubt, with an imaginary crock of gold. Well, the latter would be useful, if only to cover the cost of the course.

'I want you to have this,' Joy said, thrusting the pink-plush pig into Anthea's hands. 'Keep him. Take him home.'

Anthea all but exploded in a plethora of 'no's'. 'No, really, I wouldn't dream of it. No, I couldn't, honestly. No, you must keep him – he's one of your props. . . .'

'He's not a prop, Anthea. He's a reminder that we can all choose joy, if we want. Remember what I told you earlier on – pain is part of life, but suffering is optional. The Dalai Lama said that, and he's an extremely wise man.'

Anthea had no intention of arguing with the Dalai Lama. It would only prolong the encounter, and she was desperate to get home. Firmly she returned the pig to Joy. 'It's kind of you, but—'

'No "buts", my love. I'm giving you Giggly-Piggly to show that you deserve the occasional treat, and to help you value yourself a wee bit more. And, after all, he knows the secret of happiness, so perhaps he'll pass it on to you! And now I must get back to the class. Goodbye. Best of luck!'

Anthea was left standing with the pig. She was tempted to put the creature in the bin, but she had an uneasy feeling that, like her mother, Joy had eyes in the back of her head. As a child, she'd assumed that her mother's second pair of eyes was hidden by her thick brown hair. And Joy, too, had a great cloud of hair that could easily conceal several pairs of all-seeing eyes.

Defeated, she stumped downstairs, trying to hide the pig beneath her coat before heading for the underground. In fact, the tube was so crowded, no one really noticed her and, once she reached her flat, she dumped the toy in the airing-cupboard. On Monday morning she'd take it to a charity shop, and perhaps some child would buy it – drive its mother demented with the noise.

As for her, she felt so fatigued, she couldn't even contemplate hoovering one room, let alone cleaning all the windows in the flat. The course had taken its toll of her, both physically and mentally. She boiled herself an egg and ate it with a small slice of toast, then retired to bed. Sleep, however, proved even more elusive than usual. Her mind was like a roller-coaster – various members of the course plunging up and down on it, shrieking in hilarity: Luke and Suzy clinging wildly to each other as they made yet another precipitous descent; Caroline showing her underclothes as she rolled around in hysterics; Toby and Aziz clutching the rail as they hurtled up a dizzying incline, only to plummet down again with more boisterous guffaws.

Exhausted, she turned over on to her front. She had never been keen on fairgrounds, least of all in the middle of the night. But the disturbances weren't over yet. Joy herself suddenly burst into the room, flung the blankets back and climbed into bed beside her, reeling off the same advice she had given at the class. 'Don't wait to laugh till you feel happy. Laugh anyway and the laughter will boost your mood.'

All very well for *her*. She probably had a lovely husband and a couple of gorgeous children, and literally hundreds of devoted friends. Not quite so easy to roar with laughter when you lived alone in a new and strange locality, with a landlord who forbade all pets, and had lost not only your job but all contact with your colleagues. She ate her meals alone these days, often switching on the radio just to hear a human voice. In fact, it had probably been extremely foolish to leave today before the end of the course. Some of the class might have gone on to a pub, or out to supper together, which meant she had lost the chance of a companionable evening – rare indeed for her. But would she have fitted in? They would have all got merry (*tiddly*) and giggled with the greatest ease, while she sat po-faced with her mineral water – the duffer on the course, the only one who couldn't laugh.

Still wide-awake at 2 a.m., she decided to take a sleeping pill. The doctor had warned her off them, but she couldn't face the prospect of tossing and turning all night, dwelling on her deficiencies. As she crept out to the bathroom, she heard the sound of muffled giggles coming from the airing-cupboard and, opening the door, she saw the pig spread-eagled on the floor. It had fallen from the shelf and landed on its stomach, which had activated its laughter-button. On impulse, she picked the creature up and took it back to bed with her. She had never slept with a cuddly toy, even as a child, and somehow, in her miserable state, the idea of it appealed. It always felt so lonely, lying on her own each night, imagining married couples lovingly entwined, or affectionate little sisters, happily sharing a bed. A pig was hardly the ideal sleeping-companion but, as her mother had always said, beggars couldn't be choosers.

She pulled the covers over her, ensuring that the pig was tucked up warm and snug. Self-consciously she held the creature close, trying to transform it into an ardent husband, but the imaginative leap was too great. Her mind went into shock at the thought of naked male genitals, or of a scratchy chin pressed against her cheek, or – worse – hot, hairy legs sweating into hers. Safer to make the pig a sister – a younger sister, born after the War, in a time of peace and plenty.

But that was every bit as difficult. She had always been an only child – it was part of her identity, part of how she saw herself, and the sister she was conjuring up was simply a mirror image of herself.

She turned the pig back into a toy again as she tried a third scenario. Her father had just returned from the War and had brought the toy as a gift for her. In fact, she had never had a present from him, since he had died before she was born. But now he was *there*, as large as life, sitting on her bed and handing her a parcel, wrapped in magical paper – blue with silver stars. Thrilled, she tore the wrappings off, to reveal a fantastic sight: a pig that actually laughed! Gently, he took it from her and pressed its tummy-button with his big, brown, capable hands. And immediately a delirious laugh resounded through the room – her *father's* laugh: a laugh of overwhelming relief because the War was over and he was back, and in one piece.

Smiling with pleasure at the scene, she kept pressing the pig's button, to perpetuate her father's laugh. And then *she* was laughing, the excited little girl – laughing with unalloyed delight because both her parents adored her and both were now alive.

The picture was so beguiling, she dared to laugh in reality, quickly pressing the pig's stomach once more, to drown the unaccustomed sound. The pig obliged with deep satisfying chuckles – her *mother's* laugh, this time, the stiff death-mask of her face cracking into an exuberant grin. And once again, *she* laughed, too, thrilled to see her mother so transformed.

And now it was Daphne's turn. Her friend had died in hospital, with a grim staff-nurse in attendance – a curmudgeon more concerned with tidying beds than easing patients' pain. Cancer of the liver wasn't exactly a joyful thing, so she pressed the pig's stomach ten times in succession, to prolong the delightful experience of her and Daphne laughing – simply laughing at the joy of being healthy, and good friends. They had never laughed in actuality. Daphne was a serious type and, even before the cancer, her life had been a trial, but now they were making up for it, rollicking and gasping in transports of genuine glee.

And what about her dog? Didn't poor, faithful, anxious Dudley deserve a little merriment? He'd been very highly strung, terrified of thunderstorms, a quivering wreck in traffic, and totally unable to sleep if she moved his basket half an inch or laundered his security blanket. But, by activating the laughter-button, she could listen to his joyful bark as all his terrors vanished. Indeed, he had cast off his starchy pedigree and become a cheerful common mutt, sniffing ecstatically round lampposts, and frolicking in the park. She reached out to stroke the pig's pink ears, as she had often stroked his long brown droopy ones. In fact, Piggly's ears and Dudley's felt very much the same – velvet-soft and smooth. Nice to have a pet. A cat or dog (and, yes, a pig) made you feel less lonesome. Perhaps she would sleep with Giggly-Piggly every night. The creature no longer seemed grotesque – instead a faithful friend. 'My love,' she whispered to it, aghast at her own temerity. Yet it wasn't so impossible to say – not once she had got the words out: extravagant, unstinting words that broke the frugal habits of a lifetime.

One last thing to change – icy Miss Sylvester, who had given her her marching orders in the summer term last year. The laughter on her own lips died as she recalled the stern-lipped Head telling her she was too old and out of touch to continue teaching at the school.

'Too *old*,' she repeated falteringly, feeling again the appalling sense of powerlessness and shame. 'And out of touch.'

The pig, however, laughed the words to scorn; laughed Miss Sylvester herself to scorn, mocking her in peals of derision.

'No!' Anthea rebuked him, suddenly remembering Joy's words. 'I need to forgive her, not resent her.'

21

'Easy!' beamed the pig, hooting with forgiving laughter. 'Just look at it in a different way. She did you a favour, really. If you were still teaching at that school, you wouldn't have time for laughter. It's a skill, you see, which needs a lot of practice. I'm so good at it myself because I practise more or less non-stop.' And, as if to demonstrate, the pig convulsed itself in giggles.

Again Anthea joined in. It was definitely getting easier. She no longer cared how stupid she might sound; she no longer cared about being wide-awake in the middle of the night; she no longer even cared about tedious Miss Sylvester. She *could* forgive her now. *And* forgive her mother for the years of grief and bitterness. Forgive her father for getting killed; forgive herself for being ill, and inhibited, and, yes, old and out of touch. The relief was so colossal, it produced a protracted burst of laughter, which amazed her in its turn. Her mouth was opening wider, her shoulders shaking convincingly, and authentic, naturally happy sounds were emerging from her throat. At any moment, the next-door-neighbours would start knocking on the wall in fury, yet it didn't even bother her. She'd *laugh* at the knock when it came; laugh at her landlord's antipathy to pets; laugh at Dr Tobin when he refused to give her drugs. She no longer needed drugs – laughter was her medicine. She could actually feel the t-cells and the lymphocytes racing through her bloodstream, the endorphins falling over themselves to heal and energize her body.

And she certainly wouldn't take a sleeping pill – not at this late stage. She must be wide-awake for tomorrow, with all her senses sharp. She would get up early and go for a nice healthy walk, before rejoining the Laughter Class on the dot of ten o'clock. Of *course* she couldn't miss the second half. She owed it to the pig to be back there in the morning and bond with her new family; show all her brothers and sisters, all her loving uncles and aunts, how well she'd learned to – ha-ha-ha-ha-ha, ho-ho-ho-ho, hee-hee-hee-hee – LAUGH.

2

THIN SKIN

It all started with toast – fingers of toast she had been given as a child to eat with her boiled egg. Nanny used to tell her that every piece not finished might well feel unloved and cry buttery toast-tears. The thought had so distressed her, she never left a single crumb.

Things got worse at school. The other children detested food like Dead Man's Leg and Frogspawn, but *she* could hear it weeping when left untouched on their plates, so of course she had no choice but to eat it. *And* the bits of fat and gristle, the bacon rinds and cheese parings. She never put on weight, though. All the surplus energy was burned off in constant worry – worry about mouldy apples discarded outside greengrocers' shops, or cracked eggs thrown in waste-bins, or even fragments of chocolate trapped inside a wrapper. Did they cry *chocolate* tears?

Sometimes, it appeared, the whole world of food was weeping, especially in hot weather: milk on the turn, bananas turning black, ice-cream dripping tragically from cones.

In adolescence, her sympathies roved further to embrace ants, moths, beetles, spiders, flies – anything killed, swatted, trodden on, or flushed cruelly down a plug-hole by other, sterner people deaf to their shrieks of pain.

'You're too thin-skinned,' Aunt Freda had reproved. 'If you want to exist in the adult world, you'll have to toughen up.'

She had peered at her skin, which did indeed look thin: the veins too near the surface; knobs of bone, with barely any covering, making strange protuberances in her hands and wrists and feet.

Then, when she'd fallen off her bike and had to have her arm stitched, the doctor had confirmed Aunt Freda's words. 'I've never seen such thin skin in my entire professional life. It's like the skin of an old woman, which at *your* age is ridiculous. I'll have to use special stitches to get them to hold at all.'

For the next few weeks, she'd been too scared to use the arm, constantly expecting the wound to gape apart. Why couldn't skin be made of steel, she wondered, to prevent it ripping and tearing? Or people have lemonade pumping through their bodies instead of frighteningly scarlet blood?

And now, at twenty-two, she still used her left arm in preference to her right, which could make things rather difficult – even minor matters like answering the doorbell. It was ringing at this very moment, insistently, aggressively.

Having picked her way between the piles of clutter, she tugged weakly at the door-handle with her scarred and shaky arm; the bell shrilling a second, louder blast, as if deploring the delay.

A dapper little man, with neatly cropped black hair and a matching toothbrush moustache was standing on the doorstep. 'Good afternoon,' he said.

Was it afternoon? Last time she had checked the time, it had been only ten past ten – unless the clock had stopped.

'My name is Austin Beamish.' He held out his identity card, which showed his face in miniature, though looking slightly younger than the flesh-and-blood equivalent. 'Environmental Health Officer.'

'Oh, do come in.' Anyone who took environmental issues seriously was welcome in her home. She often lay awake at night, worrying about climate change and holes in ozone layers. 'I'm sorry about the mess,' she said, leading him a zigzag path between the various obstacles, towards the only chair. 'Please sit down.'

'Aren't *you* going to sit?'

'I'm afraid I can't.' She gave an embarrassed laugh. 'I won't go into details, but it's best for me to stand.' That wretched bike again. After years of cycling, the skin at the base of her coccyx had finally worn through, leaving a raw red area, which was extremely painful if she put any pressure on it. Simply sitting on a chair could make it start to bleed. In fact, much the same had happened in the middle of her back, where pressure from the fastening of her bra had rubbed another raw place. Her body needed patching, like she patched the frayed knees of her jeans, but, alas, extra pieces of human skin weren't as easy to come by as offcuts of blue denim. 'Can I get you a coffee?' she offered, wincing as a pain shot through her arm. Neither she (nor it) had ever really recovered from the fall.

'No, thank you.' He cleared his throat. 'This is not a social visit, Miss Mackenzie.'

'Do call me Daisy,' she urged, crouching down beside his chair, so that they were on roughly the same level. A pity about the moustache. It made him look both sinister and comic, and the combination was just a shade unsettling.

He removed a large beige folder from his briefcase and sat tapping a pen against it. 'I'm afraid there's been a complaint from one of your neighbours.'

'A complaint?' No one could make less noise than her. She didn't own a radio or television, and, as for parties, the very idea was laughable. Her friends were so thin on the ground these days that, were she to drop down dead tomorrow, the only guests at her funeral would be the bats living in the bell-tower and the mournful crows that pecked around the churchyard – both conveniently black-garbed.

'I believe,' said Mr Beamish, surveying the room with an expression of distaste, 'you have an infestation of mice.'

'Oh, the *mice!* God love them. They're no trouble.'

'Mice are vermin, Miss Mack . . . er, Daisy. And most definitely a health hazard.'

'No, mine aren't.' She could hardly hear a sound from them at present – not a rustle, not the faintest scrabble – but then they were always scared by strangers, and Mr Beamish's deep yet querulous voice would have had them all quivering in their lair behind the skirting-board.

His frown intensified, cutting a ravine between his brows. 'They carry diseases – serious diseases such as leptospirosis, and salmonellosis, which are transmitted onto food and drink in their excrement. And their continual dribble of urine causes contamination of food.'

Offended, she drew herself up to her full height again. The mice shared her life, for heaven's sake, so to have this man revile them was, to say the least, insulting.

'They also constitute a fire hazard because they can gnaw

through electric cables. I don't know whether you realize, but their incisor teeth grow significantly each year.'

'Of course I realize. In fact, I'm quite concerned about it. If their teeth get too long, the poor things find it difficult to eat. But I give them stuff to chew on – blocks of wood and dog biscuits – and that keeps their teeth nicely short and sharp.'

He gave her a look that combined horror with incredulity. 'But, that way, you *encourage* them, which is the last thing you should do. I have no wish to be rude, Miss Mackenzie, but the conditions in this room leave a lot to be desired.'

She tried to see the place through his eyes. Yes, it was dirty, but mice liked a bit of grime; yes, it was dark, but mice were nocturnal creatures and, by keeping the curtains drawn, she was gradually giving them confidence to come out in the daytime as well as just at night. Besides, the late December weather was so depressingly cold and dank, she preferred to block it out.

'For one thing, it smells extremely bad.'

'Oh, you get used to that in time. In any case, the smell is probably nice to them. You know, like dogs who sniff round lampposts or roll in steaming cowpats. I don't think it's actually right for us to judge what's good or bad for other species.'

As if she hadn't spoken, he continued in his condemnatory tone. 'And there are droppings everywhere.'

'They're not all droppings.' She glanced down at the floor, where tiny moist black rod-things alternated with minuscule white scales. 'Some of them are bits of my skin.'

'I beg your pardon?'

'It's started flaking off. It's very thin, you see, and . . .' No, he *didn't* see, judging by his expression. Most people failed to realize what peculiar stuff skin was – even normal skin that didn't wear away. It had to be strong enough – resilient and waterproof – to provide a barrier against the outside world, yet on the other hand, it was agonizingly sensitive to the slightest sensation of touch. And it varied so dramatically from place to place on the body: gossamer-frail on the eyelids, sandpaper-rough on the heels, padded over the buttocks, wrinkly-loose on the elbows, taut across the shins. And wasn't it rather extraordinary that hundreds of millions of skin cells should die off every day, to be replaced by new cells, sneaking up behind them? Sometimes, when she tuned in to the process, she could hear the screech of the dying cells competing with the triumphant whoops of the new, and the din in her head became so overwhelming she lay sleepless for nights at a stretch.

'Miss *Mackenzie!*'

She started. He'd been saying something and she hadn't heard a word.

'I've asked you – twice – if you would allow me to examine the premises. I need to make a detailed report.'

Hardly a question of 'allowing' him. He was already prowling around the bed-sit, as if he owned the place, opening cupboards, peering under units.

'This kitchen area is particularly worrying. I can see teeth-marks on the cereal packets.'

'Of course you can – the cereal is *theirs*. I buy it for them specially. Their favourites are Cheerios and Grape Nuts. I can't help it if they eat the boxes as well.'

'I'd appreciate it, Miss Mackenzie, if you could try to take this seriously. I'm endeavouring to do a job of work and your facetious attitude doesn't help the process.'

'I *am* taking it seriously.' So seriously, in fact, she could feel his harsh words piercing through her body – poisoned arrows, now sticking in her flesh.

'The more you feed the mice, the more you'll be landed with.'

'Yes, that's what Sudu found.'

'*Sudu?* Who's Sudu?'

'A girl I met at work – last year, when I *did* work. She's a Buddhist, so she's forbidden to kill a single living creature – not so much as a house-fly or an ant. The problem is she's terrified of mice, but her Buddhist teacher, the Venerable thingamajig, said she had to strive to love them rather than fear them. So she tried leaving them food, but, of course, more and more turned up, and she got into the most awful state, and was tempted to ditch her Buddhist principles and simply put down mouse-traps. In the end, I offered to swap flats with her, which we did three months ago. And the mice are miles happier, because now they're *truly* loved.'

Mr Beamish paused in his examination of a hole in the skirting-board to fix her with a reproving stare. 'I cannot impress upon you too strongly, Miss Mackenzie, that mice are *not*, I repeat not, objects of affection. If you carry on like this, you'll be completely overrun.

Female house mice reach sexual maturity at forty-two days old, and can give birth as often as every month. They don't even have to wait until they've weaned their young before they can conceive again. In fact, one breeding pair used in a research study produced over a million descendants in a period of just eighteen months.'

If he wanted to bandy statistics about, well, that was his prerogative, but personally she found it distressing that he should discuss such intimate matters without a trace of fellow feeling for the mice. It must be extremely hard on the females to be pregnant or lactating for so much of their short lives. *She* had no desire to give birth, having seen what it involved.

'Good God! There's a nest right here.' He was now investigating her bottom dresser drawer, which she deliberately kept open a few inches, to provide air for Alexandra. The poor mouse leapt out in terror at the monster-man's approach, and fled back behind the skirting-board.

'*Now* look – you've upset her, and she's about to give birth any second.'

He shut the drawer with a bang, then wiped his hands on his handkerchief, as if they'd been polluted. 'This really is appallingly unhygienic. You'll get ill, you know, if you live like this.'

She shrugged. There was little point in arguing with someone so completely blind to the beauty of a mouse's nest. Alexandra had fashioned hers out of torn-up bits of newspaper, lined it with chewed and softened string, and spent considerable time and trouble making it a safe and cosy haven for her young. She had even proved her keen intelligence by choosing the drawer that housed the tea-towels – soft absorbent fabric on hand to cushion her babies' tender skin.

Mr Beamish made a note on his pad, wrinkling his nose against the smell again. Next he inspected her bed, and the crate she used as a bedside table. OK, neither was exactly pristine, but the needs of the mice must come first.

'You'll have to call in Pest Control and arrange for these vermin to be exterminated.'

'*Hitler*,' she muttered, outraged. The moustache made perfect sense now. He was nothing more than a one-man death machine. Thank God he hadn't brought himself to use her Christian name. She had no desire to be friendly with someone who consigned her tiny room-mates to the gas chamber.

'I'll leave you a list of Pest Control Operatives, so you can phone them right away.'

'I'm sorry,' she said, 'but I've no intention of phoning anyone.'

'Are you telling me you refuse to deal with the problem?'

'It's *not* a problem, OK? The mice are perfectly happy.'

'And your neighbours are most *un*happy.'

'It's nothing to do with them.'

'Yes, it most certainly is.' He put his pad down to wag a bony finger at her. 'The mice are going under the floorboards from here to other flats. They can squeeze through a gap the size of a pen or pencil, and you have gaps much larger than that.'

'But why should they *want* to go to other flats, when I give them all they need? Not just lots of cereal, but treats like chocolate HobNobs and boxes of Newberry Fruits. I know all their special favourites. And they need to eat a great deal. They have a very high metabolic rate.'

Mr Beamish pursed his lips. 'I'm well aware of that. What *you* are not aware of, or perhaps refuse to take on board, is that you're risking your health and safety, and that of other people who happen to live in this same block.' He strode back to his chair and began making more extensive notes, his pen ripping into the paper, as if it, too, were furious. At length, he bunged the folder back into his brief-case and snapped the briefcase shut. 'I'm afraid I shall have to take this further. You'll be hearing from the council in due course.'

'I can't wait,' she mumbled, finally closing the door on him. All the noise and upheaval would have seriously disturbed the mice. And *she* was literally shaking. The poisoned arrows had gone much deeper now, skewering her heart and lungs.

Too agitated to rest, she paced up and down the room, trying to work out what to do. If she decided to fight the council, she would need a proper action plan, and would have to clear the whole place up, as part of her general strategy. These people were so blinkered, they judged everything in terms of tidiness. In fact, while the mice were lying low, she had better dispose of all the crates and boxes left over from the flat-swap. Then, if some officious type should call, at least his first impression would be favourable.

She stacked half-a-dozen boxes together and carried them down to the wheelie-bin in the backyard of the flats. With difficulty, and using her left arm, she prised open the heavy metal lid and stood peering at the contents: broken toys, old newspapers, empty cans and bottles – all classed as junk, discarded. How could she leave her own stuff here? Battered cardboard boxes probably suffered from feelings of rejection as much as did bruised fruit and mouldy cheese.

Plunging her arm inside the metal container, she retrieved a balding teddy bear. How miserable it looked, with its one remaining eye, its tattered, scruffy fur. And even the newspaper it was lying on aroused her sympathy – the once high-status *Sunday Times* now considered unworthy even of wrapping fish and chips. Her hand closed round a ketchup bottle weeping thick red tears. Easy to call it 'empty', consign it to oblivion, but if plants could suffer – and there was now scientific proof of that – then why not glass or paper? Most people refused to countenance the prospect that what they regarded as brute matter might actually be sensitive, and capable of feeling. Yet, at this very moment, she herself was actually tuning in to the low but keen lament of these unloved, unwanted objects: the heartache of a fishbone, too spiky to be swallowed; the humiliation of teabags, left damp and soggy on top of potato peelings still trembling from the insult of the knife; the pathos of a broken eggcup, regarded as too trivial to mend.

She sank down on to the concrete floor, knowing she must stay – all night, if necessary – hold a solemn vigil in honour of these things, share their pain, their sense of failure. The mice could manage on their own – they had plenty of supplies. Her first duty was down here.

Yet after only half an hour, her bottom was so sore, she had to change position and, even then, the same problem of her thinning skin arose. If she tried to kneel, her knees bled; if she leant on her elbows, they, too, began to fray. Sighing, she got up again, to see what other victims she might succour. It never failed to disturb her that in tossing away their 'trash', people destroyed their personal history, and often with barely a backward glance. Those clothes or letters or CDs they junked so casually, constituted their past in tangible form. The shirt or dress, for instance, they were wearing at the time of their first kiss; the books that traced their reading arc from *Peter Rabbit* to Tolstoy; the record they were listening to when they realized God was dead; the postcard from a partner missing (or betraying) them.

Having salvaged a volume of poetry, badly torn and stained, she was further shocked to come across some old photos in gilt frames. These were someone's relatives – mothers, fathers, spouses, siblings – real people who had once lived and loved. Yet they'd been jettisoned with no concern for the precious bonds and blood-ties, or even for the soul of the person that might linger on in a likeness.

If only dustbins worked like compost-heaps: garden waste and kitchen waste going down into the dark, in order to spring up again in new green fertile growth. A similar thing had happened in her own life – her bitter days and wasted years composting into the deep mulch of compassion. Yet there would be no such resurrection here; only snuff-out in a landfill-site. Indeed, she was appalled at her own negligence in not considering the plight of dustbins *earlier* in her life. Given the scale of the problem, she had no excuse at all. Tons and tons of so-called waste must be thrown out every day, and that in just the British Isles alone.

In fact, why was she keeping vigil by this one insignificant wheelie-bin in this one small block of flats, when there was a much larger rubbish dump down the lane by the overgrown allotments? She must go there straight away – never mind the cold, the clammy grey mist already blurring landmarks and heralding the night – she must show her solidarity with all things ditched, scrapped, spurned, disdained, cast out.

Returning to her flat, at last, she had no idea what date it was, let alone what day. Everything was blurred, as if that clammy mist had never lifted, but sunk deep into her brain. Vaguely, she remembered being ill, lying sweating and delirious beside the rubbish dump. Though the fever must have abated, because she recalled crawling down a path, to take refuge in an empty shed, once used by the allotment-owners. She had stayed there ever since, living on scraps of foodstuffs from the dump.

Now, recovered, and trudging down her familiar street, her overwhelming concern was for the mice. They'd probably had enough food in her absence to manage fairly comfortably, but she preferred to *be* there with them, as mother and provider. She was also worried that while she'd been away, Christmas might have come and gone, and the thought of 'losing' Christmas seemed somehow deeply remiss. She had planned to make it special for them – lay on their

31

own Christmas pudding, dense with fruits and nuts, and mince pies, of course, and marzipan, and a box or two of chocolate brazils. Perhaps she could celebrate it late, but if, as she suspected, it were January already, there'd be nothing Christmassy left in the shops.

As she approached her block of flats, several of her neighbours glanced at her with ill-concealed distaste. She knew she must look a sight, with tousled hair and filthy clothes, but those were only surface things. She'd once met a man, equally unkempt, who wrote astounding poetry and who, in his youth, had hitchhiked to Calcutta and helped beggars build new lives. Yet self-styled 'decent' people shunned him as a tramp, as *she* was shunned, at present.

Inserting her key in the lock, she pushed open the front door, only to stop in disbelief at the sight that met her eyes. The bedsit was completely bare – no stick of furniture remained, no rag-rugs on the floor, no curtains at the windows, no crates or clutter anywhere, no cereal, no biscuits, no well-nibbled Newberry Fruits. And there was a completely different smell in the air – not the pungent scent she had come to know and love, but the harsh reek of lethal chemicals gagging in her nostrils.

Hitler, she thought! He and his henchmen must have been here, aided and abetted by her hostile, hateful landlord; taken advantage of her absence to destroy her only friends. Aghast, she got down on her hands and knees, to peer into the holes in the skirting, where the mice retreated to sleep. There *were* no holes. Every one had been filled or boarded up. Beyond would be only corpses – pathetic, hapless victims.

Fighting a wave of nausea, she dashed back through the open door and continued running, running, down the street, along the lane, until she reached the rubbish dump and the safety of the shed. And, curling herself into a small ball at the back, she sobbed her grief and outrage to the cold, uncaring universe.

She was woken by a familiar rustle. Alexandra? Zeena? No, they and all their tender tribe would now be rotting under the floorboards. Opening her eyes, she was surprised to see a slightly larger mouse than those, with bigger ears, bulbous eyes, and different coloured fur. It was sitting on its haunches, watching her with both fear and curiosity, its long tail twitching, its small pink nose aquiver.

'It's all right,' she whispered gently. 'There's room for both of us.'

She shut her eyes again, pretending to go back to sleep, so that her nervous shed-mate wouldn't be disturbed. However, after half an hour of lying almost motionless she was forced to get up for the sake of her complaining skin.

Although there was no sign of the mouse, she eventually traced it, after a thorough search, to an old Wellington boot lying on its side in one corner of the shed. Inside the boot was a nest, and inside the nest was a brood of eight – only a few days old, she guessed, judging by their hairless coats. She gazed at them, enchanted. How remarkable, extraordinary, that once again she was sharing a home with mice, when her own had been so recently exterminated. These were field mice, not house mice, but in essence the two species were the same. Surely it must be *meant*; arranged by some benevolent Fate to appease her for her loss. Already she had nine companions and, if she fed and tended them, the nine would reproduce in their turn, until she had a shedful. She must go out now, catch the shops before they shut, lay in stocks of nuts and seeds, fresh vegetables, fresh fruit. She wasn't sure if field mice had a sweet tooth, but she would find out soon enough.

She tiptoed to the door, shivering in the evening air. Twilight was just falling, the sky barred with grey and gold. As she crept along the narrow path that skirted the rubbish dump, she stopped to stare, in surprised delight, at the contents of the pile. Arriving here this morning, there had been nothing that she hadn't seen before, but now, resplendent on the top, lay a tall, impressive Christmas tree, still planted in its sturdy scarlet tub. Its branches were browning a little, and one or two had snapped off, but it was in fine shape overall. And, strewn across it, was a tangled heap of decorations – tinsel, paper streamers, golden baubles, silver stars. Excitedly, she climbed the slope to the dump, crouching on her hands and knees to explore its treasures further. A half-eaten Christmas pudding had been casually tossed away, along with the remnants of a Christmas cake, stuffed into a plastic bag. And next to that, a carton of mince pies, with at least a couple left in it, and a red string bag of tangerines, not all of which were mouldy. Some wealthy family had obviously dumped their leftovers, though that again was strange. Wouldn't she have heard them during the day – the noise of a car engine, raised voices, tramping feet? And why had they brought their rubbish to this derelict place instead of to the official dump?

Hardly anyone ventured down this uneven rutted track, yet here were all the ingredients for a full-scale family Christmas – and hers for the taking, at no expense, no cost. Yes, it was obvious now, some Force must be concerned for her, working for her benefit and that of her new friends. She would decorate the tree for them, share the Christmas food with them, restore a sense of harmony.

Piling her arms with provisions – cake, pudding, mince pies, tangerines – she carried them in to the shed, putting them down as gently as she could, so as not to alarm the mice. Then she went back for the Christmas tree, first disentangling the pile of decorations. As she tugged at yards of tinsel, the sky dramatically lightened, and a three-quarters moon bellied out from behind the clump of trees. She stood gazing at it, humbled. Now she had the gift of light, along with all the rest.

As she craned her neck to keep the orb in view, she was aware of scaly patches on its surface, dark encrusted areas, discoloration, lesions. How familiar they looked, like the lesions on her back, the blood-encrusted sore place just below her coccyx, the abrasion on her arm, where the skin was still discoloured. Could the *moon* be thin-skinned, too – that pale ship on the dark sea of the night foundering as it sailed the broken world?

The thought was oddly consoling, and, watched by its unblinking eye, she slipped back into the shed, to celebrate the, perhaps, first happy Christmas of her life.

3

SHIP OF THE ROAD

'Would you kindly shut the door, dear?'

'I'm sorry, ma'am, we have to keep it wedged like that. When we're shifting heavy stuff, we can't be opening and shutting doors all day.'

'But everything's blowing in.' Mary gazed in dismay at the dead brown leaves lying adrift in the hall, and the splatter of red berries trodden into the Persian rug. Even small pebbles from the driveway had found their way inside.

'There's bound to be a bit of a mess,' said the youngest of the removal men – a tall, shaven-headed lad, with a snake tattoo on his arm. 'But don't worry, ma'am, you're leaving this behind. It'll be nice and tidy where you're going.'

Mary kept her eyes on the snake. It seemed to uncoil, rear up high – and strike.

'Why don't you take it easy?' the older man put in. 'Have a nice cup of tea and leave all this to us.'

'I don't drink tea,' she retorted tartly, refusing to be patronized. Of course, they'd see her as a poor old soul, no use for anything. 'But if *you'd* like another cup. . . .'

'Wouldn't say no,' grinned Snake-Arm, rolling up the rug – berries, leaves and all – and heaving it on to his shoulder, to take out to the van.

The three men had introduced themselves as Kevin, Jack and Tony, but although she remembered the names, she wasn't entirely certain which belonged to whom. She collected up the dirty cups and took them into the kitchen, where the third member of the trio was packing china into boxes.

'Are you Jack?' she asked.

'No, Tony.'

35

'Is Jack the tall one?'

'No, that's Kevin.'

She jotted the three names on her shopping list, with a description after each: 'snake', 'freckled', 'dark brown hair'. Old she might be, but not gaga – yet. 'And you all take sugar. Three for you and two for Kevin and Jack.'

'Spot on! By the way, ma'am, you do realize, don't you, half these plates are cracked?'

'Yes,' she said stiffly. The china had survived for decades. Small wonder, then, if it was showing signs of wear.

'We have to point out any damage,' he explained, wrapping the plates in large sheets of coarse blue paper, 'so you don't hold us responsible. And both these vases are chipped – see?'

'Yes, I see.'

'And that teapot's lost its spout.'

She kept the teapot for sentimental reasons. It had been Frank's favourite – white china with black splodges, made in the shape of a cow, with its tail as the handle and its now amputated head as the spout. 'How did you get into this line of business?' she asked, trying to distract the lad from pointing out further casualties.

He stopped work for a moment, and sat chewing his lower lip. 'Well, I left school at sixteen, with no GCSEs or anything. Then I tried all sorts of jobs, but nothing really grabbed me. Until one day, Kevin – he's my mate – asked if I could help him out on this removals lark, and that was it. I took to it like a bee to a flower.'

'Like a bee to a flower,' she repeated wonderingly. The sort of poetic phrase Frank might have used, not this unschooled lad. She looked at him with new regard.

'And today I opted for the packing job. It's boring but it's easier, and to tell the truth I'm feeling a bit worse for wear. Too much partying last night!'

'Oh, where did you go?' The word party brought back memories – dressing up in silly shoes, stumbling back in the early hours, leaning on Frank's arm.

'Drinking with the lads. But we got a bit carried away and stayed out far too late.' He picked up a black marker pen and wrote 'FRAGILE' on the box, then sealed it with brown sticky tape. 'Do you live alone here?'

'*Now* I do,' she said.

'Nice house, isn't it?'

'Very nice.' She filled the kettle, switched it on. After six months on her own, it was good to prepare a proper tea-tray, instead of one lone cup. And Tony seemed a sensitive soul, handling her possessions with a respectful tenderness; even taking an interest in her life.

'Are those your children in the photo?'

She glanced at the chubby faces, blond curls, guileless smiles. 'Yes, though that was taken ages ago. They're grown up now.' He was probably wondering where they were – with reason. Julian she could forgive – he could hardly come all the way from Sydney – but Isabel . . . 'My daughter should be here soon. She's been delayed. A crisis at work.'

'Oh?' Tony assembled another box, deftly folding down the cardboard flaps and sealing the joins with tape. 'What sort of work would that be?'

'She runs her own employment agency – Cameron Recruitment. One of her managers phoned in sick this morning, so she has to man that department herself. She promised to come as soon as things calm down.'

'Don't worry – there's plenty of time. We'll be a while yet with all the stuff you've got here.'

'Yes, my husband . . .' – she paused – '*late* husband, was something of a collector. He liked nice furniture.'

'Will there be room for it where you're going?'

'I'm afraid not.' Frank's furniture was large-boned, like himself, and wouldn't fit the poky little rooms at Marlborough Court. A ridiculously pretentious name for an ugly modern complex, overlooking a scruffy recreation ground. 'It's going to my daughter's. She'll keep what she wants and sell the rest. Now, I'd better get on with this tea.' She scoured the dirty cups with unnecessary force, as if trying to dismantle Marlborough Court. 'Here's yours, Tony. And a slice of my special ginger cake.'

'Ta ever so much. You're spoiling us.'

Nice to have someone to spoil – a son who still lived at home; a son like Tony, who would sit with her sometimes and let her talk about Frank.

He put the roll of tape down. 'I'll take the tray out to the others, shall I?'

'*I* can manage.' She carried it into the hall. Jack and Kevin were manhandling Frank's Victorian desk, bumping it along the passage and out through the front door. The hall looked worse than ever – more withered leaves, more gravel from the drive. It was as if the outside was coming in, to compensate for the inside going out. In a couple of hours *she* would go out; leave this place for ever.

She stood motionless a moment, looking for somewhere to put the tray. The hall table had already gone and, when she walked into the living-room, that, too, was joltingly bare. There were strange, brighter patches on the carpet where the sofa and armchairs had been; trails of cobwebby dust on the walls, once hidden by the pictures.

Still holding the tray, she traversed her steps to the hall. 'Tea!' she called, but no one came, so she ventured out to the driveway and saw Jack and Kevin sitting in the removal van, sneaking a cigarette. The van was loaded with her stuff, yet it was *their* territory, not hers. They had turned it into a temporary home, with Thermoses and lunch-boxes, even a couple of magazines. The word 'home' was on her mind. Marlborough Court would never be home. She had detested the place, from the start. No proper families lived there, and hardly any couples. It was mostly women, and mostly widows, and everybody *old*. All the electric sockets were at waist-level, in case you couldn't bend, and all the flats had call-buttons, in the event of a stroke or heart attack. Pets were forbidden, noise was forbidden and, as for parties, it seemed highly unlikely that any resident would have either health or spirit enough to send out invitations, order food and wine. Sheltered housing had been Isabel's idea, of course. 'You'll be so much safer, Mum. I won't need to worry any more.'

Mary stepped back inside as she saw Jack and Kevin making their way to the house, carrying more boxes, taller ones this time. 'Here's your tea,' she said. 'I hope it hasn't gone cold.'

Jack drained his at a gulp. 'We're going to start upstairs now,' he said. 'Is it OK if we clear the wardrobes?'

She had intended doing that herself, but Isabel had advised her to wait till she arrived. She had promised to bring suitcases and boxes, and spare her mother the trouble of packing. Mary glanced at her watch. She had been waiting now two hours. '*I'll* do it,' she told Kevin.

'Don't worry, ma'am. It won't take us long. These boxes are specially made with a rail at the top, so your clothes can be hung up. That way, they don't get creased.'

It wasn't the creases that worried her, rather the thought of her unfashionable clothes being revealed to the public gaze. And – worse – her undergarments. She took the stairs as fast as she could, the men tramping up behind her.

Standing at the bedroom door, she suddenly saw Frank lying in their double bed in his stripy blue pyjamas. She closed her eyes to perpetuate the vision: to feel the warmth of his body thawing her chilly feet; the scratchy caress of his chin against her cheek; smell his autumn tang of bonfire smoke. She would miss the bonfires – *and* the garden: the shaggy-haired chrysanthemums and good-natured Michaelmas daisies that came up every year, without any fuss or bother; the straggly, stoical roses that resigned themselves to never being pruned because she was too busy planting broad beans. The so-called grounds at Marlborough Court had no vegetables at all, and fewer flowers than benches – benches for the frail and the infirm. She had seen people on those benches: solitary figures, whiling away the empty hours, staring into space.

'I hope we're not in your way,' said Kevin, striding over to the bed and stripping it of sheets and blankets.

'No. I'm in yours,' she replied, watching Frank disappear in a tangled shroud of bedding. Quickly she opened drawers and cupboards and grabbed nightgowns, bloomers, brassieres and bed-socks, and a shameful tube of denture-cleaner. (Frank had kept his own teeth – beautiful teeth, small and evenly spaced.) Clasping the bundle to her chest, she hurried downstairs and crammed the lot into her capacious overnight bag, before returning to the kitchen, where Tony was now packing pots and pans. They, too, looked old and vulnerable, burnt inside and blackened at the bottom. Frank had sometimes helped her with the cooking, fancying himself as a celebrity chef and always turning the gas up recklessly high. It had annoyed her at the time, but now she longed to see him charring food and ruining saucepans with the same flamboyant abandon, oblivious to the acrid smell of burning. He wouldn't have lasted a day at Marlborough Court. Their indignant smoke alarms would have hounded him from the premises before he'd so much as heated the oil.

'D'you know,' said Tony, ripping a sheet of blue paper in half. 'I once spent three whole days packing up nothing else but saucepans. It was for an Asian lady, and she must have had a cooking fetish. There were at least a hundred different pans, stowed away in every nook and cranny.'

'Good gracious!' Mary said. This young lad had met so many people – all in transit, all displaced; nomads on the run.

'Listen! Isn't that the phone?'

'So it is.' She went into the hall, where the phone was sitting on the floor, next to the empty teacups. 'Hallo? . . . Oh, Isabel! What's happening? . . . I see. . . . Don't worry, darling. I understand. Yes, of *course* I know you meant to come. It's quite all right – I'm fine. The men are marvellous. They're taking care of everything.'

'My daughter,' she explained to Tony, rejoining him in the kitchen. 'Another crisis, I'm afraid.'

'It sounds like it's a high-powered job.'

'Most definitely.' Isabel had always been ambitious, even in her cot. When other babies were content to lie and gurgle, she would be shaking the bars and trying to climb out, as if keen to embark on the serious business of life, and not waste time puking and drooling.

'And how about your son? What line of work is he in?'

'Oh, he's a high flier, too. He went out to Australia soon after he left Cambridge, and now he's the Area Manager for Intex International.'

'Brilliant!' Tony said. 'You must be proud of them.'

She nodded, wondering for the umpteenth time why neither of them had married. She and Frank had longed to be grandparents, but the subject was never mentioned by either of their offspring. Instead they talked business – monthly trade figures, marketing trends, profit and loss accounts.

Tony passed her a crippled pan. 'You do know that handle's broken off.'

'Yes, we used it as a dog-bowl. I suppose I ought to throw it out, now Skipper's passed away.' Six deaths within a year, counting the dog and cat. She stood up purposefully – self-pity was a crime. 'I'm going to make a little tour of the house. My daughter's just advised me to make sure I don't leave anything behind – you know, things I might miss, like adapter plugs.'

'Good idea.'

She wandered from Frank's study to the dining-room, hardly recognizing the rooms in their denuded state. All that remained of the furniture was chair-leg-indentations on the carpet and a faint furring of dust and fluff. And the only ornaments on the mantelpiece were strips of cardboard and rolls of sticky tape. A *Daily Mirror* lay abandoned on the floor, along with a crumpled cigarette packet. The rugs were criss-crossed with dirty footmarks; the empty bookshelves gaped. The books had been promised to Isabel – not that she had time to read. No doubt, with her sharp business sense, she would sell them to a dealer. All Frank's love of literature, his interest in ancient Greece, offloaded to a stranger.

She could hear the two men overhead, bumping furniture about, their loud male voices reminding her of Frank – again. She forced herself to concentrate, searching for forgotten plugs, peering into cupboards to check that they were empty. The Robinsons would be moving in tomorrow, their four young boys rushing round the garden, the cupboards full of *their* stuff.

Jack and Kevin appeared in the hall, groaning under the weight of the double bed. 'We're nearly done,' said Jack, pausing to mop his sweaty face. 'Once we've got this in the van, we should only be another fifteen minutes. What do you want to do, ma'am?'

'*Do?*'

'Well, I know you said your daughter was going to drive you, but seeing as she hasn't turned up....'

'Oh. I see.' It wouldn't be very practicable to wait here on her own. There wasn't so much as a chair in the house; not even a book to read, to pass the time.

'You could come with us, if you like. We can take you to your daughter's, so long as you've got a key.'

She nodded. She used the key when Isabel was away – re-stocked her daughter's freezer, watered the exotic plants. 'Well, if you're sure it's no trouble. And I won't be under your feet?'

'Far from it. It would be a help to have you there the other end, so you can tell us what goes where.'

'Fine,' she said, forcing a smile. She had to admit she couldn't picture Isabel's house cluttered with Frank's furniture, wherever it was put. No doubt it would go the way of the books.

'OK, that's settled, then. You can sit up in the cab with me and Kevin, and we'll shove Tony in the back.'

She disappeared into the cloakroom, to comb her hair and apply a coat of lipstick, in preparation for the unexpected adventure of travelling with three men. 'Ready,' she announced, re-emerging in her hat and coat, and clutching her overnight bag. As she locked up for the final time, she refused to say goodbye to the house, refused to cry, refused to feel a thing.

'Your carriage awaits you, ma'am,' joked Kevin, helping her into the cab. Even with his sturdy arm, it was a big step up and made her legs complain. But once settled between him and Jack, the van felt surprisingly safe, despite the bumpy ride. It was good to have a man on either side, their bulk ready to support her. To tell the truth, she did feel rather faint, but probably best to ignore it. Hypochondria was as pernicious as self-pity. 'You must find this job extremely tiring,' she remarked. Focus on other people – that was the trick.

'You get used to it,' Jack replied, shouting above the engine noise. 'Pianos are the worst, though. I put my back out recently, shifting an old upright. Between you and me, it looked ready for the scrapheap, but the way the owner carried on, you'd imagine it was a Steinway grand!'

She laughed, glancing right and left of her from her vantage-point upfront. It was gratifying being so high up, and in such an imposing vehicle, lording it over paltry little cars.

'I think we'll take the motorway,' Jack remarked, braking at the lights, 'just for three or four miles. That'll avoid the town centre. It always seems to be jammed, whatever the time of day. We'll get off again at junction eight, and it's only another mile from there.' He leaned across and passed her a packet of fruit drops.

She took a red one, sucked it vigorously. Only five miles to Isabel's. She wished it were five hundred. She had no desire to sit there on her own, once the men had gone, waiting again, perhaps till late at night.

'So when do you move in to the new place?' Jack enquired.

'Tomorrow morning. My daughter's taking me over in the car.' *If* there were no more crises.

'It'll be nice for you there.'

'Yes,' she said half-heartedly, wondering if anyone would call at Marlborough Court – the milkman, maybe, or the vicar.

'Is it far from your daughter's place?'

'No, only twenty minutes in the car.' Not that Isabel would visit very often. It couldn't be expected when she had so much on her plate – the agency, her sailing club, her frequent trips abroad. Julian would come, though, on his annual summer leave. Unless he went to New York instead – a possibility he'd mentioned on the phone.

She crunched the remains of her sweet. Fruit drops reminded her of childhood: the big house in the country, the sisters, brothers, aunties, the two sets of grandparents. No one lived alone then – old folk were taken in. 'Oh, look!' she said, 'a hitchhiker.' She gazed with interest at the wiry little man standing by the slip road to the motorway, festooned with rucksacks and cameras, and holding up a large printed card, saying INVERNESS. She and Frank had always planned to go to Inverness, hire a holiday cottage, do a bit of fishing in the loch. But the plan had never materialized, and then Frank had had his heart attack and. . . .

She swivelled in her seat to watch the tiny figure of the hitch-hiker, now fading to a blur. 'I hope someone offers him a lift. He's got quite some way to go!'

'I'm afraid we're not allowed to,' Jack explained. 'Our insurance doesn't cover it. And even if we were, it wouldn't be worth his while. We're turning off in less than a mile.'

'I used to hitchhike.' Mary took another fruit drop – a cheerful yellow one.

Both men turned to gaze at her in surprise. 'You never!' Kevin said, looking almost shocked.

'Yes, I was quite a girl in my time. And anyway, it wasn't so dangerous then. There weren't all these stories about murders and assaults.'

'So where did you go?' asked Jack, hooting at a brazen MG overtaking with only inches to spare.

'All over the place. Funnily enough, my first trip was to Scotland, though I never got as far as Inverness. Then I went down to Devon, and on from there to Wales. And I hitchhiked in France and Italy, as well.'

'What, all on your own?'

'Yes.'

'Weren't you scared?'

'Not in the least. Anyway, I didn't have much money then, and since I was really keen to travel, that was often the only way.' And often the best way, she thought – taking your chance with a driver (would he be surly or charming?); taking your chance with the car (bumpy old crock or purring limousine?); the exhilarating sense of speed, the inability to plan. You might be stuck for hours on the roadside, or involved in a puncture or a breakdown, or reach your destination far sooner than you thought. And you struck up instant friendships with fascinating people – eccentrics and free spirits – quite different from her narrow circle at home.

The memories were returning as they rattled along the M1; fields and bridges flashing past, other cars flashing past, everybody purposeful, headed for a destination. This was quite a spree, she thought, allowing the years to slip away until she was a young untrammelled girl again, the whole of her life ahead; her horizons wide, unbounded.

'It's a wonder you got lifts,' said Kevin, still regarding her with interest. 'I mean, in them days there weren't so many cars.'

'You'd be surprised! And anyway there were always plenty of lorries. I remember, once, flagging down a huge pantechnicon. The driver was a lovely man – as big and solid as an ox, but basically a gentle soul. It was getting really late, and he must have noticed how tired I was because he suggested that I stretch out in the back of the cab and try to get some sleep. But, I wouldn't hear of it. I was too keyed up even to close my eyes! So I sat in the front beside him, just as I'm doing now, and stared out for hours at the dark mysterious night. The lorry felt like a ship – a great big powerful ship, sailing the sea of the road, and I imagined I was a seafarer, voyaging out to some new exotic land.'

'You're quite poetic, ma'am, if I may say so,' Jack observed.

'Yes, I used to write poetry once – long ago, when—' Quickly she broke off. That beguiling phrase, 'long ago', ought to be avoided.

And, at that moment, they rounded a corner so sharply, she was tipped almost into Kevin's lap. They both laughed and righted themselves, although she was disappointed that they were now turning off the motorway, indeed slowing to a halt as they hit a tailback of traffic.

She sat in silence, while Jack started-stopped, started-stopped, along a succession of dreary roads, until at last they reached the High Street.

'Good,' he said, releasing the brake. 'The traffic's moving at last.'

She peered out of the window at the familiar row of shops: Safeway's, Superdrug, the Indian takeaway. They were now only a mile from Isabel's; less than eighteen hours from Marlborough Court. 'Excuse me,' she said suddenly. 'Could you let me off? I need to do some shopping for my daughter. She won't have a thing in the house.'

'I'm sorry, ma'am, I can't stop here. I'll get a ticket.'

'Just for a second, to allow me to get out.'

'You mean you don't want us to wait for you?'

'Oh, no. I'll take the bus to Isabel's. It's only a couple of stops.'

'But how will we get in?'

'With this,' she said, extracting the key from her bag. 'Just leave everything in the hall, until I arrive. I won't be long.'

'Hold on!' said Jack, slowing down reluctantly. 'Is there a burglar alarm, or a vicious dog or anything?'

'No, nothing like that. Just turn the key.'

Jack pulled in to the side of the road, and Kevin opened his door and helped her down the step. 'See you soon,' he said.

'Yes, see you soon.'

She crossed the road and walked briskly into Safeway's, in case the men were watching. But once the van had disappeared from sight, she left the shop and stood looking back the way they'd come, her stomach lurching violently as she was cast adrift on a wild sea of indecision. Huge breakers seemed to be crashing in her head – waves of longing and rebellion, counteracted by undercurrents of duty, guilt, misgiving. But the exhilarating roar of the waves was drowning out the undercurrents, and great champagne-spumes of spray began fizzing through her bloodstream, dispelling any doubts. Why *shouldn't* she see Inverness, even at this late stage? She still had life ahead of her, and, if she chose, could still widen her horizons. Frank would approve – she knew he would. She could take him with her in spirit, call on his strength to keep her courage high. Sixty years ago, on her first hitchhiking trip, the lorry had stopped at Oban and she hadn't succeeded in getting another lift, so she had cut her losses and hitchhiked back again. This time she might be luckier – luckier in several ways. After all, houses would be much cheaper in the Highlands, cheaper than Marlborough Court. She could bid goodbye to wardens, stair-lifts, panic-buttons . . . It would be much too far for Isabel to visit, but who wanted duty visits? If a daughter couldn't come out of genuine affection, then better not to see her at all.

Decisively, she seized her overnight bag, which she'd left resting on the pavement, and began striding back towards the motorway. Despite her age, she was still a seasoned walker and, if she really put a spurt on, she might catch up with that wiry little fellow on the slip road. The removal men had reminded her how pleasing it was to have a bit of company – male company especially. Her heart was pounding fiercely, as if she were indeed sailing uncharted seas, yet if she braved the storms, a Ship of the Road might bring her safely to port.

As she'd told the men, she was quite a girl.

And not frightened in the least.

4

WITH ROSEBUDS IN HER HAIR

'Sorry,' Alan mumbled, as he tried to squeeze into the crowded carriage, pressing his hot, perspiring body against the people already jammed inside the doors. There was hardly room for a babe in arms, let alone for a man his size. He was conscious of people shrinking from him, frowning in disapproval at his massive thighs and protuberant belly, as if they viewed his bulk as a personal affront. He only hoped he didn't smell. His usual application of three different deodorants (daubed one on top of the other) couldn't be relied on in such relentless heat. The temperature had climbed to 32° outside and, even underground, he felt like a huge leg of pork spluttering and sizzling in an oven.

The train lurched to a halt at Victoria, where scores of passengers struggled to get out, regarding him as an obstruction that could be pushed and shoved with impunity. He was assaulted on all sides by briefcases and bags; jabbed in the legs by an arrogant young tourist loaded down with two knapsacks and a bedroll. But at least some seats were free now, and, as he lowered himself with difficulty into the narrow red-plush cage, he smiled apologetically at his neighbours on either side. Anyone obese had to apologize continually – for taking up too much space, being aesthetically unpleasing, a drain on the National Health Service and, ultimately, a loser. He glanced up at the advertisements, which often offered solace: the promise of fun-packed holidays, or low rates on car insurance. He didn't own a car, or ever go on holiday, but it was nice to know these things existed, at least for other people.

'Losing your cool? We can help.'

Ah, he thought, a new and stronger deodorant; just the thing he needed. But, peering at the smaller print, he saw it was nothing of the sort – instead a plug for Anger Management courses, claiming to save your marriage and career. Again, not for him, alas. He didn't have a girlfriend, let alone a wife, and his tinpot job could hardly be classed as a 'career'. Besides, anger was rarely a problem for the seriously overweight. It required confidence to lose your temper, and every excess pound you carried whittled away that confidence, making you more inclined to placate people, rather than let fly.

'This is the Victoria Line to Walthamstow Central,' a recorded voice informed him. 'The next station is Green Park.'

Another influx of people fought their way into the carriage, one of them a striking young girl, carrying a sheaf of pale pink rosebuds incongruously wrapped in brown paper. As he lumbered up to offer her his seat, she flashed him a smile of such gratitude and charm, his legs turned to semolina. He had to grab the rail to prevent himself from falling but, even as he clung there, decidedly weak at the knees, he found it nigh impossible to wrest his eyes away from her. Never before had he seen such an enchanting creature – though rather bizarrely dressed, he had to admit. There were more rosebuds in her long, dark, tousled hair, pinned along the front and sides. And all her clothes were pink, to match the flowers: an old lace party frock, with a raggedy, uneven hem, pink trainers, tied with polka-dotted laces, and shell-pink tights, embroidered with deeper puce-pink hearts. Her skin was porcelain-pale, which only served to emphasize the dark lustre of her eyes. Her lips were a perfect Cupid's bow; her nails varnished sugar-pink. He tried to guess her age. Nineteen, perhaps, or twenty, though her girlish figure and childlike air made her seem far younger. She sat staring straight ahead, lost in her own world, unaware of him or anyone else, and apparently impervious to the heat.

His gaze moved from her pert breasts to the clumsily wrapped bunch of flowers. Where had she bought such delicate rosebuds? – he had never seen such things in an ordinary florist's shop. And who were they for, he wondered? Perhaps a patient in hospital, or a dinner-party hostess. He ached to know everything about her; longed to thrust a questionnaire into her slender little hands, and ask her to fill in her name, address, date of birth, occupation, marital status. . . .

47

'The next station is Oxford Circus. Change here for the Bakerloo and Central Lines.'

The recorded voice broke into his thoughts, and reluctantly he moved towards the doors. It was late-night shopping in Oxford Street, and he was on his way to buy some short-sleeved shirts. But as he stepped on to the platform, he suddenly changed his mind and blundered back into the carriage just as the doors were closing. The short-sleeved shirts could wait. His need for the girl was greater. He elbowed his way towards her and stood feasting his eyes again, eager to drink her down to the dregs, like a delicious strawberry milkshake, pink, nutritious and most definitely addictive.

At Warren Street, he was rewarded with an empty seat right opposite and, forgetting his usual good manners, he hastily scrambled into it, beating two other contenders. Why should anyone else have the privilege of sitting face to face with her, breathing in her fondant-pink smell; maybe even catching her eye and being honoured with another radiant smile?

But, no, to her he was invisible – just another anonymous passenger. She hadn't even noticed his girth, which most people did immediately, nor did she seem to realize that *he* was studying *her*. Her hair, in particular, was a source of fascination. It rippled past her shoulders in such a luxurious mass, it seemed alive in its own right, gleamingly dark and excitingly dishevelled, as if she had just got out of bed. He imagined reaching out and touching it, or, better still, burying his face in that silky, shining mane, and submitting himself to an ecstasy of pleasure. Never, in the whole of his life, had he touched a woman's hair, yet now he was experiencing a deep and almost painful urge to wind a strand around his fingers, feel its glossy texture, cover it with kisses. Though he would have to take the greatest care not to dislodge the rosebuds, which were so utterly bewitching they made her seem like a Flower-Fairy from one of his childhood books. Had they come from someone's garden? Or were they a present from an admirer? Or perhaps she was an artist and intended to paint them as a still-life. If only he were younger and thinner, he could strike up a conversation, comment on the weather, or on the semi-finals at Wimbledon, and that might lead to . . . His mind explored the possibilities: a drink, a date, a summer ball, a wedding on a sun-kissed beach, an exotic honeymoon. Or if he were a rose-grower, he could talk knowledgeably about her flowers, casually let fall their Latin name, impress her with his expertise.

They were just pulling into King's Cross. He prayed she wouldn't get off. He'd gladly follow her to the end of the line – indeed, to the ends of the earth. Yes, they had come back from their honeymoon and were now celebrating their first Christmas in another romantic island paradise. Then, as spring burst forth, their first child was born, amidst coral reefs and banyan trees – a daughter as pink and pretty as its mother. And now they were lying on warm silver sand on their first wedding anniversary, toasting each other in gigantic ice-cream sundaes, topped with mango, pawpaw, passion fruit . . . He anchored himself to the armrest as the train rattled along the track. It seemed exceptionally bumpy, shaking him like a monster blancmange. No matter. He turned it into a camel – he and his young bride astride a Mongolian dromedary, as they traversed the desert, beneath a shimmering sky.

'This is King's Cross. Change here for the Northern and Metropolitan Lines, and for National Rail Services. . . .'

Would her voice be as refined as that, as softly feminine? He would have to take elocution lessons, in order to be worthy of her. And buy some different clothes. His white shirt, navy trousers and timid squiggly tie were so boringly conservative. And what could be done about his hair, which was neither fair nor dark, but a sort of indecisive amalgam of them both, with a little grey admingled, to make it drabber still? The conventional wisdom that appearances didn't matter was a blatant lie – like so much else in life. *His* appearance was a huge brick wall, which stopped anyone from recognizing the sensitive and skinny man behind it. But this girl might be different; might pierce his gigantic carapace and bore through to the mollusc skulking modestly inside.

He was still supping on her rapturously – sipping from her lips, nibbling on her skin, then licking slowly down her legs, alluringly defined by the clingy nylon tights. His tongue traced the outline of one of the embroidered hearts, which exploded in a sugar-rush – pink-sherbet fizz pulsating through his mouth. His own heart, he felt, was every bit as turbulent, so smitten with the girl that it had leapt clean out of his chest, and was now hovering in mid-air, in view of all the passengers. And a heart far braver than *he* was, beating with such force the whole train must hear its exultant boom-boom-boom, and now actually daring to *speak* to the girl, with equal confidence.

'I *love* you,' it declared. 'I never believed in love at first sight, but now I know it's possible. I'll do anything you want, take any risk on your behalf, face any peril, including death itself.'

He added his own more modest plea, speaking in an undertone and flushing at his impertinence. 'Oh, I realize I'm not in your league, but don't judge by my exterior, I beg you. Give me a chance, at least. I'll buy a puce-pink tie. I'll grow my hair. I'll dye it. . . .'

She hadn't heard a word, so bemused by her own thoughts that even a rampant heart and its owner could make no impact on her. Most of the other passengers seemed irritable and stressed, fanning themselves with newspapers, or restlessly tapping their feet. Only *she* sat serene – a pink princess on her red plush throne. He yearned to be her prince, almost willing her to faint, so that he could pick her up and carry her home, tuck her up tenderly in bed, while he lay panting beside her, ready to obey her every whim. He closed his eyes, imagining what she might ask of him. To feed her with fresh figs, fan her feverish skin, undo the buttons on her blouse. . . .

When he opened his eyes, she had gone. Oh, *no*, he all but shouted, fighting shock, horror, desperation, in hideous succession. 'Stand clear of the closing doors,' the relentless voice was warning. With unaccustomed speed, he levered himself out of his seat and forced his cumbersome body through the doors a scant second before they closed. But suppose he was too late? She'd probably been swallowed up in the crowd, lost to him for ever. No – suddenly he glimpsed her, striding down the platform towards the exit sign. He stumbled in pursuit, managing to catch her up on the escalator, although once she was in sight, he deliberately hung back, not wishing to make it obvious he was following.

He had no idea of his whereabouts until he reached the street and saw the sign outside the tube: Seven Sisters – a place he'd never been to in his life. She, too, seemed slightly bemused, looking around uncertainly and shifting from foot to foot. Perhaps she was meeting someone who hadn't yet turned up. He had a sudden image of her seven sisters, all rushing up to greet her, all dressed in pink, with rosebuds in their hair. Once the honeymoon was over, he'd invite them all to stay – seven gorgeous sisters-in-law, to compensate for his dearth of females to date. No woman ever looked at him – or only to grimace in disgust.

The girl hadn't moved a step, but was still glancing to right and left, as if taking in her surroundings. Following her gaze, he noticed an African hair salon, advertising 'weaves and braiding', a South American café, a Spanish Music Centre and a Lebanese Kebab House, all within fifty yards of each other. Seven Sisters was truly cosmopolitan. In fact, it wasn't hard to imagine that he and the girl had already jetted off from Heathrow and arrived in some enticing tropical clime. All the people passing looked wonderfully exotic: an African woman in a jungle-print dress and matching turban, a handsome young Latino flashing his white teeth, a Jamaican girl with, yes, braided hair, and a bearded Arab in an ankle-length white robe. If only *he* could wear a robe, to conceal his gruesome bulges, and grow a bushy beard like that, to deflect attention from his double chin. Then he could approach the girl, saunter nonchalantly up to her, declare his love, hold her close.

But, all at once, she made a move herself, setting off along the High Road, the flowers clutched firmly in both hands. He followed a safe distance behind, keeping his focus on the pink lace dress, which was lapping in a seductive manner against the pale pink tights. The white flash on her pink trainers was like a beacon leading him on, past a luggage shop, a hardware store, a cheap café and a clothing bazaar.

Soon he was panting from the effort, rivulets of sweat trickling down his face and back. She, however, continued to stride on, regardless of the sun's fierce glare. The flowers must be wilting in this ferocious heat – needed water, as *he* did. 'Stop!' he begged her under his breath. 'Let's sit down and rest, have a drink together.'

And, miraculously, she *did* stop – outside an impressive red-brick edifice, with iron railings in the front. A hospital, he thought. She must be taking the flowers to a patient, as he'd originally assumed. But, on closer inspection, it turned out to be a block of flats. Was this where she lived, or her friend lived – the one hosting the dinner party? It certainly looked elegant, with tall shady trees, bay windows and its own decorative iron gates – nothing like his dreary basement bedsit.

Plucking up his courage, he took a step towards her. He must confront her *now* – this instant – before she disappeared inside. But instead of entering the flats, she walked over to a litter-bin just beyond the railings, and peered into its depths. He often did the same, hoping to find a half-eaten doughnut or carton of French fries.

Perhaps, miracle of miracles, she shared his eating habits: preferred food which was left in waste-bins or abandoned on park benches, free for the taking, if you didn't mind a germ or two. How wonderful, incredible, if they had that trait in common. No one else had ever understood, but simply damned the practice as disgusting, if not downright weird. What they failed to realize was that he felt less guilty (and less gluttonous) eating food he hadn't bought himself, and that if it was stale or even dirty, that assuaged the guilt still more. The girl could truly be a soul mate if she felt the same as he did; believed in a God of Failures, who mercifully provided for those who dreaded food-stores where shoppers were on public view. If he piled his trolley in Tesco's with pizzas, pasties, pastries, he was aware of people curling their lips and whispering cruel gibes. 'Can't that tub of lard live on his own fat-stores, instead of buying even more?'

But his life would be transformed if, everywhere they travelled, he and the girl could root for their provisions in rubbish heaps and garbage bins, share the triumph of trawling gutters and lighting on a squashed cheese roll, or the last beguiling fragments of a Twix bar, or a few delectable crisps (prawn-flavoured or cheese and onion) lurking at the bottom of a bag. Such food was free in every sense. It cost nothing and it didn't fatten – well, not as much as normal meals. And he would gladly divide all his spoils in half. Indeed, if there was only half a crisp left, or one pathetic peanut, *she* should have it, not he.

He ventured a little closer to the bin. Was she sussing it out with a trained professional eye, disregarding the newspapers and other soulless debris, and going straight for the comestibles – the toffee packets, popcorn bags, the greasy fish and chips wrappings?

No, her eyes were fixed on the pavement, not on the bin at all. Which meant something must have fallen to the ground – a chip, a piece of popcorn? He was too far away to see, and dared not move any closer. She might recognize him from the tube and accuse him of being a stalker.

Then suddenly, and shockingly, she flung the sheaf of rosebuds in the bin, turned on her heel and veered off down a side street. He rubbed his eyes in flagrant disbelief. How *could* she throw them away – those exquisitely delicate rosebuds? He rushed up to the bin and retrieved the hapless flowers, cradling them in his arms. Only then did he notice a tiny white card pushed deep down into the bunch. He extracted it with difficulty, pricking his fat fingers on the thorns. 'All my love, darling,' was written in a flamboyant script, 'from your devoted A.'

The blood rushed to his face. 'A' was *his* initial. These rosebuds were her bridal bouquet, and yet she had hurled them into a litter-bin, along with his devotion. He had never found it easy to run, but indignation lent him strength, and, plunging down the side street, he finally caught up with her by a stretch of derelict houses, boarded-up and marked for demolition.

'How *dare* you!' he shouted, all the suppressed anger of his forty years suddenly bursting forth like a torrent of hot lava from a volcano long-quiescent. He thrust the bouquet back into her arms, which left his own hands free to grab her by the shoulders and shake her till her teeth rattled, shake her till her body sagged, shake her till she lost her footing and slumped leaden to the ground. Despite her screams, he continued to berate her. No one could hear them – no one was around.

'I loved you,' he yelled. 'And this is how you treat me! I bought new clothes to please you. I took you everywhere, saved you all the titbits, starved myself so *you* could eat your fill.'

He kicked out at her body, targeting her legs, with their false and treacherous hearts; slapped her scheming little face, punched her in the ribs. Tears were streaming down her cheeks – and his. The rose-buds in her hair had fallen out and were lying mangled on the pavement. His weight had crushed the bunch of flowers, broken all the stems. They, too, were strewn in disarray, beside the girl, his bride – she and they mere wreckage now, mere dross.

He fell to his knees in front of her, sobbing out his shame and grief in great racking, hurting gasps.

Once again, he had destroyed the thing he loved.

5

HOTEL NORFOLK

'Mr and Mrs Gonzalez,' Stuart announced, leaning one elbow casually on the reception desk.

'*Barnes*,' hissed Melanie, too late. They had spent twenty minutes choosing an inconspicuous name, and now he'd gone and blown it. The receptionist would probably turn them away. Not that she seemed particularly bothered – too busy filing her nails.

'Sign here,' she said, putting the file down with obvious reluctance, and reaching across for the register. 'And print your name and address underneath.'

'*I'll* do it.' Melanie pushed forward. If she left it to Stuart, he'd put something stupid like Wormwood Scrubs. She paused for a second, sucking the end of the pen. Then, 'Appletree Cottage,' she wrote, picturing it in her mind – a cosy little dream-home, with a thatched roof and a duck-pond, and Cox's Orange Pippins piled higgledy-piggledy on the scrubbed-pine kitchen table. 'Wroxham, Norfolk,' she added, with a flourish. Norfolk was where she used to go in childhood, on her imaginary holidays, with her imaginary Dad, on an imaginary boat on the Broads.

'And I'll need your car registration number,' the receptionist put in, returning to her manicure.

'We don't have a car.' Stuart had the occasional loan of his brother's motorbike. She had her student bus-pass.

'Well, just leave it blank.'

Blank was how she felt. Not nervous any more. Last night the nerves had been so bad, she had hardly closed her eyes.

'That'll be fifty pounds.'

Stuart handed over a bundle of notes, fastened with a rubber band. It was all she could do not to snatch them for herself. Fifty pounds was halfway to an iPod.

The receptionist counted the money suspiciously, appearing almost disappointed to find it was correct 'Room 507,' she said, fumbling for the key and banging it down on the desk. 'Breakfast is between seven-thirty and nine. It's included in the price.'

Breakfast! Stuart was due at work this evening – they had a scant two hours together. Anyway, even the *thought* of bacon and eggs was enough to turn her stomach. Which meant her nerves had come back. Yes, horribly.

Stuart led the way up the narrow stairs, flattening himself against the wall to make room for a group of people coming down – all men, all swarthy-dark and bearded, and all loaded with serious baggage. Their own small suitcase was empty. She had insisted on a case, though, for the sake of appearances. Stuart said no one gave a shit these days, even if you booked in with another bloke or a twelve-year-old nymphet. It was all very well for Stuart – he hadn't been brought up strict Catholic, with a mother who thought sex was not just a sin, but messy, vulgar and, on the whole, unnecessary.

The foreign contingent was still lumbering down the stairs, talking loudly and belligerently, as if arguing with each other. She caught a whiff of sweat as the largest of the group pushed past her – an old guy in a loose black robe, with what looked like his wife's slippers on his feet. Once the party had squeezed by, she and Stuart continued up three more flights. She noticed with a sort of desolate interest that the stair-carpet changed pattern every dozen steps or so. They must have used a batch of cheap offcuts, and – judging by the fraying patches – saved the most threadbare for the final floor.

'This is us,' said Stuart, inserting the key in the door. The lock refused to budge, however, despite further frantic attempts.

That's God's *doing, Melanie. He's barring the door, for the specific purpose of saving you from Hell.*

Mum, please don't start, she pleaded silently.

'That stupid cow must have given us the wrong key. You wait here, and I'll go down and give her a bellyful.'

'No, *I'll* go.' Couldn't she just slip away, phone Stuart later, on his mobile, and say she'd felt sick and had to go to the chemist. She *did* feel sick – it wasn't a lie.

'Hang on, I've done it now. And cut myself in the process. That bloody lock needs fixing.'

Every time a person swears, they personally make Jesus cry.

'Go *away*, Mum,' she begged.

'What did you say?' asked Stuart.

'Nothing.'

'Look, are you OK?' Stuart turned back to face her, sucking his bleeding thumb.

She nodded.

'You do want to do this, don't you?'

'Yeah. 'Course.'

'Give us a kiss, then.'

'Wait till we're inside. Someone might see.'

'Who? We're on our tod up here. Which suits me fine. We can make as much bloody racket as we like.'

He took her hand and led her into the room. 'Hm,' he said, frowning. 'It's not exactly the fucking Ritz.'

Nervously she glanced around. The bed took up almost all the space – a large, low divan, covered with an old-fashioned satin eiderdown, whose shell-pink cabbage roses seemed to shrink from his black leather gear. There were bare boards on the floor, and a flimsy paper blind at the tiny attic window. All she could see were rooftops, gleaming in the rain. Her mouth was dry and her legs felt weak and trembly. No chance of a get-out now. They were here – alone – a couple.

'So how about that kiss, then?'

'In a sec.' She escaped into the bathroom – not that there was room for a bath, only a miniscule shower, a tiny half-basin, and a toilet jammed into the corner, with barely room for one's knees. She supposed she ought to wash. That book she'd borrowed, *Sensuous Sex*, advised a long leisurely bath together, soaping each other's bodies and sipping champagne from the tooth-mug. They couldn't afford champagne, and anyway Stuart wouldn't waste time in a bath. He was always in a hurry – even now pounding on the door.

'Get a move on, darling. We haven't got all night.'

'Coming.' She ran the hot tap, which stayed obstinately cold. There was no sign of soap or flannel, so she wetted the end of the towel and dabbed it between her legs. She could hear her stomach rumbling as she patted herself dry. According to the book, it was good to get into the mood by sharing a romantic meal – sexy foods like oysters and fresh figs – eaten to the accompaniment of soft, seductive music, in the glow of candlelight. Stuart had bolted a cheeseburger in the glare of a cheap caff, to the accompaniment of the racing results. She had eaten nothing.

'Mel, come and help me out. My cock's as stiff as a plank.'

Shivering, she emerged into the bedroom. Stuart was sprawled naked on the bed. He had yanked off the eiderdown and was lying on a grubby blue nylon sheet – his body pale, huge and terrifying. She averted her eyes from his ... his ... All the words were so crude.

'Get your kit off, darling.'

He was meant to undress her, so the book said, teasingly and sensuously, one garment at a time. And she shouldn't be wearing jeans, but something loose and silky that slipped off in a trice. She *had* bought a new Wonder-bra but, once she took it off, her fake cleavage would collapse. And the bra was lacy black and so didn't match her plain white boring pants. It had been a case of one or the other. The black lace pants cost £15.99.

She fumbled with the top button of her shirt, aware of the goose-flesh on her arms. The old electric heater had rusting bars and a dodgy-looking flex. If the Fire Brigade arrived, they'd discover her in bed with Stuart. And a hotel fire might get into the papers – her mother's *Daily Mail*.

She undid the next three buttons, wondering where to put her clothes. There was neither chair nor wardrobe, so she presumed she just dropped them on the floor.

Stuart solved the problem for her by leaping up from the bed, dragging the shirt over her head and tossing it behind him, then tugging down her jeans.

'You're beautiful,' he murmured, unhooking her bra and fiercely kissing her breasts.

She should never have agreed to come. Except Kate had said 'Go for it!' and lent her the book and everything. Kate had done it – dozens of times. All the others had.

Stuart was kissing her on the lips now, thrusting his tongue right inside her mouth. He tasted of onion from his burger, plus an over-lay of stale beer. His teeth were dangerously sharp – shark-like teeth that felt too big for his mouth.

Then he laid her on the bed, on her back, and began kissing her
. . . her . . . There were no words for that either, and they were going
miles too fast. She was still fighting off her mother – who had plenty
of words, all wildly disapproving. Stuart's tongue was sort of jabbing
deep inside her – which was peculiar, and had to be wrong. And
suppose she tasted funny? She should have brought her own soap,
but books didn't tell you things like that – only how to give your
man a massage or pass grapes from your mouth to his.

He pulled away a moment, his mouth slimy from her . . . her. . .
'Kiss my cock,' he said.

She gazed at him, aghast. They had explained that in the book,
but it sounded really off-putting, and difficult as well.

'Kneel between my legs.' Stuart got up and stood beside the bed.
His thing looked dreadfully big, sticking out so stiffly it pushed right
against his stomach. He guided it into her mouth, but immediately
she gagged. Fighting panic, she tried to remember what she'd read.
You had to co-ordinate your hand and mouth movements, control
your touch and speed. But how on earth could she do all that when
she was almost being choked?

'Ouch!' Stuart yelped. 'Suck, don't bite.'

She spat him out, blushing with embarrassment yet gasping in
relief. 'I . . . I'm sorry, Stuart. I . . . I need to take things slower.' She
rubbed her dirty knees. 'Couldn't we just cuddle for a bit?'

He lay beside her on the bed, but he could see he was put out. She
tried to stroke his thing instead, forcing herself to look at it. You
were meant to tell the guy how beautiful it was, but it didn't look
beautiful at all, only angry and inflamed, with a horrid, wrinkled,
lumpy bit dangling underneath, all covered in coarse hairs. She
didn't even know how hard to touch. The book said, 'Hold it firmly
like a tennis racquet,' but she was as clueless about tennis as about
sex.

Stuart was trying to help. His hand was steering hers, demon-
strating what he liked. She felt terribly ashamed. She ought to
know, by instinct, as Kate and all the others did.

'I've just got to fuck you, darling. You've got a wonderful firm little
arse. And I love your tits – they're . . .' His voice had gone all gaspy
and he was breathing very heavily.

He fumbled under the pillow, withdrew a small foil packet, tore it
open and turned his back a second. When he faced her again, his

thing was all but bursting from a shiny yellowish skin.

He knelt above her on the bed, flicking her nipples with his thumb. 'Relax – I'll take it slowly. I don't want to hurt you, Mel, OK?'

'OK.'

'And I want you to come. It's a turn-on for the bloke to know the woman likes it.'

'OK.'

She shut her eyes. Better not to see. It didn't hurt – not really – but she left the room for safety's sake, and floated out of London, up to Norfolk and the Broads. Yes, the breeze was in her hair now, the tang of salt on her lips, the water rippling gently, and the huge dappled sky arching overhead. She was on her father's boat. He had come back, at last, to find her. He had never meant to go away; never meant to hurt her.

They were on their own, the two of them – no mother, no new wife. He was showing her the countryside, pointing out a cormorant, marsh marigolds, a swallowtail. And then he put his arms around her and held her strong and close, blocking out the terrors, making her feel safe.

'Can I come home?' he whispered, as the boat vanished in the mist. And she took his hand and led him to their cottage – the cosy little cottage with the apples on the table and the roses round the door. They sat together by the fire, listening to its crackle and to the soft spitting of the logs. And he fed her cakes, big creamy cakes, and a mug of foaming chocolate. And the warmth and froth seeped into her until she seemed to lose her body and melt sweetly into his. And he was kissing her and kissing her, telling her he loved her – no – shouting it out loud, making such a noise the whole cottage seemed to leap and shake, juddering with joy.

And she was crying out, 'I love you, Dad, I love you,' and she heard him say, very deep and true, 'I love you too, my darling.'

And then there was silence – peaceful, waiting silence, like a sleepy Norfolk river stirring into dawn.

'Was it good for you?' he murmered.

'Oh, *yes*,' she whispered, holding him still closer. 'Better than I could have dreamed.'

6

WISTERIA

'Forty years? You're joking!'

'No, honestly, it's true.' Nell paused to count on her fingers. 'In fact, it's even longer – nearer forty-one.'

Pauline put her wineglass down and crossed her arms with almost an aggressive air. 'Let's get this straight. You haven't seen the guy for forty-one years and now he's asking you out?'

'Not out. To his house. For dinner.'

'Well, he's obviously got devious designs on you. And how old is he, for God's sake – a hundred?'

Nell forced a laugh, wishing now she hadn't brought the subject up. Pauline would only mock – was maybe even jealous. Yet she longed to discuss the matter, if only to sort out her feelings, which mixed fear and curiosity with interest and desire. 'He must be roughly my age. We were both in our early twenties when we first met at BGP.'

'And were you an item then?'

'Oh, no, far from it. We were completely unalike. I was fresh out of art school and quite a swinger in my modest way, whereas he was frightfully formal and correct – rolled umbrella, well-cut suit, unfailingly polite.'

'So you never got it together, you mean?'

Nell shook her head emphatically. 'He seemed to like me, but nothing ever *happened*. I went round to his flat a couple of times, expecting a bit of— you know – but he didn't so much as kiss me. Actually, I suspected he was gay. In those days, advertising agencies attracted loads of gays – still do, no doubt.'

Pauline forked in more spaghetti. 'How did he manage to track you down, though, after all this time?'

Was she really interested, Nell wondered, or just asking questions so she could pass on spicy gossip to their other mutual friends? With Pauline, you could never tell. 'Well, the weird thing is he's always kept in touch. Every year at Christmas I'd get this fabulous card – handmade and *huge* – but with just his name, Errol.'

'Errol?' Pauline raised her eyes to heaven. 'I might have guessed he'd have a film star's name.'

'Actually it suited him. It means "noble", and he *was*, rather. And it's sort of old-fashioned, which is right for him as well. Anyway, back to the Christmas cards. He never wrote a message on them, or any news of what he was doing. And there'd never be a wife's name bracketed with his, just Errol short and sweet. Well, I always sent a card in return, simply to be polite. And, would you believe, that went on for forty years – all the time I was living in the Highlands. Then, this last Christmas, I got his usual card, but instead of reciprocating with one of mine, I scribbled him a note and told him I was moving back to London. That did it! He replied by return of post, said he'd love to see me, and he'd actually never stopped thinking about me during all these years.'

'Mr Romantic, obviously.'

Nell registered the snide tone. 'To tell the truth, I'm not sure whether I ought to go. He might be – you know – weird.'

'So what? It's only one evening. If it doesn't work out, you need never see him again. What's he like to look at, by the way?'

'Oh, no complaints on that score. Quite a heartthrob, really. Tall and slim, with dark hair and deep blue eyes. And he always wore these gorgeous clothes – handmade shirts, suits that must have cost a bomb, silk ties from Italy that looked like works of art.'

'It sounds better by the minute. Maybe he's always fancied you, but was just too shy to say.'

'I suppose it's quite a thrill having any man interested at all. Once Sam walked out, I thought that's it – nothing left but a celibate old age.'

'Come off it!' Pauline scoffed. 'You've only been without a bloke for a matter of six months. It may have slipped your mind, dear, but *I've* been living like a nun for seven and a half years.'

End of subject, Nell thought. If she wanted helpful advice, then best to confide in her cat.

*

'Go on, *ring* the bell,' she told herself. 'You can't stand on the step all night.'

Glancing quickly to right and left, she got out her handbag-mirror and sneaked a quick glance at herself. The new blonde highlights were definitely a success and the preposterously pricey make-up had actually done what it promised and made her skin look younger and more glowing. Yet she wasn't sure about the sleeveless dress. Was it wise at her age to reveal too much upper arm? If only it weren't so swelteringly hot, she could have worn her blue, but that was a touch matronly, and Errol would remember her in micro-skirts and knee-length boots, with extravagantly false eyelashes and hair down to her waist. Still, he could hardly expect micro-skirts now that she'd got her bus pass, and at least she had a cleavage, emphasized with a string of amber beads.

'Look, are you going to ring or aren't you? You're already late, and he's probably still a stickler for punctuality.'

Taking a deep breath in, she pressed the bell – and instantly regretted it. She should have phoned to say she wasn't well; called the whole thing off. Her anxiety increased as the seconds ticked determinedly on, but no one came to the door. Had she got the day wrong? Had he changed his mind? She was just about to ring again when the door was opened gingerly and there stood. . . .

She stared in disbelief. *Could* it be Errol – this cuddly-plump old man, dressed in a white T-shirt and baggy chain-store slacks, with a jowly face and sparse grey hair? Where was the rangy figure? The Jermyn Street suit? The crop of raven hair? Even his eyes had faded; their once Mediterranean blue now a wishy-washy English-summer sky. Quickly trying to hide her shock, she returned his formal handshake. His hand was hot and clammy, when he had always been ice-cool.

'How lovely to see you,' he said, with a gracious smile. At least his voice was the same – the sort of mellow, velvety voice used in brandy commercials, suggesting maturity, high-status and tradition.

'Yes, lovely,' she repeated, distracted by the furnishings as he led her through the house. How could it be so different from the elegant flat she still recalled from the Sixties? – everything in tasteful shades of brown and beige and cream, sophisticated lighting, impressive modern paintings on the walls. Here, the carpet was mauve (*mauve!*), and she was catching glimpses of hideous china ornaments, frilly dolls on frilly chairs, heart-shaped cushions, a table-lamp in the shape of a crinolined lady.

'I thought we'd have drinks in the garden,' he said, ushering her through the French doors in the lounge, on to a small paved patio.

Again, she had to disguise her dismay. Interspersed with tubs of begonias, stood the very worst in kitsch: two simpering cherubs sculpted in fake marble, with mops of tousled curls and cutesy little wings.

'Do sit down,' he urged, courteous as ever. 'What can I get you to drink?'

A triple gin, she bit back. 'What are *you* having?'

'I don't drink,' he said, with another of his smiles. 'So it'll just be fruit juice for me.'

Fruit juice! In those heady days at Bartlett, Grange and Price, they had all been as high as kites – if not on LSD then certainly on hooch. Yes, even decorous Errol had liked his drink – or three. 'Er, fruit juice will be fine.'

'Raspberry and cranberry? Or mango and papaya? And I've also got Brazilian water-melon, and Capri Sun – that's a sort of pineapple, with a tang of coconut. Or there's Berry Blast, which, as it says, is mainly various berries.'

She fought an overpowering urge to laugh. He sounded like a waiter, trying to impress. What about plain, common and garden orange juice? And still she couldn't reconcile herself to the change in his appearance. Of course he wouldn't look the same as when he was in his twenties – any more than she did – but somehow she had never imagined *jowls*, or that dreadful casual T-shirt. She'd been expecting *Saga* man – slim, distinguished, greying at the temples, perfectly attired. 'Raspberry and cranberry, please,' she said, suddenly realizing he was waiting for an answer.

While he went to fetch it, she tried to take in her surroundings. The ugly yellow-brick house was squashed between its neighbours and totally undistinguished. The whole area was basically suburban and thus seemed wrong for Errol, who had once lived in suave Belgravia. The only attractive thing in sight was the cascade of purple wisteria that covered the entire back wall of the house and was magnificently in bloom.

'I love your wisteria,' she said, when he reappeared with the drinks.

He gave a fastidious frown. 'It's actually doing a lot of damage. The branches are fiendishly strong and force their way between the brick and the roof-tiles, and that causes leaks in the roof. The top floor's noticeably damp. But . . .' He shrugged in an almost hopeless fashion, as if the problem were too much for him. Perhaps he'd been ill and couldn't cope. Perhaps he'd inherited the place from a dead parent, and was living here against his will. Perhaps, perhaps, perhaps. She still knew nothing about him.

'Well,' she said, plunging in, 'what's been happening all these years? We've so much to catch up on.'

'Absolutely. But I want to hear about *you*. You were married, weren't you, Nell?'

'Twice.' She gave a casual laugh. It had become second nature now, making thirty wasted years sound little more than a bad-hair day. 'Both mistakes.'

'Oh, dear, I'm really sorry to hear that. And do you have children?'

'Yes, three – two boys and a girl. How about you?'

'No. No children. Absolutely not.' He gave the words such vehemence, he made offspring sound as noxious as crack cocaine. 'And what brought you back to London after all these years?'

She noted the change of subject, remembering from the past how he had preferred the role of questioner to that of questionee. 'Oh, several different things. I got a bit fed up living in the wilds. And then my second marriage broke up. And, worst of all, I had to retire from teaching and I loathed not being busy. So what really clinched it for me was that I was offered a new job running an art department at a private London college. It was just too good to turn down, especially at my advanced age when I thought I was on the scrap heap.'

'Congratulations! That's wonderful.'

'Well, at least it keeps the wolf from the door. And do *you* still work?'

'A little.' The same wary look, and nothing given away, of course. 'Will you excuse me a moment. I'd better check on the dinner.'

'Can I help?'

'No, I wouldn't dream of it. You sit and enjoy the sun.'

The sun was, in fact, too blisteringly hot to enjoy, and seemed to be glaring down on her with almost a sense of spite, as if determined to melt her make-up or tarnish her blonded hair. She moved her chair closer to the wall, in an attempt to find some shade. The smell of the wisteria was mellifluously sweet; the flowers so lushly profuse they formed a purple waterfall flowing down the house. How could anything so pretty be a menace? Perhaps the roof was leaking from some completely different cause. She had never heard of wisteria doing structural damage.

Reluctantly she sipped her juice. It was the colour and consistency of blood, and tasted somehow sour and sweet at once. She shifted in the uncomfortable wicker chair, feeling far too restless to relax. In any case, wasn't it rather selfish to leave Errol to get dinner on his own? Most men, in her experience, were clueless in the kitchen and, whatever he said to the contrary, he would probably appreciate some help.

She walked back through the lounge, surprised to hear the sound of voices. *Voices?* Who was there? She tracked the sound to the kitchen and peered in through the half-open door. An extremely young, extremely pretty Oriental girl – Thai, or Filipino, maybe – was standing at the sink, dishing something up. She looked little more than seventeen, with a mane of long dark glossy hair rippling down her back. Errol must have hired some help for the evening. Filipino agencies were springing up all over the place, offering cleaners, cooks, domestics – at a price, of course.

'I'm sorry,' she said, venturing into the kitchen, 'I was coming to lend a hand, but . . .' Her voice trailed off as Errol took the girl by the arm and steered her away from the sink.

'Nell, meet my wife, Mali.'

'Your . . . your *wife?*' Nell was all but speechless. The age-gap must be fifty years. And in all other respects, the contrast was grotesque. While the girl was barely four-foot-ten and as slender as a flower-stalk, he not only towered above her but looked as if he'd crush her, were he to enfold her in an embrace. And where *he* was grey and faded, *she* was in the bloom of youth and dressed in soft mauve silk, like the radiant wisteria. 'I . . . I'm sorry,' she stuttered. 'I didn't catch your name.'

'Mali,' Errol repeated. 'It means "flower".'

Indeed. Nell herself felt suddenly too large – a stonking great weed overpowering a delicate little blossom – and with too much ageing flesh on display. This child had tiny buds for breasts, modestly covered by her high-necked dress. And her skin glowed from within, not courtesy of Estée Lauder.

'Mali comes from Tak Fah,' Errol said, 'a village near Lopburi.'

'Oh, yes,' Nell said politely, wishing she hadn't failed geography at school. Neither Tak Fah nor Lopburi meant anything at all.

'It's about seventy miles north of Bangkok,' he added, as if he'd read her mind.

She nodded, looking up expectantly in the hope of further details. How had they actually *met?* On holiday? On a business trip? Or had he simply ordered Mali from one of those meretricious Internet sites offering instant Thai brides – young girls like lambs to the slaughter, purchased by randy old men? But, judging by his expression, he was giving nothing else away, and Mali herself had uttered not a single word.

As Nell gazed at the mismatched man and wife, anger and disappointment battled in her head. How could she have been so ludicrously vain as to imagine he might fancy her, when he already had the perfect woman in his house, his bed, his life? But why hadn't he *said*, for heaven's sake, when he had first invited her? 'My wife and I would like you to come to dinner,' would have sounded perfectly reasonable, but there hadn't been the slightest mention of any wife or partner. And wasn't it also rather strange that Mali hadn't come to greet her, either in the hall or in the garden? Was he trying to keep her secret? Perhaps she was just his wife in name, but actually worked as his housekeeper.

Suddenly remembering her manners, she held out her hand to the girl. Ignoring the gesture, Mali placed her palms together and gave a deep submissive bow. Thrown, Nell started to babble: how great it was to meet her; how kind of her to cook dinner; wasn't it blazingly hot this evening; what a pretty dress!

Finally drying up, she was met with total silence. The girl looked worried, almost threatened.

'I'm afraid Mali doesn't speak English,' Errol said. 'I'm endeavouring to learn Thai, but it's one of the most difficult languages for Westerners to master. It's what they call tonal, so that the meaning of a single syllable can be altered in five different ways, according to which of five different tones is used.'

She had no idea what he meant, and was more concerned, in any case, with how wife and husband managed to communicate when neither spoke the other's language.

'Thai script is even more confusing,' Errol went on to explain. 'It's derived from Sanskrit and has forty-four consonants to represent twenty-one consonant sounds, and thirty-two vowels to deal with forty-eight different vowel sounds.'

'Really?' In her present state, she could barely recall what vowels and consonants *were*, let alone grasp the complicated maths involved.

It was a relief when Errol announced that dinner was served, and ushered her into the dining-room. The room was tiny and stifling, with only one small window. Although the sun was shut out by a ruched, beribboned blind, the heat had built up relentlessly, so that the air was now as thick as viscous soup. However, the table had been beautifully laid, with a posy of purple flowers at each place, and purple napkins folded into flower-shapes.

'Mauve is Mali's favourite colour,' Errol remarked, pulling out a chair for her.

Hence the choice of carpet, Nell supposed – the same mauve as in the sitting-room. It seemed odd, though, that he should allow his shy child-bride to dictate the colour scheme, when he himself had such impeccable taste.

'Do let me get you some wine. Would you prefer white or red?'

'Which does Mali like?'

'Mali doesn't drink. In fact, it was she who talked me into giving it up.'

'Oh, I see.' She *didn't* see. Could it be some religious thing? Perhaps Mali was a Muslim and thus abhorred all alcohol. But Thais were largely Buddhist, as far as she could recall. 'I'll have red,' she said defiantly. She just had to have a drink to help her get through this ordeal. What she couldn't understand was why Errol had invited her at all, and how he had described her to his wife: as a ghost from the past, an ex-colleague, or an artist he had once admired? No, none of those – he didn't have the language.

She was grateful when he poured her wine, though she had to restrain herself from gulping it until Mali had rejoined them. Fortunately the girl appeared within a couple of minutes, and carrying a dish of small, round, khaki-coloured things. Nell eyed them anxiously. Was this the Thai equivalent of dinner? There were barely two apiece, and she was absolutely ravenous, having deliberately not eaten lunch, to leave room for a substantial evening meal.

'These are one of Mali's specialities,' Errol explained in his vintage-brandy voice. 'Fishcakes made from cod and shrimp, with a seasoning of ginger and fresh lime leaves. Do help yourself.'

Mali handed her a serving spoon, and stood hovering beside her chair as she did as she was told and took a couple.

Clearly a mistake. When Errol was passed the dish, he restricted himself to one, and the smallest one at that.

'Please start,' he urged, picking up his own fork.

'Isn't Mali going to join us?' she asked, aware that the girl was now standing deferentially between the table and the door, apparently more the servant than the hostess.

'She will in a while. It's the custom in her country for women to look after their men – and any guests, of course. They see that as an honour, not a chore. And Mali in particular likes to be absolutely sure that everything's under control before she sits down herself.'

Nell took his words almost as a rebuke. Wouldn't any man want a wife like that: unselfish and submissive, and putting her own needs last? And wouldn't Western women seem monsters in comparison: self-centred and demanding and out for what they could get? Mali did indeed look the picture of subservience, hands folded, dark eyes watchful, ready to spring to attention should anything be required. Part irritated, part ashamed, Nell forked in her first mouthful, taking the smallest possible bites, so as to spin the fishcakes out and not appear too gluttonous.

Barely had she finished, however, when Mali glided out of the room, returning with two other dishes, which she set down on the table.

'This is what we call *Popia To*,' Errol said, in his role as food interpreter. 'They're like spring rolls, but served with a plum sauce. And the other one is *Tung Tong*. That's minced pork and vegetables, wrapped in filo pastry and deep-fried. But you're probably quite familiar with Thai cuisine. It's become so widespread now.'

'Not in the wilds of Scotland it hasn't! Even our nearest pub was miles away and only served bar snacks.'

'Well, do try these starters. I think you'll find them good.'

Ah, these were simply starters, which meant more food must be forthcoming, so at least she wouldn't starve. None the less, she still felt rather uncomfortable tucking in while Mali waited on her, and Errol, for his part, sat toying with a fragment of spring roll. Had he always had such a delicate appetite? She couldn't remember; didn't recall them actually having a meal together, only drinks, and more drinks.

She opened her mouth to ask Mali where she bought her Thai ingredients, only to realize that the girl wouldn't understand. Her natural inclination was to be friendly, but all the opening gambits that rose spontaneously to her lips – how long have you lived in England? How did you meet Errol? Do you work at all? – had to be rejected on grounds of basic comprehension. And it seemed rude to put such questions to Errol himself, as if she was prying into his private life. Fortunately he came to the rescue, asking if she ever heard from any of the old crowd at BGP.

'No, I lost touch with them all, years and years ago. I can't even remember their names now.'

'Roger Masters,' Errol prompted. 'David Rothenstein. Anne-Marie O'Reilly, Simon Lancaster.'

'Lord, yes! It's all coming back. You must have a marvellous memory.' Had he sent them *all* Christmas cards for the last forty-odd years? And would he invite them all here in turn, to admire his obsequious little bride? 'Simon was quite a goer. I remember he threw a party once, at his place, and he painted the whole place silver just for that one night. Even the food was silver, though God knows how he managed that!'

She was aware that they were excluding Mali, but the girl seemed quite content, preoccupied as she clearly was with the progress of the meal. The minute the plates were empty, she slipped out to the kitchen again, bringing back a heavy tray loaded with an array of food – rice, chicken, prawns, beanshoots and a host of other delicacies.

'Oh, it all looks quite delicious,' Nell exclaimed. 'You shouldn't have gone to so much trouble.' *Damn*, she thought, breaking off, this is double Dutch to her. She smiled instead to express her gratitude and, although the smile felt false and forced, it was instantly returned. Mali had a radiant smile, displaying small white pearly teeth. They would simply have to communicate with constant fatuous grins. At least the story would appeal to Pauline, who would also be secretly pleased, no doubt, that all prospect of romance had been killed stone-cold dead. Pauline never liked her friends to enjoy what was lacking in her own life. But perhaps that was true of everyone except the greatest saints.

Mali hovered by her chair once more, urging her in dumbshow to help herself to the food. Nell wasn't sure of the etiquette. Did she stick to one dish at a time, or take a little of everything. She decided on the latter, which seemed to be correct, since Mali nodded her encouragement and passed more serving spoons. However, when Errol followed suit, his wife suddenly sprang forward and, with what sounded like a curse, snatched the spoon from his hand, transferring most of the food he'd taken from his plate to her own.

Nell recoiled in shock. What on earth had happened to the respectful, servile bride? And how could Errol allow himself to be treated so imperiously? He was staring down at the floor, as if he wished it would swallow him up.

'Mali likes me to watch my weight,' he murmured. 'I'm afraid I'm on a diet at the moment.'

'Oh, dear,' Nell muttered back. Plump he might be, but there was little chance of him gaining any *further* weight on Mali's strict regime. All she had left him to eat was a sliver of chicken, a teaspoonful of rice, and a small green puddle of some vegetable or other. 'Errol, listen,' she said softly, 'could you please persuade Mali to sit down and eat with us? I'd feel a lot more comfortable that way.'

There followed an exchange between husband and wife in what sounded like an extremely alien tongue. The upshot was that Mali *did* sit down, but only with undisguised reluctance.

'Well, *bon appetit!*' Nell said, in an attempt to lighten the atmosphere.

'*Bon appetit!*' Errol rejoined, though he made no attempt to eat, perhaps fearing another outburst should he dare to swallow a mouthful. And indeed Mali was still fixated on his plate, as if defying him to take another morsel, and showing not the slightest interest in sampling the food herself.

Nell looked from one to the other. With her loaded plate and brimming glass, she was obviously Ms Greedy-Guts, flanked by two ascetics. She loathed drinking on her own, and the two tumblersful of mineral water seemed to cast reproachful glances at her wineglass. 'Do *you* cook, Errol?' she asked, trying to distract attention from herself.

'No, Mali prefers me to keep out of the kitchen. It's *her* domain.'

And so is the whole house, Nell thought, eyeing a second crop of hideous china ornaments displayed on top of the sideboard. However much Errol might have changed, no way would he have bought such things himself. Yet it still seemed quite extraordinary that he should have allowed this girl such power. Buying and furnishing a house was surely a *joint* endeavour and, though it might involve some compromise, a total climb-down by one partner was odd in the extreme. But perhaps in Errol's case, it was part of some unspoken pact. In return for beauty, youth and servility, he ceded his young bride this unattractive suburban house, complete with hideous mauve carpets, schmaltzy china dogs, ersatz marble cherubs and hazardous wisteria. 'This chicken's really tasty,' she remarked, suddenly aware that she'd been lost in her own thoughts.

'Yes,' said Errol, putting down his tumbler. 'It's cooked with lemongrass and coconut milk, so the flavours are very delicate. And Thai cuisine is extremely healthy – low-fat, high-fibre, lots of fruit and vegetables – all the things the medicos advise.'

'So couldn't you get away with eating a bit more?' she asked, glancing at his meagre rations.

'No, no.' Frowning deeply, he raised his hand, as if to silence her. 'It's a bit of a tricky issue between us.'

Hurt, she lapsed back into silence. In any case, every word she addressed to Errol seemed to shut out Mali. However, the girl was staking her claim to him in other, less direct ways. Her eyes, in fact, never left his face, watching his every mouthful like a controlling mother or restrictive dietician. How could he submit to such surveillance? Lacking any answer, Nell took refuge in her wine again. Errol had already refilled it, so she was probably drinking too fast. But what the hell. . . .

'More rice?' asked Errol, offering her the dish.

'Yes, please.' She helped herself, then, half in jest, placed a little on his plate as well.

'*Mai tum!*' Mali barked, immediately leaning across to remove the offending rice.

Nell flushed. Was this frail but steely girl trying to kill her husband by means of slow starvation? Indeed, both host and hostess appeared to be indulging in some religious fast. Mali had eaten almost nothing and Errol had chopped his scrap of chicken into even smaller shreds, which he was now pushing round his plate. Well, there was nothing for it – if this appetizing spread was not to end up in the waste-bin, she had better eat for all three of them.

With a determined smile, she reached out for the beanshoots, only to knock her wineglass over in the process. She watched in horror as a dark red stain spread into the cloth, and wine began dripping on to the carpet.

Mali leapt to her feet with an anxious cry and rushed out of the room, returning with a floor cloth and a bucket, while Errol used a wad of paper napkins to mop up the mess on the table.

'I'm sorry,' Nell kept repeating. 'I'm really terribly sorry. It was just a stupid accident. Look, let me help. If you can find another cloth, I'll give Mali a hand with the carpet.'

'No, *please*,' Errol murmured, obviously embarrassed beyond measure, 'she'd rather do it herself.' He lowered his voice still further. 'Don't worry, Nell. It's just that Mali's very house-proud. In fact, it was she who chose this house. She fell in love with the wisteria.'

'Wisteria,' Mali repeated in heavily accented English, as she continued to scour the carpet.

'It's the only word she knows. No, that's not quite true. She knows "diet", too.'

Was Errol joking, Nell wondered? He looked anything but jocular, as he cast anguished glances at his wife, who was still rubbing at the wine-stain.

'I do hope I haven't done any permanent damage,' she said, following his gaze. At least the carpet wasn't pristine white, unlike the tablecloth. Red on purple couldn't show that much. Anyway, it was surely the height of bad manners to make one's guests feel guilty and ashamed.

'Of course not.' Errol said. Then, still seeking to reassure her, he made a deliberate effort to relax back in his chair, and returned to the innocuous subject of the house. 'When we first bought this place, there was wisteria all over the front, as well, but the surveyor advised us to get rid of it because it was forcing the tiles apart. In fact, he thought we ought to remove the whole damn lot, back and front, but Mali wouldn't hear of it.'

'Wisteria,' Mali said again, obviously picking up on the conversation.

Nell had a sudden uneasy feeling that perhaps she understood far more than she let on. Maybe she *did* speak English but, for some unfathomable reason, preferred to pretend she didn't. She cast a surreptitious glance at the girl, who had got up from her knees, at last, apparently satisfied with her labours on the carpet. But there was still no hope of continuing the meal, as next she turned her attention to the table, clearing everything off it on to the sideboard, in order to remove the dirty cloth. Then, extracting a clean one from the bottom sideboard drawer, she elaborately relaid the table, refusing all offers of help. Nell felt more and more uncomfortable as she witnessed the whole palaver, and Errol, too, seemed equally on edge. Just at that moment the phone rang, shrilling through the silence. 'Do excuse me,' he said, getting up to answer it.

Nell longed to trot out after him, simply to avoid being left alone with Mali, who was now sitting at the table again. The girl was smiling at her, but the smile seemed totally bogus: just a charming façade disguising what she *really* felt: that her English guest was clumsy, careless, greedy and uncouth. So, when Mali offered her more food, she resolutely declined. Not only were the dishes tepid and congealing, she had lost her former appetite and frankly longed to be back home, sprawled in front of the television and nursing a double gin. Her wine, she noted with annoyance, had not been replaced. Indeed, both glass and bottle had mysteriously disappeared, as if she were not to be trusted with another drop of alcohol. So there was no chance now of getting slightly tiddly and surviving the evening in a pleasantly boozy haze.

With nothing to eat or drink, and no way to converse, the silence seemed to gape and stretch, and she began to feel disturbingly cut off, as if marooned on a desert island with no kindly passing ships. And the island was a torrid one, with equatorial temperatures. Her hands were clammy, her face was flushed, and beads of perspiration began snailing down her back. Yet while she sat sweltering in the heat, Mali looked as cool and fresh as a flower.

The girl suddenly got up, though – perhaps to fetch her husband, or to find out who had phoned. But no, she was back in seconds, with a large white padded photograph-album clasped against her chest. 'Our Wedding' was written on the front, tooled into the leather in gold italic script. Laying it on the table, she opened it with an air of pride, to reveal several dozen pictures of her and Errol as exotic bride and groom. And *recent* pictures, clearly. This groom was plump and grey, not the slim Adonis Nell had known at BGP. She stared in shock at his wedding outfit: baggy white pyjamas, with a wide purple sash looped from shoulder to waist, and a purple flower-wreath dangling round his neck. In her mind, she added the rolled umbrella she remembered from the sixties, the monogrammed black leather briefcase and highly polished black calfskin shoes. The resultant image was so absurd, it was all she could do not to laugh.

Quickly she shifted her gaze to the bride, who was arrayed in a mauve silk gown, with a flower-wreath identical to Errol's, and more luxuriant purple flowers pinned to her dark hair. She was smiling almost triumphantly, whereas *he* looked, frankly, diffident. In fact, in almost every picture, his expression hardly varied from wary to resigned. Had he simply felt self-conscious about being photographed, or could he have actually married against his will? Perhaps he'd got Mali pregnant and been forced to do the decent thing. No – her figure was so girlishly slim, that was out of the question. Unless she'd already had the baby, but given it up for adoption, or left it with her mother, or. . . .

As she leafed on through the album, her natural curiosity began to clash with a deep unease. Other people's wedding photos were invariably distressing – the hopes and expectations that, given time, would doubtless crumble to dust; the vast amount of labour and expense poured out for just one illusory day.

Mali, however, seemed totally absorbed, now pointing out the pictures of the wedding guests: a bevy of mainly females, of assorted ages and shapes, but all with the same dark eyes and hair. Since no commentary was possible, Nell was left to wonder who they were – girlfriends, sisters, workmates, aunts? And the location of the wedding was equally unclear: somewhere oriental – that was obvious from the backgrounds – but was it Mali's village or a garden in Bangkok?

Nell swung round at a sudden exclamation from behind her. Errol was standing in the doorway, looking anything but pleased.

'For goodness' sake,' he said, the silken voice now steely. 'You don't want to see all those.'

'No, actually I'm interested. Is this Mali's family?'

'Yes, she comes from a very large one.' He gave a brief but disconcerting laugh. 'They say when you marry a Thai girl, you marry her whole tribe as well.'

'But surely you can't see them very often – not if they're so far away.'

'It's not a question of *seeing* them,' he muttered enigmatically, shutting the album firmly and putting it out of reach.

What on earth did he mean? Was he supporting them financially: sending regular handouts to Mali's elderly parents, or to idle siblings, venial hangers-on? And why was there no sign of *his* family in any of the photographs? And – most intriguing of all – how had he met Mali in the first place? But his grim expression precluded any questions. He seemed as taut as a guitar string, which, if plucked, might give off a discordant wail. And his wife was palpably angry with him for removing the precious photographs. With an indecipherable outburst, she stalked over to the sideboard, picked up the album and marched out of the room.

The snick of the closing door appeared to remind Errol of his manners. 'I'm so sorry about the phone-call,' he confided, returning to his chair and to usual courteous tone. 'It was my elder brother ringing, with news about his hip-replacement, so I couldn't cut him short. But let's finish dinner, shall we?'

'I couldn't eat another morsel, honestly.'

'But Mali's prepared dessert.'

'Oh, dear, I'm really sorry, but . . .' Her voice tailed off. Mali had just come in again and the unspoken tension between man and wife hung in the air like a mushroom cloud. Anyway, she just couldn't face a third course – ploughing through more delicacies while the other two ate nothing. In fact, she was feeling so demoralized she just *had* to make her escape, even at the expense of being seriously rude. 'Gosh! Is that the time?' she said with mock surprise, making an elaborate pretence of checking her watch. 'I'm terribly sorry to have to rush off, but I promised my friend Pauline I'd pop in to see her tonight. She's extremely unwell . . . lives alone . . . no one to look after her . . . may be worse by now . . .' The lies kept coming, coming, yet she couldn't seem to stop, desperate to excuse herself without causing deep offence. 'It was so kind of you to invite me . . . enjoyed myself immensely . . . just hadn't realized how late it . . . daren't leave my friend any longer . . . do hope you understand. . . .'

As the words dried up, at last, she was aware of their futility. Mali *couldn't* understand, and Errol probably didn't. Yet her overwhelming impulse was to leave this house – and fast. 'Forgive me, Errol,' she implored. 'And could you please explain to your wife.'

Errol said a word or two in Thai. On hearing Mali's shrill response, Nell felt still more guilt-stricken. The girl had every reason to be hurt – it was both cavalier and boorish to leave before the end of the meal, and Mali had obviously taken trouble preparing the desserts. Yet, cavalier or no, she felt driven by a sense of almost panic, which, even now, was propelling her to her feet and steering her out of the room.

Errol, darting in pursuit, caught up with her in the hall. 'Are you sure I can't persuade you to stay?'

She shook her head. 'No, really.'

'But there's so much we haven't talked about. I wanted to hear about your children – how old they are, what they're doing – and how you're enjoying your new job, and whether you're still painting or. . . .'

'Errol,' she said tersely, 'I *have* to go. OK?' Deliberately she restrained herself from elaborating further. More excuses and untruths would only make things worse, and he was looking pretty gutted as it was.

Reluctantly he opened the front door and, as she made her hasty exit, she was surprised to see that it wasn't dark at all. The dining-room had been so gloomy, she assumed that night had fallen, but she was stepping into a balmy mid-June evening, still gilded by the last rays of the sun. Had she over-reacted? Everything out here seemed so innocent, so peaceful: serene blue sky, gold-tinged clouds, white froth of fragile orange blossom perfuming the air.

As she turned to say a less incoherent goodbye, Errol suddenly lunged forward and gripped her by the arm, as if to claw her back by force into the house. '*Nell!*' he breathed, gazing at her intently.

She was startled by the gesture and by his urgent, tremulous tone. This was the first time he had touched her, or looked directly into her eyes. And *his* eyes seemed to plead with her, expressing extremes of emotion she had never seen before. 'What?' she said. 'What is it?'

But, in place of a reply, he took a slip of paper from his pocket and slid it into her palm, closing her fingers round it, with an almost furtive air. Then, without another word, he stepped back into the house and closed the door.

She stood, bewildered, on the path, clutching the piece of paper. Whatever could it be? Some sort of invitation to meet up with him again? All at once, Pauline's words re-echoed in her head: 'Maybe he's always fancied you, but was just too shy to say.' Could this be an intimate note, entrusting onto paper what he couldn't verbalize? But how on earth would she respond, now that he had Mali in his life?

Still speculating, she unfolded the note. Just five words were written on it, in hasty, sprawling capitals: HELP – PLEASE HELP ME, NELL!

Deeply shaken, she began to walk away – *away* from the closed door, *away* from the urgent plea; back to home and safety. Yet after only a dozen yards, her steps slackened to a stop. Wasn't she being callous – ignoring someone from the past who was now in desperate straits? If she had any shred of feeling for him, she really ought to go back. He might be watching from a window, signalling to her, even; desperate for some response.

But, as she turned to look at the house, shoots of baneful wisteria began spiralling up the walls, snaking round and round; the intransigent, tenacious stems seeking a firm claw-hold in the brick. The plant was growing before her eyes, writhing and twining as it laid siege to the building, throttling the inhabitants, obstructing all the light, suffocating, choking, hideously determined.

Then, suddenly, explosively, it erupted into flower; long toxic purple tassels swooping down to engulf the doors and windows; their subtle, honeyed fragrance intensifying to a noxious reek. And, as she watched, the tiny yellow open eye at the base of each mauve floret fixed her with a virulent stare, as if to say 'Keep Out! Keep Off!'

She broke into a run, racing back along the street and on towards the tube. If she didn't escape, she, too, would be smothered. Already she could feel the tendrils coiling round her heart and lungs, tightening their insidious grip, preventing her from breathing, strangling her and stifling her. 'I'm sorry, Errol,' she cried aloud, all but tripping in her haste. 'I can't help. I can't. I *can't!*'

She knew her limitations.

Purple was too perilous.

7

MATTHEW, MARK, LUKE AND

Matthew, Mark, Luke and John
Bless this bed I lie upon.
Four white angels round my bed;
Two at the foot and two at the head. . . .

'Amen,' she said, as always, closing her eyes to picture her four friends. Matthew first, of course, although the fact he'd been a tax collector made her invariably uneasy. Her own father had been jailed for some shady business never quite made clear, but whatever the disreputable details, strict St Matthew would have cracked down on him hard. Matthew had also been a martyr, so he would have little patience with her petty aches and ailments. She imagined him shrugging off savage sword-blows and agonizing spear-thrusts as if they were mere midge-bites, and continuing to write his Gospel even in the process of expiring.

'Goodnight, St Matthew,' she said a little nervously. 'And please remember, whatever Father may have done, *I* always paid my taxes.'

She turned over on her other side, so she could see her dear St Mark. He had also been martyred, but she liked to think he'd made a bit more fuss about it, maybe even groaned aloud when subjected to extremes of torture. In her *Book of Saints* he was described as 'stump-fingered' – a phrase that left her baffled, though she suspected that he suffered from arthritis. Her own fingers weren't exactly stumps, but they were extremely stiff and swollen, which made it very difficult to write. She could barely scribble a few words on a postcard, let alone transcribe a full-blown Gospel. Yet Mark had managed somehow, and that always gave her comfort.

'Goodnight, St Mark,' she whispered. 'Keep exercising your hands. It won't cure the arthritis, but it does help to keep them flexible.'

She half sat up, so she could peer down at the end of the bed, where Saints Luke and John took up their respective posts. Luke had always been her favourite, right from early childhood when, every night without exception, her mother had tucked her into bed, reciting the consoling verse just before the goodnight kiss. Of course, as a tiny child, she hadn't known the word 'Evangelist', but she *had* grasped the basic concept of Heavenly Protectors, who would stay with her all night, save her from lying frightened in the dark. Even in those far-off days, she spent much time awake, worrying about her absent father; haunted by the prospect of her mother disappearing, too, behind some prison wall. So it had seemed only natural to confide in her four Guardians – a habit she'd continued through her troubled teens, her shell-shocked twenties, and on through all the decades until now, at eighty-seven, it was simply part of her routine. Not that she had ever told a soul. People would regard her as seriously disturbed, if not downright deranged, if she admitted that she talked out loud to four imaginary saints.

Though 'imaginary' was an ambiguous word. Matthew, Mark, Luke and John seemed actually more substantial than the few flesh-and-blood people still remaining in her life. Family members had always been distressingly scarce, and as for darling Desmond, all she had left of him was her engagement ring, a photograph and his posthumous award for gallantry. After his horrific death, St Luke had been her only comfort. Friends had proved quite useless, either saying the wrong thing, or avoiding the subject altogether in the hope that it might go away. But Luke had seemed to comprehend that she, too, felt annihilated, when her fiancé's ship was torpedoed in the North Atlantic, and that part of *her* had perished in that barbarous explosion; been incinerated, wrecked, expunged.

If Luke and Desmond had met in ordinary life, they would have hit if off immediately, she felt. As the patron saint of both doctors and artists, Luke must have been a most accomplished man. In all her life, she had never met an artist who also practised as a doctor, or a medical man who painted. Most doctors, in her experience, were far too busy to mess around with paints. In fact, her own GP, the steely Dr Cunningham, was usually too busy even to say 'Good morning.' When you entered his consulting room, he'd be staring at the computer screen, probably trying to remember who you were.

'Goodnight, St Luke,' she murmured. 'Don't work too hard. If you're called out in the early hours, then try to catch up on your sleep at the weekend.'

Now there was just John to come and, since she had seen his picture in so many leading galleries, he was the easiest to visualize. Of course, all four of the Evangelists featured in religious art, but John was depicted more often than the others, on account of the fact that he'd been closest to Christ, both through kinship and emotionally. Domenichino, in particular, had painted him a score of times, and she especially liked the version in the Brera, which showed the saint in a state of almost ecstasy, kneeling before the Madonna, pen in hand. Those days seemed like a mirage now, when, spry and able-bodied, she had been on art tours with friends now mostly dead: Christmas in St Petersburg, Easter in Vienna, August touring France and Spain, weekends devoted solely to the Louvre or the Uffizi. . . .

'*Concentrate*,' she urged herself, anxious because St John remained a blank. He simply wasn't coming into focus, despite the fact she knew his face so well: the mobile, sensitive mouth, the compassionate brown eyes, the wide intellectual brow. She felt a certain bond with John, since her own personal way of coping with life's burdens was to keep determinedly busy, and he, too, was a workaholic, with endless calls on his time. As patron of writers, on the one hand, and theologians, on the other, and all who worked in book production thrown in for good measure, he must be besieged with requests from every corner of the globe, at all hours of the day and night. Yet he never failed to keep his vigil by her bed and, having done so uncomplainingly for the best part of a century, it seemed all the more upsetting that he should abandon her tonight. But he *wasn't* there – she knew it. Even in the dark, she could tell who was present, who not. On three sides she was guarded, safe from nightmares and night terrors, but the fourth side remained a vacuum, precarious, exposed.

Even his symbol was missing – the haughty eagle that normally hovered just above his head, representing his soaring inspiration. In truth, she had always found the eagle somewhat inappropriate.

Wouldn't a peaceful, gentle dove have been eminently more suitable for peaceful, gentle John than a cruel bird of prey with bloodstained talons and murderous beak? Even when the eagle wore a halo, as he did in several of the paintings (and also in her bedroom), it seemed little more convincing than if Attila the Hun had been depicted with an olive branch. The other Evangelists' symbols were less incongruous. Mark's lion looked positively amiable in Tintoretto's version – a smiling vegetarian rather than a snarling carnivore, and complete with a pair of rather fetching wings. And she'd seen Luke's ox depicted as a sweet, obliging creature contentedly chewing the cud. Even so, the symbols left her cold. It was the men themselves she warmed to: their solidity, their decency, their combination of kindness and strict principles – so different from her father, who'd been convicted for domestic violence as well as for embezzlement. And, of the four, John was the most reliable, which made it all the more distressing that he wasn't actually here.

Well, there was nothing for it – she would have to take a sleeping pill. Sleep was elusive enough in the ordinary way, let alone without her fourth custodian. She fumbled for the light switch and snapped it on, blinking in the glare, then reached for the tiny pill-bottle she kept in the bedside drawer. Unscrewing the obstinate cap, she sent up a prayer to the God Who Rarely Heard. 'Saint John, come back. I need you.'

The following night she went to bed much earlier. The day had dragged interminably, mainly because she detested being useless. After compulsory retirement, at least she'd had her voluntary work and, when that dried up, she still continued to keep busy, knitting blankets for orphans in Romania and making greetings cards to sell for the Red Cross. But, year by year, arthritis had put paid to all her hobbies and, in the last twelve months, she hadn't raised a single penny for a single charity. In fact it was just a question nowadays of getting through the empty hours without having to ask anyone for help. She dreaded the thought of being a burden or – worse – landing in a Care Home. Which is why she never breathed a word about her nightly ritual with Matthew, Mark and co. Give anyone the slightest suspicion that you were a candidate for Alzheimer's, and they'd cage you up in Belvedere or Holly Bank – innocuous sounding places that were really only prisons in disguise.

Once she'd cleaned her teeth and had a shower – baths were nigh impossible, since she could get neither in nor out – she buttoned up her nightdress and sat resting on the bed a moment. Surprising how the simplest things had become peculiarly exhausting. A shower was like a marathon run, and even climbing the stairs to bed required courage, perseverance. But finally she was ready – alarm clock wound, glass of water poured, Desmond's photo tucked beneath her pillow – so she clambered into bed, pulled the blankets over her and switched off the bedside lamp.

'Matthew, Mark, Luke and John,' she recited in a whisper, as soon as her eyes had adjusted to the dark.

Matthew appeared with his usual brisk efficiency, and Mark followed close behind, taking up their positions on either side of the headboard. But Luke – where was steadfast Luke? Nervously she fixed her whole attention on his persona, calling up his attributes: the physician's skills, the artist's flair, his empathy with the bereaved. No use. He failed to emerge, as did his trusty ox – no farm-yard smells, no sound of gentle lowing. And John was absent, too, still. Frantically summoning him once more, she was met with heavy silence, closing in around her like clammy autumnal fog. And with neither Luke nor John there, the entire foot of the bed was unprotected territory. Spectres might slip in – shades of her dead father, not to mention all the bogeymen left over from her childhood.

Her heart was beating worryingly fast, yet she dared not resort to sleeping pills again. She had only a couple left, and heartless Dr Cunningham refused to renew her prescription. 'Those tablets lower your blood pressure, which is already very low. You might suffer a fall, and *then* what?'

What indeed? There was certainly no one around to pick her up from the floor. So she decided, on reflection, to spend the night read-ing, which, if nothing else, would distract her from her fears. Fortunately she had some books to hand. She had learned long ago, when the sharp claws of arthritis began gripping tighter, tighter, to keep everything within easy reach.

Turning on the light, she reached for *The Return of Sherlock Holmes*. Holmes was nothing like as powerful as the Evangelists, but he did help to pass the time. And she had always had a soft spot for Conan Doyle himself, who had trained and worked as a doctor before finding his true calling. In fact, she often wished she could have joined his practice instead of Dr Cunningham's. She was sure he'd be more generous in dishing out the Mogadon, since he suffered from insomnia himself. Another thing they had in common was the loss of someone precious in a war. (Doyle's son had died from influenza, but only because he was already severely weakened from wounds incurred on the Somme.) And the great man believed in spiritualism and fairies, so he certainly wouldn't scoff at her parleys with the Evangelists.

Thursday night was wet. The rain beating on the bedroom window reminded her that winter must have risen from its lair and be striding on its inexorable way towards the dead end of the year, threatening her with chilblains and burst pipes. The fiery blaze of October had already dulled and faded, and every evening now was punctuated by the cruel ack-ack of fireworks. These days, Guy Fawkes seemed to last a fortnight and get noisier each year. And, like Christmas, it was a bad time to be childless. Guys and bonfires, along with Christmas trees, Christmas stockings and Santa Claus himself, had meaning only for families, not for spinsters living on their own.

Still, self-pity was despicable, and she must simply trust that Luke and John would be back on duty, along with their confrères. So, having ensured that all the windows were shut, and found an extra blanket, she lay in the dark, quietly intoning her mantra.

'Matthew, Mark, Luke and John, bless this bed I lie upon. . . .'

Matthew bodied forth, thank God, but her relief in his obedient presence was ominously short-lived. However much she might implore, Mark refused to join him, as did the stubborn lion. And since Luke and John continued to absent themselves, Matthew remained obstinately alone, guarding one small corner of the bed, with all the rest open to malaise. She lay in terror, listening to the death throes of Desmond's valiant crew, and then the glug-glug of the gloating waves feasting on their corpses.

No night had ever seemed so long and, when she finally rose to a grey, reluctant dawn, she actually felt ill from lack of sleep. Yet, haunted by what might lie in store, she vowed not to go to bed at all tonight. If the pattern of the last three nights repeated itself, then Matthew, too, would fail to keep his tryst, leaving her totally unprotected for the first time in her life. The thought was so alarming, she was tempted to ring the health visitor, or Mrs Mills next door, just to hear another human voice. But the health visitor would fob her off with a leaflet about pneumonia jabs, and Mrs Mills had her hands full with three children under five. Best not to make a fuss. If she settled down with a jigsaw puzzle, that would keep her busy, especially the fiendishly difficult one she'd avoided up to now, in which almost all the pieces were the same confusing blue: blue sea, blue sky, blue-shadowed hills, misty blue horizon. Jigsaws and arthritis didn't go too well together. You needed deft and flexible fingers to fit the fiddly pieces together, whereas hers were more like spatulas and refused to bend at the joints. But at least time was not a problem – all day stretched before her, followed by all night – and if she kept her mind on summer blue, it might block out winter's black and toothless grin.

By seven the following morning, she had completed much of the sea and sky, and was working on the hills. Her back ached, her fingers throbbed, but she refused to call a halt. As she'd feared, Matthew had kept his distance, not appearing for a single minute during the long and painful night, but she had no desire to dwell on the fact. She was simply waiting for the dawn to break, which always made things easier.

Yet, as the minutes ticked on – and on, and on – there still was not the faintest lightening in the sky. Normally at this time, the black paled to dusky charcoal, then to gunmetal grey and finally to pearly-white or tremulous jigsaw-blue. She had watched the sequence so often, it seemed distinctly worrying that it wasn't happening now. She pulled the curtains further back and peered out at the garden. The darkness was completely solid, like the blackout in the war. And there were no other signs of morning – no blackbird's trill or robin's tweet, no comforting clash of bottles, or chuntering of the milkman's float. Could her watch be wrong? It said 7.55, which meant it should most definitely be light.

Abandoning her puzzle, she struggled up the stairs to check the bedroom clock, which was radio-controlled and thus utterly reliable. Halfway up, she paused to catch her breath. The stairs seemed steeper every time she climbed them, but at last she reached the top. Before switching on the light, she stood nervous at the bedroom door, conscious of the still impenetrable darkness. The curtains were undrawn, and black-cat night pressed its dense, unlucky fur against the windowpane. Yet the clock on the bedside table said one minute to eight. It was surely inconceivable that both her watch and *this* clock would have gone wrong simultaneously. Unless it was 7.55 in the *evening*. But how could she have lost a day? Days weren't like keys or spectacles, which you could put down and mislay. And anyway she had been working on the jigsaw for the last twenty-hours, with all her wits about her, and wretchedly aware of each leaden, crawling minute.

Again she went to the window and stood gazing out, desperate for some sign of dawn: glints of sunlight, streaks of pink, the flapping of a pigeon's wings as it stirred from its night-roost. She knew it must be morning, yet everything was conspiring to convince her it was night – both the silence and the darkness unrelenting, absolute. It was like being trapped in solitary confinement, in a small and unlit cell, while the rest of the world continued with its normal life: washing, dressing, making breakfast, setting off to work. Between that busy world and *her* world reared a prison wall of darkness, confining and entombing her.

Gripped by mounting terror, she stretched out on the bed. Surely in this extremity the Evangelists would come. In all the years she had called on them, her need had never been so great. 'Matthew, Mark, Luke and John,' she entreated, repeating their names again, again, as if that would somehow rouse them.

No response. No action. No one there at all. She lay staring at the still uncurtained windows, *willing* dawn to break. The sun must rise, it *must* do; it always had for eighty-seven years.

Minutes limped and stumbled past with excruciating slowness, but the darkness only deepened, along with her sense of panic. She was only a speck, a pinprick, in the great mysterious scheme of things, with no control whatever over dawn or day or light. Yet her four Advocates had power. In their lifetimes they had been hailed as wonder-workers who could calm storms, heal the sick. And it wasn't even a miracle she needed – just break of blessèd day.

Summoning up the last dregs of her strength, she called on her friends once more. 'Matthew, Mark, Luke and . . .' It was difficult to speak now, the words guttering in her throat.

But, suddenly, an answering voice took over from her faltering tone – her mother's voice, as melodious and comforting as it had been in her childhood. She lay back in delight, transported to those

early years when her mother bent to kiss her – the scent of laven-
der and caraway cake; the caress of the verse itself.

> Matthew, Mark, Luke and John,
> Bless this bed I lie upon.
> Four white angels round my bed;
> Two at the foot and two at the head. . . .

'Amen', she struggled to respond, reaching out to grip the strong,
safe hand. But her mother's voice continued, adding two more lines
she had never heard before:

> One to watch, and one to pray,
> And two to bear my soul away.

With a shuddering sigh, she closed her eyes. *Now* she understood
– dawn would never break for her, morning never come. But her
Guardians had returned, at last; two stepping forward to claim her
soul, escort it through the long eternal night.

'Amen,' she whispered, her body sinking down, down, down to
nothingness, decay.

'Amen.'

'Amen.'

'Amen.'

8

NOT IN YOUR SIZE, MADAM

'I'm sorry, Madam,' the salesgirl said, with a pitying look. 'We don't stock them in size ten.'

Robin stored the look in the cupboard of her mind, along with the tasteless jokes, the sniggers, even the occasional snort of contemptuous disbelief. 'Well, could you get them for me?' she asked, 'on special order?'

'No, I'm afraid they're not made bigger than a seven. We *do* have the seven in stock, though, if you'd like to see it.'

No,' she said abruptly. How did this brainless girl think she'd fit into a seven? By amputating her toes?

Wearily she left the shop and continued along Oxford Street. At least shoe-shops were plentiful here – though all horrendously crowded on a Saturday. In fact, the next one she tried, with a 'Summer Madness Sale' in full swing, required courage to join the fray. Aggressive music was pounding at full volume, and the customers seemed equally belligerent as they jostled each other in the hope of finding bargains. All the sale shoes had been put out on display in a series of special racks, clearly labelled by size: three and a half to seven. Nothing *her* size, of course, so she sank down on a chair, waiting until an assistant was free to serve her, and trying, as always, to tuck her feet out of sight. She passed the time by watching normal women with normal feet riffling through the racks, blithely unaware of how fortunate they were – indeed considering it their natural right to have a choice of colours and styles.

At last, a salesgirl approached, a redhead with a perfect complexion, marred only by her sullen expression.

'I need some shoes for my wedding,' Robin said, lowering her voice, as if she were in the confessional. 'White, size ten.'

'I'm sorry, can you speak up.'

She began again, louder, uncomfortably aware of the couple sitting beside her, who couldn't fail to hear. 'I need some wedding shoes. Size ten.'

'*Ten?*' The tone expressed alarm this time. Women with big feet were dangerous now, as well as simply grotesque.

'Yes,' she repeated. 'Ten.'

The couple were listening with interest. Welcome to the freak-show, Robin thought, aware that she was blushing. Well, at least she hadn't burst into tears, as she used to as a child. Yes, the problem had started early. At age nine, she was wearing sevens; at twelve, she had reached her present size, which brought malicious gibes from her schoolmates.

The salesgirl gave a shrug. 'We don't do ladies' shoes in that size. You'd need to try the men's department.'

Men's shoes for her wedding? 'They're not likely to have white, are they?'

'Well, they might have slip-ons, seeing that it's summer. And they'd certainly have trainers.'

Trainers she had plenty of, but they would hardly go with a lace and satin wedding dress. 'I was actually hoping for a court shoe, with a reasonably high heel.'

'You won't find *that* in a ten. Unless you have it specially made. There are places that do made-to-measure.'

If you've got £500 to spare, Robin refrained from saying. The dress alone had put a considerable strain on her finances, and several more expenses were looming on the near horizon. She couldn't expect Stephen to shell out for any more. He was already paying for the reception *and* the honeymoon. What she needed was a father – a generous, solvent Daddy who would defray the cost of the whole affair, in return for the privilege of leading her up the aisle. But all her father had bequeathed her (before vanishing into the aether) was the gene for oversized feet. 'I'm afraid I can't afford that sort of thing. Is there another ordinary shop I could try?'

The girl looked dubious. 'Well, there's a new place opposite Debenhams. They might have something, but . . .' Her voice tailed away, as if it had reached the end of the line.

'Thanks,' said Robin, standing up. Her feet were healthy and functional, with well-formed arches and straight, unbunioned toes. On a man they'd be admired, whereas for a female they were a source of deepest shame. Large feet were inherently unfeminine, as well as totally unsexy. She even tried to hide them from Stephen – not exactly easy when they were about to be man and wife.

Once out in the street, she squeezed her way between hordes of shoppers; dodging pushchairs, parcels and hazardous umbrellas. August it might be, but it was raining with freakish glee – size ten rain drenching her light sweater.

She found the shop: a boutique called Shoe Box, which looked anything but promising. In the window were tiny, dainty shoes, arranged on silken cushions, with – worryingly – no price tags. She went in, none the less. The wedding was just two weeks away, and she was becoming increasingly anxious about her lack of suitable footwear.

She stood nervously in the doorway, taking in her surroundings: plush purple carpet, embossed gold and purple wallpaper and ornate gold display-tables. All the assistants were male, and dressed to reflect the colour scheme, in striped gold and purple shirts, with matching purple ties. The one gliding up to serve her was a frail and willowy creature, whose own feet were so mincingly small, they looked as if they'd been bound since birth.

'Can I help you, madam?'

She repeated her request. The man did little more than raise an eyebrow, but the gesture was enough to make her feet grow larger still – each now the size of an ocean liner, confronted with a delicate Tom Thumb.

'No, absolutely not, madam.' Tom Thumb shook his head vigorously, as if to emphasize the absurdity of such unconscionably large feet. 'There's nothing in the shop above an eight.'

Well, eight was an advance on seven. But why should either be the cut-off point? If you were unlucky enough to wear eight and a half, were you automatically banished to some limbo for monsters and misfits? 'So what are people with big feet meant to *do*?'

'I'm sorry, madam, I wouldn't know.' He looked offended, as if she had asked him something indiscreet, such as the details of his sex-life.

Another salesman had stopped to listen. He, too, was small and graceful. Perhaps all the staff who worked here were selected for their elfin feet. 'Have you tried the big department stores?' he asked.

'Most of them, I think.' London was unknown territory, and the array of shops she had visited so far was already blurring in her mind. She tried to tick off the names in her head: John Lewis, House of Fraser, Marks and Spencer, Debenhams – none of them with a single shoe larger than an eight. She had only come up here in the first place because Karen had assured her it was a veritable Mecca for shopping. Yet she might as well have saved her fare.

'Including Selfridges?'

'Er, no,' she said uncertainly.

'Well, their shoe department's huge, so you might find what you're looking for. And it's just a hundred yards from here.'

'Thanks,' she said, rallying her strength to face the crowds again. Living in a tiny village left you totally unprepared for the sheer press and crush of bodies; the sense of being a dowdy provincial amidst a sea of streetwise trend-setters. Karen had offered to come with her, relishing the prospect of a London shopping spree. But 'spree' was not the appropriate word when it came to buying shoes. Besides, she balked at the idea of even a close friend witnessing her humiliation. Karen wore size three.

Just outside the Shoe Box, a stretch of pavement had been cordoned off for repair. Robin zigzagged through the remaining narrow walkway, in an attempt to avoid the puddles. It was a relief to reach Selfridges, if only to be in the dry. Taking the escalator to the second floor, she was greeted by canned music so jaunty and self-satisfied, it seemed to be blowing a fanfare to the shoe department itself, which was ostentatiously stylish, with trendy decor, dramatic lighting and snooty-looking sales assistants.

She dithered for a moment, feeling overwhelmed by the sense of wealth and privilege. The department comprised a dozen or more mini-boutiques, all with designer names: Yves St Laurent, Prada, Dior, Dolce and Gabbana, Gucci, Jimmy Choo. And the shoes themselves, arranged on elegant tables, were pampered aristocrats; some so exclusive they'd been placed in locked glass cabinets like priceless museum exhibits. And priceless was the word: £300 appeared to be the basic starting price. She was tempted simply to leave. Only the thought of walking barefoot down the aisle made her approach a saleswoman – one from Kurt Geiger, whose range of footwear seemed at least a little cheaper than the rest.

'No, I'm sorry, madam, not in ten. We do have a couple of styles in nine, but they're very clunky, I'm afraid.'

The word went straight into her mind-cupboard, along with the other epithets she'd amassed in fifteen years: bizarre, ungainly, hulking, gross, preposterous. 'Is it worth trying all these others?' she asked, gesturing to the galaxy of mini-shops.

'For size ten? Definitely not. Nine's the absolute maximum, and even those are thin on the ground. Bally do a few, for instance, and so do Chloe and Prada, but there's very little choice of style.'

'Thank you,' Robin muttered, turning miserably away. Clunky was how she felt – a great lumbering elephant, lowering the tone of this exquisitely tasteful establishment.

'Just a moment, madam.' The saleswoman was calling after her, obviously pitying her dejected state. 'You *can* get larger sizes in the States.'

'That's rather a long way to go.'

'Not really,' the woman replied, oblivious of Robin's irony. 'I went to New York myself last month, just for the weekend.'

Her own weekends were spent mostly with her invalid mother, or with Stephen's widowed father, and, even had she managed to give both aged parents the slip, there was still the little matter of the air fare to New York. 'Well, thanks for the suggestion,' she said, casting an envious glance at a pair of shoes on display, in softest, whitest calfskin, with deliciously dainty heels.

Back in Oxford Street again, she stood soaked to the skin, wondering where to go next. Maybe she should swallow her pride and try a men's department, as that salesgirl had advised. It was clearly time to compromise, to forget court shoes and high heels, and settle for a man's white slip-on.

A few doors down, she found Clark's, which looked mercifully unpretentious, with prices that didn't require a remortgage. Ignoring the women's section, with its slingbacks and stilettos, she went purposefully downstairs to the men's.

'Yes, I know I'm in the wrong department,' she told the salesman, before he could get in first. At least this guy was large – a great hunk of a male, with feet to match. 'But I'm afraid my feet are man-sized.' Best to adopt a jokey manner. And she certainly wouldn't mention the wedding – that would be too incongruous. 'I need something in white, for my, er, work.' If he assumed she was a nurse, it might gain her sympathy. She'd had enough of pity and contempt.

'What style did you have in mind?'

'Nothing too hulking. A slip-on would be fine.' She cleared her throat. 'Size . . . ten,' she said self-consciously.

He made no reaction beyond a friendly smile. 'Well, in men's shoes, that's probably nine and a half, or even nine. I'll see what I can find.'

How incredible, she thought, to have suddenly gone down a size. Nines were positively petite. They were even sold in Selfridges.

However, the longer he was gone, the more her spirits drooped. He was probably having difficulties finding something in white. None of the men she knew would ever wear white shoes – certainly not Stephen, who would condemn them as effeminate. She did a quick check on the male customers sitting in the department: two in trainers, two in black lace-ups, one in brown moccasins, and one in beige suede boots. The owner of the moccasins was staring at her curiously, doubtless wondering what she was doing in the men's department.

Quickly she unfolded her *Independent*, and tried to hide behind it. An article on torture in Darfur caught her eye. Just the thing to help her get things in proportion. Here she was, living in the free world, with no thumbscrews or torture racks, no imprisonment without trial, and she dared complain about something as petty as her feet.

At last, the salesman returned, with three – yes, *three*, boxes stacked up in his arms. A spark of hope flared in her head, as if someone had struck a match in a dark cave. She watched him set the boxes down, remove the lid of the first, and withdraw a pair of large white shoes. Large was the operative word. These were ridiculously wide, and totally unsuited to her ultra-skinny feet. Her feet were like her body, which was built in beanstalk mode, measuring five foot ten, with no excess flesh or curves.

However, she allowed the man to help her on with the shoes, still desperate to believe that somehow they might fit. But as she stood up tentatively, they instantly slipped off.

'Your feet are so narrow!' he exclaimed. 'They must be double A.'

'Triple A, actually.'

'Oh, dear.' He sounded truly concerned. 'We only stock standard widths – E or double E. So I'm afraid you'll find these other two pairs just as wide.'

'Can I try them all the same?' OK – she was clutching at straws, but there might be some solution. A special insole? Straps to hold them on?

If anything, the next two pairs were wider still. She couldn't walk a single step without them falling off.

The man was looking increasingly dismayed. 'Where did you get your present shoes?' he asked.

'Oh, these are ages old. I bought them when I was on holiday in Spain. It was a real stroke of luck. They were the only pair in the shop.'

'They don't *look* old,' he said, picking one up to examine it.

'That's because I keep them for best. Most of the time I stick to trainers, even at work. Lord knows what I'll do when these wear out.'

'You can have shoes specially made, you know. There's a very good place in Mayfair.'

With Mayfair prices, no doubt. If only she could put custom-made shoes on her wedding-present list, along with sheets and saucepans. They would be far more use, though also far more expensive, of course. Her friends didn't have that sort of money – any more than she did. 'My funds won't run to it at present,' she explained, wishing now she had spent less on the dress. But it had seemed only fair to Stephen to opt for something glamorous. After all, if you were lanky and unfeminine, it was as difficult to find a man as to acquire a pair of shoes.

'I don't want to insult you . . .' The man broke off with an embarrassed laugh.

She tensed. What now? Since the age of twelve, insults had come thick and fast, but each new one really hurt.

'But, well, you could try a charity shop.'

'Actually, that's a very good idea. I hadn't even thought of it.'

His face relaxed. 'Sometimes you come across all sorts of treasures. Just last week, my sister bought a wet-suit in Oxfam. And I've been pretty lucky myself. I got this marvellous leather jacket for only a tenner.'

'Do they have charity shops in Oxford Street?' she asked.

'I've never heard of any. But there are quite a few where *I* live – in Pimlico.'

'Where's that?' It sounded worryingly foreign and was probably miles away.

'Three stops on the tube. Just walk back to Oxford Circus station and take the Victoria line.'

As he expanded on the instructions and even drew her a little sketch-map, she was tempted to give him a hug, not only for his help, but for being genuinely compassionate – not the suspicion of a sneer.

She sorted through the rack with an increasing sense of hopelessness – several pairs of lace-ups in navy, brown and black, a pair of purple winklepickers, assorted court shoes, mainly in dark colours, and a variety of sandals, ranging from strappy-smart to flat, earthmother types. But absolutely nothing in white, and nothing bigger than size six. Beside the rack was a cardboard box containing mules and flip-flops. It would certainly be daring to team a classic wedding gown with yellow plastic flip-flops or fluffy fake-fur slippers, but Stephen would never forgive her.

She'd have to face it – it was time to cut her losses and give up. This was the fourth and last charity shop in Pimlico, and the only size-ten footwear she had found so far in all of them was a pair of stout green wellington boots. Yet somehow she was reluctant to go home. Her tiny cottage would feel damp and claustrophobic, and Stephen was away, so she couldn't invite him for his usual home-cooked supper. Knowing her, she would sit there stuffing crisps – and worrying, of course: the only bride in the history of humanity to wear green wellies on her wedding day.

She turned her back on the shoes, and began trying on some crazy hats, to divert herself from feet. The grey silk toque, complete with length of veiling, transformed her into a dowager duchess, while the dirty white fedora gave her a slightly menacing air, like a seedy American crook. The only one that appealed to her was a wide-brimmed Panama, luxuriant with an overgrowth of flowers: poppies, roses, lilies, snowdrops, all extravagantly blooming, regardless of the season. If only she could carry off such an exuberant hat, but she had learned, when only a schoolgirl, never to draw attention to her height.

The other shelves were piled with ancient tat: cracked LPs, old hockey sticks, well-worn sports bags, naked dolls. This shop was full

of things, like her, that didn't fit society's high standards: unfashionable clothes, scuffed shoes, well-thumbed books, cups with no
saucers, tasteless ornaments. Here, she wasn't a freak – just someone slightly wanting, marked down for quick sale. And she certainly
felt more comfortable than in those pretentious West End stores. For
one thing, there were no condescending, super-sexy salesgirls – just
a grey-haired matron, wearing granny-specs and a baggy home-
knitted cardigan.

'Can I help you with anything?' she asked, catching Robin's eye.

'No, thanks.' Robin was reluctant to go through the whole saga
again. If necessary, she would postpone the wedding until she won
the lottery, or backed a rank outsider who went on to win at Aintree.
Then she could jet off to Manhattan and buy every single size-ten
shoe in every New York store, or summon the royal cobbler to her
cottage, to take her individual measurements, and deliver back the
finished shoes in less than twenty-four hours. 'I'm just having a
general look-round, OK?'

'Yes, of course. Go ahead.' The woman was folding plastic bags.
They, too, were mongrels: crumpled bags from Sainsbury, Tesco,
British Home Stores, recycled for use here.

Robin moved to the rails of clothes. Despite her failure with the
shoes, she could still buy something else. She checked through all the
hangers and eventually lighted on a blue silk blouse with sleeves
that actually reached her wrists, rather than stopping short at her
forearms, and an elegant matching skirt that, miraculously, was long
enough. Stephen was bound to disapprove of her wearing 'germy
cast-offs', but need he ever know? 'Can I try these on?' she asked.

'The fitting-room's just here.' The woman pointed to a curtained
alcove adjacent to the counter. 'But someone's in it already. If you
don't mind waiting a few minutes. . . .'

'Or you can share,' said a voice from behind the curtain. 'It's a bit
of a squeeze, but do come in.'

Robin tensed. This was taking matiness too far. Besides, she was
invariably uneasy about strangers eyeing her body – noting its
length, its angularity, its lack of hips and breasts. 'It's OK. I'll wait.'

The girl popped her head out and gave Robin an engaging smile.
'I may be quite a while, I'm afraid. I'm trying to find something for
my wedding.'

'Gosh! So am I.'

95

'What, a dress?'

'No, shoes.'

'Oh, shoes are easy-peasy. It's the dress that really matters, and I just can't find a thing. Apparently, a gorgeous silk creation arrived in here last week, complete with a veil and train and everything, and was snapped up within the hour. I went ballistic when I heard. I've been hunting around for ages, and my wedding's only two weeks' away.'

'I can't believe it! So is mine.'

'What date?'

'September 3.'

'Same here! Wow, this is quite extraordinary. We're obviously two of a kind.' The girl drew the curtain back and beckoned Robin over. 'I'd like your help, actually, so long as you don't mind. I've tried on so much stuff, I can't judge it any more. You see, I've given up all hope of a proper wedding dress, so now I'm scraping the barrel, considering anything and everything. What do you think of this, for instance?' She struck a theatrical pose, then twirled around to show Robin what she was wearing – a full-length evening dress, in an unflattering shade of greyish-green, that suggested mould on cheese.

'It's not . . . quite right,' said Robin haltingly. She hated being rude, but the girl looked barely twenty, and this dress was frumpish through and through.

'Yeah, you're right, it's shit. I'm getting desperate, that's the trouble. There's this black thing here.' She held it up on its hanger, for Robin to inspect.

'You can't wear *black* for your wedding.' Robin surprised herself by sounding so vehement. But it was vital to be honest – weddings were important. 'Isn't there anything in cream, or even a pale gold?'

'No. Bugger all! I've tried every charity shop for miles around. Some do have wedding dresses, they said, but August's a bad month, because everyone's away. But what about *you?* Why such a problem with shoes?'

If Robin paused, it was only for a second. This girl was so friendly and outgoing, she found herself confiding in her with barely a shred of embarrassment. Besides, the girl was tall herself – five-foot-eight, she'd guess, with endearingly large feet – nowhere near size ten, of course, but still big enough to prevent invidious comparisons.

'Hell, I'm sorry,' the girl said, pulling the green dress over her head to reveal a boyish figure, clad in grubby underwear, the bra fastened with a safety-pin. 'I know exactly how you feel. Why are weddings so outrageously expensive? Bill and I were tempted to elope, but his family would go berserk. I'm Annie, by the way.'

'And I'm Robin.' She grimaced. 'I'm afraid my name's completely wrong for someone tall, with hulking feet. Robins are such *spindly* little birds. They should have called me Ostrich.'

Annie laughed, pulling on a pair of ragged jeans. 'Well, nice to meet you, Ostrich. Hey, if you've got time, why don't we have a coffee together? You'd be doing me a favour, just getting me out of here, before I cough up twenty quid for some disaster of a dress!'

Robin smiled. The smile relaxed her face, which, she realized only now, had been set in a grim mask since she had first set out this morning in a chilly, rain-lashed dawn. 'I'd love to,' she replied. 'In fact, let's make it something stronger and drink to both our weddings.'

She picked up the machete and, gritting her teeth in terror, brought it swingeing down against her anklebone. The pain was indescribable as she slashed through tender flesh and gristly tendon. Blood was gushing out profusely from the wound. She felt faint at the very sight of it, but somehow managed to summon the strength to lop the foot completely off. It was the only solution, if she wanted to salvage the wedding, along with Stephen's respect.

Although weak from loss of blood, she hacked into the second foot, sawing away relentlessly until at last the bone was severed. Once both feet were finally dismembered, she lay back ashen-pale on the bed. The agony was worth it, especially as she had lost not only her feet, but also a couple of inches in height. Now she would be shorter than the groom, which would save him both annoyance and embarrassment.

'Stephen!' she called, her voice a jagged whimper, her hands clenched against the pain, which was rising in intensity, threatening to overwhelm her.

He was there in seconds, his face appalled.

'But I did it for *you*,' she sobbed. 'I didn't want you to be ashamed.'

'Ashamed? I'm mortified. You can't expect me to marry an amputee.'

'But surely if you love me. . . .'

'Love's got nothing to do with it. It's over. Finished. I don't ever want to see you again.'

She opened her eyes, pushed the tangled sheets off the bed and stared down at her feet – both still there, uninjured. No blood, no gore, no Stephen. He was away in Frankfurt, on business, and wasn't expected back until next weekend.

'Love's got nothing to do with it,' she repeated slowly, amazed at the truth of the words – a truth she had totally hidden from herself. She *didn't* love him – never had. All this time she'd been living an illusion, mistaking gratitude for love. Women with beanstalk bodies and size ten feet belonged on the scrap-heap and could never hope for romance. So when Stephen proposed, she had accepted with alacrity, thrilled that someone was actually willing to wed her after all. How could she have allowed her feet to dictate her future? Better to be alone than marry a man she didn't love. And he didn't love her either, as he had stated in the dream. Only now did it dawn on her that he, too, had his reasons for the marriage – reasons which, like hers, had little to do with amour: he *liked* her being grateful, indebted to him, submissive, a doormat of a partner.

She scrambled out of bed, aghast to see it was already half-past eight. She would be late for work, in trouble with her boss. Too bad. There was something more important that had to be done first. She opened the wardrobe and took out her wedding dress on its padded velvet hanger. She held it up against her, admiring the sweetheart neckline, the long, tight sleeves fastened with tiny pearl buttons, the sweeping train flowing out behind. The perfect dress for the perfect wedding.

Laying it carefully on the bed, she went to fetch the veil; magnificent in real French lace, and held in place with a circlet of flowers. She arranged it on her head and took a few steps round the room, grinning at her reflection in the mirror: a blushing bride in men's blue-striped pyjamas, topped with frothy lace.

After a final promenade, she refolded the veil in its layers of tissue paper and replaced it in its box, squashing it down as flat as it would go, so the dress would fit on top. That, too, she wrapped in tissue, making sure it wouldn't crease too much. Then she took the box downstairs to the kitchen and hunted around for some packaging. Fortunately, Stephen was a hoarder, squirreling away anything and everything that might one day come in handy – jam-jars, bits of wood, rubber bands, old newspapers. His own flat was chockablock, and now he had appropriated *her* place as a further source of storage. Using his string and his brown paper, she parcelled up the box, found the torn-off piece of menu-card on which Annie had scrawled her address, and copied it onto the parcel.

She dashed back upstairs and, after a perfunctory wash, threw on her clothes, and was out of the front door by five to nine. Clutching the bulky parcel awkwardly against her chest, she jogged down the lane to the village shops, determined to be first in line at the post office. Annie would need time to alter the dress, or, if she was hopeless with a needle, to find someone else to do so. It was only really the hem that needed taking up – the rest would fit her, more or less. And even if she botched the hem, the dress would still look infinitely better than a mould-green frumpish frock or one in funereal black.

She was bubbling with excitement as she handed the box across the post-office counter, imagining Annie's reaction, her amazement when she opened it.

'Not at work today?' the postmaster inquired.

'Yes, I should be, but I overslept. Listen,' she said, returning him to the matter in hand. 'I want this sent by registered post.'

'It'll cost you,' he warned, 'something that size.'

'I don't care what it costs.' From this day on, her finances were her own affair. Stephen could no longer nag her about what he called her 'extravagance'. She was free to waste money on outlandish things; free to give away a brand new wedding dress, without him telling her she was 'headstrong' and 'irresponsible', and must return it immediately to the bridal shop for a refund.

And as for the matter of September 3 – her should-be wedding day – she had plans for that as well. She would be guest instead of bride; invite herself to Annie's wedding instead of presiding at her own. No problems about what to wear: her charity-shop blue skirt and blouse, teamed with that frivolous cottage-garden of a hat Annie had talked her into buying, and the most outlandish pair of trainers she could find.

9

QUEEN OF CHOLESTEROL

'Mind if I join you?'

'Er, no.' Laura was embarrassed to see a mountainously fat woman looming over the table – so big she blocked the light.

With much puffing and straining she lowered herself into the chair, her buttocks overflowing the seat each side. 'You're new, aren't you?' she enquired.

'Yes,' said Laura tersely. People were staring. The poor thing must be twenty stone, and wore a violent purple tracksuit that only emphasized her bulk.

'Nice to meet you. I'm Beryl.'

Laura gave a brief nod of acknowledgement. She had been hoping to remain anonymous, at least until she got her bearings.

But Beryl was not to be deterred. 'And what's your name?' Her blue eyes were her best feature – what could be seen of them through the folds of her cheeks.

'Laura.'

'How long are you here for?'

'Just the weekend.' Doubtless intended as friendly chit-chat, the questions seemed intrusive. What would it be next? Her age? Her weight? How she'd voted in the last election?

Beryl gave a sudden laugh, which set her three chins quivering. 'I've been here a month already. Doctor's orders.'

'Heavens! You must be . . .' She was about to say 'a glutton for punishment' but quickly changed it into 'tired of the place.'

Before Beryl could respond, a waitress bustled up: a slender girl, barely out of her teens. All the staff, Laura noticed, seemed to be enviably thin – an exemplar to the guests, perhaps. 'Good afternoon, ladies. Could I have your room numbers?'

'Fifty-three.' Laura kept her voice to a murmur, not relishing the prospect of uninvited visitors.

Beryl flicked back her long, untidy hair. 'And I'm in the Grosvenor Suite.'

In which case, Laura thought unkindly, she could afford a decent haircut.

The waitress consulted her list. 'Miss Spencer and Miss Robinson. You're both on the fruit diet, I see.'

Beryl made a face. 'Yes, worse luck! I'm sick of fruit. Couldn't I have a jacket potato? Just a teeny-weeny one?'

'I'm afraid I can't authorize any changes. You'll need to see the dietician.'

'No fear! She'd have me on nothing but water if she could.'

'Which reminds me, what can I get you ladies to drink?'

'A Bacardi and Coke,' Beryl grinned. 'And I wouldn't say no to a strawberry milk-shake. With oodles of whipped cream.'

'Mineral water for me, please.' Laura was increasingly aware of the surreptitious glances cast in their direction. It was only natural that Claremont Grange would cater for the overweight, but Beryl was truly gargantuan. She seemed oblivious, however, of the attention she was attracting, and continued blithely bantering with the waitress: where were the rolls and butter? And how about some garlic bread as a starter?

Laura stared down at the tablecloth, wishing some fairy godmother would swathe her in a cloak of invisibility. To be honest, though, her feelings about Beryl were ambivalent: horror that a fellow human could become so grossly fat, and envy at her lack of shame about it. She herself, with only a stone to lose, found her appearance deeply depressing, and was amazed that someone the size of a beached whale could be so downright cheerful.

'I'm treating myself to a doughnut!' Beryl reached out to an imaginary plate and took a bite of empty air. 'I'd kill for one, wouldn't you, Laura?'

'Well, no, I don't think I'd go that far. . . .'

Fortunately the real food now arrived – not the single apple or orange Laura had expected, but a veritable cornucopia: two halves of cantaloupe melon filled with redcurrants and raspberries, and decorated with mint leaves and slivers of fresh peach. Around the edge of the plate were arranged interlapping slices of mango, star-fruits, nectarine and papaya, with a final border of lychees and black grapes.

'Pass the cream!' joked Beryl, cramming a handful of raspberries into her mouth. 'At home I put cream on everything – cornflakes, spaghetti, scrambled eggs, mashed potato.'

'And where *is* home?' asked Laura, hoping to steer the conversation away from food.

'New Malden. I'm lucky – I live right near the big Tesco's. They've got their own bakery, and there's an Indian take-away and a café and a pizza bar. I adore pizza, don't you?'

'Well, I wouldn't say—'

'That's my trouble, Laura.' Somehow Beryl managed to keep chewing all the time she was speaking. 'I'm seriously into junk food. I mean, who in their right mind would want to eat a stick of celery? What these dieticians don't understand is that it's not just a matter of calories and stuff, but what the food feels like in your mouth. Take a chocolate Flake . . .' She gnawed the flesh from a slice of papaya, then devoured the rind as well. 'When you bite into a Flake, it crumbles on your tongue and the flaky bits stick all round your teeth. And when you suck them off, they're wonderfully velvety and—' She interrupted herself to mop a rivulet of papaya juice from her chin. Laura watched, appalled. Eating with one's fingers had been a grave sin in her childhood, akin to murder or adultery. She was only glad her mother wasn't here.

'Actually, chocolate's my main weakness. I only buy the small bars, but once I've had a couple I just have to go on and on. Do you find that, Laura?'

'I . . . I don't eat chocolate.'

'*Really?* Does it give you migraine?'

'No . . .' She could hardly say she was trying to lose weight: compared to Beryl she was skeletal. 'Tell me about this place,' she said, determined to change the subject. 'What are the treatments like?'

Beryl shrugged. 'Haven't a clue. They won't let me in the steam cabinet because my blood pressure's sky-high. And I'm too heavy for the massage couch. And too big to fit in the bath. They don't cater for the likes of us. Discrimination, I call it. Perhaps I should go on a march, with a placard saying "Bigger baths" – and free chocolate while they're about it.' She gave a yelp of laughter. 'Boxes, not bars. Those big fancy ones with bows on the top and pictures on the inside of the lid showing the different fillings. That's the sort of job I'd like – inventing the names for chocolates: Coconut Kiss, Forbidden Fruit . . .' She made a smacking noise with her lips. 'I'm sure I'd be brilliant at it.'

'And what *is* your job?'

'Well, eating, I suppose. In fact, there's nothing more important when you come to think of it. If we didn't eat, we'd die. Anyway I'm greedy – I make no bones about it. I went to Weight Watchers once and the people there all said they were fat because of their hormones or their genes. It really pissed me off. Why couldn't they be honest and admit they just liked pigging out?'

Laura picked up her knife and fork and cut a sliver of mango. Greed had been another sin; meals a duty rather than a pleasure, and hedged about with rules: Take the cake nearest you, not the one you'd like. Think of the starving children in India. Finish everything on your plate (and no exceptions made for eyes in potatoes or gristle on meat). 'So why bother to go to Weight Watchers?' she asked with a hint of impatience.

'Oh, that was my GP again. He's such a misery-guts. And as thin as a bloody rake. He even sent me to this outfit called Loaves and Fishes.'

'What's that?' Laura tried to avert her eyes from Beryl's gigantic bosom, which merged with her stomach into an amorphous mass of flesh.

'Sort of Weight Watchers with religion thrown in. It started in the States, of course. "God keeps the pounds off, and steers you away from the cookie jar". Except He wasn't very successful in my particular case. You're supposed to imagine His all-seeing eye watching when you cheat, but it made me feel so creepy I ate more than ever, just for comfort. Mm, this is nice – really sweet and juicy.' Having demolished its lavish contents, Beryl was now attacking one of the melon halves, tearing great holes in the rind in her determination to scrape out every scrap of flesh.

Laura put her fork down, wishing she could lose herself in a book, like the man at the next table, who had a paperback propped against the water jug and was eating plain boiled rice. Other people,

too, seemed to be on diets that were weird in the extreme – a plate-
ful of raw spinach, for instance, served with a revolting brown
concoction in a glass. The dress code was equally variable, ranging
from leotards and tracksuits to towelling dressing-gowns. Dressing-
gowns at lunchtime! Her mother would be scandalized. As a child,
she assumed her parents went to bed fully clothed. Nighties and
pyjamas seemed just too indolent to feature in their lives. And she
had never seen their sheets dishevelled or their blankets
disarranged. Even first thing in the morning, the heavy maroon
counterpane was clamped rigorously in place, as if neither they nor
their bedclothes had moved an inch all night.

Beryl hiccuped suddenly. 'Oops! Pardon me,' she giggled, pulling
at the waistband of her tracksuit-bottoms. 'This wretched thing's too
tight. It stops the food going down.'

'Haven't you got anything . . . looser?'

'Well, to tell the truth I get a kick from wearing sports clothes.
Since I left school I've never set foot in a gym but, kitted out like
this, I can make believe that I'm about to break the record for the
high jump! Here, take a look at these.' She heaved herself sideways
and stuck her foot out at an angle, for Laura to inspect. 'The latest
Nikes, with heel supports and air pads and what-have-you. Just the
thing to run a marathon!'

Laura forced a smile. Although less than half the size of Beryl,
she felt a fraud in a tracksuit, and had chosen a self-effacing shade
of grey. Louder colours like bright purple were better confined to the
ultra-thin and ultra-young.

'You're a slow eater, aren't you?' Beryl remarked, looking specu-
latively at Laura's untouched plate.

Laura flushed. Memories of meals at home had put her off her
food: her mother hovering, flannel at the ready, to scour her face
clean the minute lunch was finished; the gale of tutting and sighing
as the crumbs around her place were gathered up; the recriminations if she left a piece of fat.

'Mind you, it's better for the digestion, Dr Crawford says. I do bolt
my food, I must admit. It probably dates from boarding-school, when
you had to eat your dinner double quick or someone else'd snaffle it.
I eat so fast at home I have to lie down afterwards to recover.'

'Do you, er, live alone?'

'God, yes! Who'd put up with me?' Another gleeful laugh. 'The trouble is, when I go to Tesco's, you'd think I was shopping for an army. I never use those mingy little baskets. I take the biggest size trolley and tell myself I'm saving time by stocking up for weeks. But when I get home I can easily polish off a month's groceries in less than a couple of hours.'

Laura could see the month's groceries swelling and jostling inside Beryl's body; pushing out her frame in unsightly bulges and excrescences, as if it simply wasn't large enough to accommodate the surplus flesh. 'Aren't you ever sick?'

'Yeah, occasionally. But I just can't relax if there's uneaten food around. I can hear it sort of . . . talking to me, saying "Eat me, Beryl – love me, Beryl. Eat me, love me, eat me, Beryl". I've even been known to sleepwalk to the fridge. In fact, the night porter here had to wake me last week at three o'clock in the morning. I was outside the kitchen, trying to force the lock.'

'You're joking!'

'No, it was quite scary, actually. I felt really peculiar when I came to.' A film of perspiration had broken out across her face, as if every mouthful she ate, even of healthy fruit, was putting an additional strain on her heart. But now she set about the other half of the melon, spattering juice on the tablecloth as she jabbed in her spoon with undiminished ardour. 'I say,' she hissed, lowering her raucous voice for once, 'see the girl that's just come in – the one in the blue top? She's here to *gain* weight, would you believe? Everybody loathes her because she's allowed all this extra food – bread, potatoes, butter, and porridge for breakfast, with cream. Someone told me she's had cancer, but I bet she's anorexic. I can't stand anorexics – starving themselves on purpose when we've been put on this earth to eat.' She picked up the melon skin and began enthusiastically sucking. 'I wonder what fruit we'll have tonight.'

Laura winced at the unpleasant slurping noises. 'Is it always different?'

'Well, they try to ring the changes, but if you've been here as long as me, you're bound to get repeats. Mind you, I've been through more exotic fruits than I even knew existed – pomegranates, persimmons, passion fruit, pomelos . . . Gosh, how odd – they all begin with p! Frankly, I'd rather have a pork pie.' She stressed the two p's with a wobble of her jowls. 'In fact if we're talking about the feel of food in the mouth. . . .'

We're *not*, Laura interjected silently.

'. . . nothing beats a pork pie. There's the lovely crunchy pastry, and that delicious layer of jelly, and the chewiness of the pork, and those little lumps of fat that dissolve on your tongue and—'

Laura gave up trying to eat. Her parents never bought pork. Not for religious reasons, but because they despised pigs of any kind.

'The only thing that comes close to it is trifle. Whoever invented trifle deserves the Nobel Prize. Just think about it, Laura – that gorgeous sherry-soaked sponge at the bottom, then those lovely silky chunks of pear or peach, then rich, smooth, yellow custard and foamy white whipped cream, with toasted almonds on the top and yummy glacé cherries. Get a load of that on your spoon and you're in heaven, wouldn't you say?' Her face wore a dreamy expression, as if she'd already gone to heaven and was feasting for all eternity.

Laura sipped her mineral water. At home, trifle was only for guests, which meant it was a case of Family Hold Back – one of the most dispiriting rules of all. You had to pretend you weren't hungry, and sit and watch the grown-ups tucking into chicken vol-au-vents or strawberry mousse or after-dinner mints.

'I can't be bothered to cook, but they do fantastic trifles at Tesco's – chilled not frozen. The frozen ones take so long to thaw, and knowing me, I'd be eating them rock hard!' She popped a couple of lychees into her mouth, followed by half-a-dozen grapes. 'Have you tried those Cadbury's mousses, Laura? They're out of this world – just cream and chocolate, basically. But the pots are ridiculously small. They don't make them in the family size. D'you know, I often get such a craving for chocolate I have it at every meal, starting with Coco-Pops for breakfast and ending with chocolate chip cookies at midnight.' Her plate was now empty save for lychee stones and a few discarded pips and rinds. She had even eaten the mint leaves. 'I read in *Slimmer's World* that you should buy biscuits you don't like, to stop you eating so many. They suggested ginger nuts instead of things like butter shortbread. But what's wrong with ginger nuts, for goodness' sake? I can't think of *any* biscuits I don't like. What are your favourites, Laura?'

Laura sat scrunching her napkin. It would sound horribly priggish to say she didn't eat biscuits either. Her mother would occasionally buy a packet of rich tea, but there was nothing rich about them – they were the dullest, plainest biscuits in the shop.

'Um . . .' She cast about desperately for a name. '. . . gypsy creams,' she said at last.

Beryl's eyes lit up. 'Ooh, yes. Scrumptious! I've often thought that if I ever had children, I'd give them biscuit names.' She guffawed loudly, startling the man at the next table. 'Why settle for Janet and John when you could call the little blighters Butter Crinkle or Currant Crisp? Have you got kids, Laura?'

'Er, no.' She had never been confident enough to believe she could avoid her parents' mistakes. Maybe forcing people to eat gristle was genetic.

'You live on your own, then, do you? – like me.'

No, *not* like you, she bit back. Her fridge was almost empty and she took enormous pains to avoid the temptation of supermarkets. The Pakistani grocer round the corner stocked most of the things she needed. Beryl was still looking at her enquiringly, so she gave a reluctant nod.

'Don't you find it lonely? That's the only advantage of this place – there's always somebody to talk to. By the way . . .' Beryl paused, frowning. 'I hope you don't mind me asking, but. . . .'

What now? Laura wondered. The state of her bowels? Her sex life?

'. . . if you're not going to finish your lunch, would you mind if I ate it? Seems an awful shame for it to end up in the pig-swill.'

'Help yourself.' Laura passed the plate across. 'But I . . . I'm afraid I'll have to dash. I've, er, booked a massage.'

'What about your pudding, though?'

'Pudding?'

'Well, yes, I agree – pudding's rather an exaggeration. It's just a tiny scoop of sorbet, so small it would fit in your eye.'

'I'm sorry, I haven't time to wait, but do have mine if you want.'

'Great! Thanks. See you around. In fact, shall we meet here for tea? It's only a cuppa, but they sometimes give you an apple if you're fainting from starvation.'

'I'm not sure what I'll be doing this afternoon.'

'Please try to make it, won't you? It's been really nice talking to you. I can see we have a lot in common.'

'Mm – well, must dash! Goodbye.'

*

Out of sight of the dining-room, Laura slowed to a walk. She *did* feel lonely – not at home, but here. Standing in the deserted hall, she found the vast house intimidating. The elaborately carved staircase seemed to say 'Keep Off!', and the bewhiskered grandees in their sumptuous gold frames eyed her with contempt. Nor did she feel at ease in her room, with its ostentatious furniture and its floor-length curtains (looped back with tasselled braids) framing a view of lake and parkland. Her entire London flat would have fitted into the floor-space.

She wandered along the passageway, passing an antique long-case clock, its dial exquisitely painted with autumnal fruits and flowers. Time was dragging – it was only half past one. Her massage wasn't in fact till four, and anyway the thought of stripping off in front of some sneery slip of a girl held very little appeal. An aerobics class would be more beneficial – if she could remember the way to the gym. The timetable listed something called Body Blitz, starting at two o'clock, and although it sounded alarming, it would be better than sitting staring at a lake.

Rounding the corner, she almost collided with a fair-haired woman, dressed in a smart black tracksuit.

'Excuse me,' Laura said, 'I've rather lost my bearings. I'm looking for the gym.'

'Don't worry, I can show you. I'm going there myself.'

'Thanks. I only arrived today so I haven't quite got the hang of things yet.'

'Oh, I'm an old hand. I come here at least three times a year.'

Laura smiled politely. 'Well, that's a good advertisement.'

'I'm not so sure! My husband thinks it's a shocking waste of money. You see, I'm really good all day and stick to salads, then by teatime I'm so ravenous I sneak off to the pub for pie and mash.'

Laura stiffened. Not another food obsessive.

'The trouble is, they've got much stricter recently. At breakfast this morning I ordered a slice of toast, and from the fuss they made you'd think I'd asked for a huge great fry-up.'

Laura maintained a deliberate silence. Wasn't there something gross about this constant preoccupation with one's stomach? Her mother would certainly think so. The function of food was to keep you alive. Beyond that lurked the perils of over-indulgence and gluttony.

'My name's Audrey, by the way.'

'I'm Laura,' she said reluctantly. She hadn't come to Claremont Grange to make tedious conversation with strangers she would never see again.

'What room are you in?'

'The, er, Grosvenor Suite.'

'Really? That's quite close to me. If you feel peckish, do give me a knock.' She lowered her voice to a conspiratorial whisper. 'I smuggled in some stuff from the pub last night – nuts and crisps and Twiglets.'

Laura muttered her thanks. Audrey's husband was right. Why pay good money to slim, then gorge yourself on the sly?

'In fact, if you're free after the class, perhaps you'd like to come to the village with me. My spies report that there's a divine new teashop serving home-made scones and French pastries.'

Laura stopped in her tracks. Everyone she met seemed to want to lure her into temptation. Of *course* she'd love a scone or a pastry (or pie and mash, or crisps) but, as her mother warned so often, every sin exacted its due punishment. Besides, one visit to the teashop might undo years of self-control. She was ever alert to the dangers: cafés, restaurants, sandwich bars, eager to entrap her; bakeries and sweetshops flaunting their treacherous wares. If she weakened this time, it might open the floodgates and drown her in a sea of forbidden foods. 'I . . . I'm afraid I can't,' she stammered. 'In fact, I've just remembered, I've got to make a phone-call. It . . . it completely slipped my mind. See you in the gym, OK?'

'Yes, fine. Turn left at the end of this passage and it's straight ahead.'

Laura doubled back to the hall and hurtled up the staircase to her room. There, she stuffed her things into her suitcase, grabbed her coat and raced down again to the car. She couldn't stay here a moment longer – it was just too hazardous.

Lolling on the sofa in her new bright purple nightdress, she prised open the carton of cream. The trifle already had whipped cream on top, but more wouldn't go amiss. She poured on a generous dollop and then dug her spoon in, swallowing slowly to savour each contrasting taste and texture: sherry-soaked sponge, silky peach and pear, velvety custard, the crunch of toasted almond. It had been a good idea to buy the family size. The Cadbury's mousses, although sublime, had definitely been on the small side. She had eaten them with the chocolate chip cookies, again enjoying the different textures. Eating was a skill she was only just beginning to master. It required experience and finesse to discover the right combinations – Coco-Pops with strawberry milk-shake, gypsy creams with chocolate Flake.

In fact, it was time for another Flake. She wobbled out to the kitchen and looked with delight at the boxes and cartons piled on every surface. At least six months' supplies just waiting their turn to pleasure her: doughnuts oozing jam and cream, twelve-inch pizzas with a wealth of different toppings, every type of cereal from Raisin Splitz to Honey Loops, bottles of strawberry milk-shake, dozens of packets of biscuits, and, of course, chocolate in every shape and form, including a five-pound box of Continental Assortment.

Returning to the sofa with a Flake bar, she removed the wrapper and stroked the rippled surface across her cheek. There was something wonderfully tantalizing about flirting with the food before she ate it; letting the bar caress her lips, slip between them for a second then teasingly withdraw, before she took an actual bite.

She gave a groan of pleasure as the chocolate crumbled on her tongue and dissolved in lingering fragments in her mouth. How could anyone imagine that living on one's own was lonely? Didn't she have the food for company? She had whispered to the Abbey Crunch how cleverly crisp they were, and how she adored the bourbons' dark, consoling filling. And now she was snuggling up with a chocolate Flake, spinning out the last seductive mouthful.

More cream, more cream, her body begged. Every food, without exception, was improved by a deluge of rich double cream – cornflakes, spaghetti, scrambled eggs, potatoes – and it was absolutely delicious eaten straight from the carton. She dipped her fingers in and slowly sucked from nail to knuckle; repeating the process in a mesmerizing rhythmic fashion until cream was drooling down her chin and making gratifying splotches on her nightie.

A hiccup took her by surprise – perhaps a sign that she needed to lie down, to allow the food to settle in her stomach. There wasn't any rush – she had all day to eat; all year. She had given in her notice, in order to concentrate on food. Eating was the most important job in life. If you didn't eat, you'd die.

With a cushion as a pillow, she stretched out luxuriously. She barely fitted on the sofa now, but that itself was a cause of satisfaction. Being more substantial increased her sense of security; gave her greater impact in the world. And, during the last few glorious weeks, she had learned that even rest-periods could be used to good account. While your tongue and jaws were recovering, your nose came into play.

Reaching out for the party-pack of pork pies, she inhaled their delirious smell. 'P – p – p,' she murmured with a quiver of her jowls. P for perfection, plenty, profusion, pleasure, promise. . . .

She couldn't wait another moment to smell the chocolates, too. Smells, like flavours and textures, could be combined in intriguing ways: the enticing whiff of gorgonzola mingling with the gingery tang of brandy snaps; the bland aroma of milky porridge countered by the piquancy of olives.

She removed the scarlet bow from the box of Continental Assortment and clipped it in her hair. Then she lifted the lid, admiring the sheer artistry of the hand-made chocolates inside. Although they nestled close together, each was an individual. Some were alluringly naked, some encased in crinkly gold foil; one was shaped like a shell, another like a heart, and a third was fashioned into a miniature crown, complete with white chocolate 'diamonds'. Several were tastefully decorated with scrolls and latticework; others formed crispy clusters bursting with nuts.

She breathed their heady chocolate smell right down into her lungs, all the while feasting on their names: Raspberry Blush, Peach Paradise, Noisettine, Romantica . . . Then she picked out a Pecan Parfait and, with her finger, gently traced its curve, enjoying its smooth hardness, before exploring the little curlicue on the top. 'You're so precious to me,' she whispered as she pressed a Praline Rosette to her lips. 'You bring such joy to my life.'

In fact, she just had to feel their velvet sweetness melting in her mouth, their centres liquefying, their hidden treasure of nut or nougat exploding on her tongue. Her hand hovered over the box, finally settling for a Cappuccino Dream. She bit into rich truffle, relishing the hint of coffee liqueur. Next she tried a Hazelnut Secret, probing its moist centre to search out the luscious nut. And how could she resist Forbidden Fruit: a tiny pyramid of plain chocolate cradling a whole maraschino cherry – succulent and juicy, as voluptuously she rolled it round her mouth.

But one cherry wasn't enough. She popped in a second, third and fourth, feverishly riffling through each layer in turn until she had tracked down every one. Then she did the same with the truffles, cramming them all in at once, and revelling in the sensation of stretched lips and bulging cheeks.

And when the box was empty, there was still plenty of food in reserve: ready-meals in the freezer, whole cheeses in the fridge, French pastries from the patisserie, quart-sized cartons of ice-cream. Never again would she be hungry, never again alone. Her children were beside her – darling Butter Crinkle, beloved Currant Crisp – and her new friends were thronging the kitchen, ready to comfort and sustain her.

Already she could hear their joyous voices calling: 'Eat me, Laura. Love me, Laura. Eat me, love me, eat me, Laura. . . .'

Life was perfect.

Sweet.

10

ELIZABETH TWO

'Foul weather for July,' he said, eyeing the angry rain-clouds brooding over the lake.

The woman standing next to him murmured vaguely in reply. He wasn't sure of the protocol here. *Should* you talk to strangers? Presumably it wasn't much of a problem for the other thousand-odd guests, who all seemed to be in groups or couples, strolling smugly arm in arm, or conversing with each other. As far as he could see, he was the only person on his own – and now compounding his sense of failure by talking about the weather, for God's sake.

He meandered back to the tea-tent, where a bevy of waiters and waitresses, liveried in black and white, were lined up to attention at the entrance to the marquee, and a further squad positioned behind each serving station. According to his watch, it was a minute past the official time for tea, but no one had yet wended their way to the tables, or made inroads into the array of cakes and sandwiches.

'Darling!' cried a familiar voice. He stopped, rooted to the spot. Elizabeth! She'd changed her mind, decided not to leave him in the lurch. He swivelled round, a smile lighting his whole face. The smile collapsed as he saw not Elizabeth, but a sultry-looking stranger in a cartwheel of a hat, trimmed extravagantly with flowers. The 'darling' wasn't his at all. She was greeting another woman, a slimly elegant creature, wearing an equally exotic hat, adorned with ostrich feathers.

'How are you, sweet?'

'Absolutely fine.'

'Is Charlie here?'

'Yes. He's gone to find us seats. Do join us, if you like.'

'Love to,' he muttered under his breath, envying their closeness, the mutual hug, the confiding little giggles. He shivered suddenly. Didn't these women feel the cold, dressed as if they were in flimsy sleeveless frocks? A spiteful wind was tugging at the frocks, mauling the flowers and feathers in their hats. The earlier showers had churned the grass to a slippery brown slush and, although there was now a lull in the rain, their spindly shoes were caked in mud. Given the weather, waterproof coats and gumboots would have been more practical garb, but everywhere he looked, both men and women were attired as for a smart society wedding. Hats were obligatory for female guests, and some of the headgear was sensational. None the less, Elizabeth's hat would have outclassed them all: an outrageous creation in the shape of a fruit-bowl, brimming with cherries and grapes. The fruit was so authentic in appearance, you felt you could bite into one of the luscious purple grapes, or pop a couple of cherries into your mouth. But what would she *do* with the hat, he wondered – return it to the shop, or wear it to delight some new admirer? There was bound to be another bloke, if not now, then soon. He'd kill the bastard. . . .

'Ah, there's Charlie,' the taller of the woman drawled. 'And headed this way, thank heavens! That means we can get our tea. I'm starving, aren't you, Clarissa?'

Yes, thought Trevor, ravenous. He was aware that he hadn't eaten since last night, but the emptiness wasn't confined to his stomach. A vast Elizabeth-sized hole had opened up inside him. How could she have been so heartless as to inform him, a mere two hours before this event, that their relationship was over, and she intended to move out?

He followed the two women, as if craving female company – any female company – to help fill that gaping hole. But suddenly a clumsy fool of a military man, dressed in full regalia, crossed his path and collided with him, all but knocking him to the ground.

'So sorry, old chap. Are you all right?'

'Yes, fine,' he lied, reeling from the impact – the second blow of the day. Elizabeth's news had punched him in the solar plexus, made him physically sick.

Once he'd recovered himself, he saw to his dismay that, in a matter of minutes, long queues had formed in front of every serving station, so that the chance of getting any tea seemed increasingly remote.

The two women had vanished, but he took his place in one of the queues, behind a man in naval uniform and his, presumably, wife – a plain matron inappropriately dressed in polka-dotted pink silk, which only served to emphasize her protuberant hips and bottom. Confronted with their backs, he felt even more alone. He shouldn't have come at all, but, even in the throes of grief, he had craved to gain admittance to the grounds of Buckingham Palace, to be there by right, hobnobbing with the Queen. The reality was different altogether. The Queen, if she were here at all, was keeping her royal distance; his head ached, his shoes squelched, and he had always hated queuing. Elizabeth would refuse to queue, on principle. In her opinion, queuing was both boring and undignified, as well as being a total waste of time. Throughout her pampered life, there had always been someone to fill her cup or bring her a plate – refill the cup, replenish the plate – while she reclined in a hammock or lorded it on a luxurious *chaise-longue*.

'Are you playing golf this Sunday?'

'Yes. Half past ten. A foursome.'

'I'm still worrying about that meeting, James. The CEO's due in from New York first thing Tuesday morning, and I just have to have the presentation ready.'

Sandwiched as he was between two sets of conversations (the pair in front and the pair behind), he tried to distract himself from Elizabeth by tuning into both couples' lives. However, the talk seemed pretty banal, especially in light of the fact that everybody here must have some particular talent, or have made some contribution to society, otherwise they wouldn't have been invited in the first place. Wrong! What had *he* ever done, apart from writing a few tedious books no one wanted to read? It was Elizabeth who had wangled the invitation, through a contact in the Society of Authors – which made it all the more ironical that she hadn't actually come.

'They're frightfully slow, aren't they?' the woman behind complained. 'What can they be doing – killing the pig for the ham sandwiches?'

'Royal protocol, maybe,' the deep male voice replied. 'Perhaps they have to curtsy between filling every cup.'

'Well, I wish they'd get a move on. My feet are killing me!'

Trevor shifted from foot to foot. At least he was lucky in that respect – his feet might be wet, but he was well-shod in sensible lace-ups, not tottering on stiletto heels. Count your blessings, his father would have said. Except his father, a republican and a socialist, would have strongly disapproved of this entire malarkey.

He shuffled forward a couple of yards, his father and Elizabeth now battling in his head. The two had always loathed each other: she despising Len's plebeian origins, while Len, for his part, dismissed her as spoilt and stuck-up.

He stared moodily at the adjoining queue, which seemed even longer and slower-moving than his, and contained an unaccountable number of clerics – a female in a dog-collar and an ankle-length burgundy robe; a short, squat man in a cassock, and an imposing figure in cardinal's red.

'Bloody papists!' he heard his father snap. 'If Jesus came back to earth, he'd abolish the Vatican, and hurl a few hand-grenades into all those fancy bishops' palaces.'

Leave me alone, Trevor pleaded. Even five years after his death, Len was still doggedly alive, spouting opinions, abolishing institutions, marching for working men's rights.

He tried to focus outwards by observing his fellow guests: a frail little chap weighed down by outsize mayoral chains; an African woman in flamboyant national dress, with a turban the size of a tea-urn adorning her statuesque head; a group of Indian women fluttering and shimmering in brilliant, gold-trimmed saris. And at last the queue was moving – indeed, the couple in front were actually serving themselves, although taking their time about it, dithering over what to choose. When they finally moved away, it was now he who was confronted with the same confusing choice: every type of sandwich, bridge rolls, mini-scones, flapjacks, almond fingers, strawberry tartlets, cream-filled gateaux and at least four different types of plainer cake.

'Tea, sir?' asked the waiter. 'Or would you prefer iced coffee? There's also lemonade and orange juice.'

More decisions. 'Er, tea,' he said.

'I'm afraid it'll be a few minutes, sir. We're just refilling the teapot.'

'Oh, right. . . .'

'But do help yourself to food.'

The plates were worryingly small. If he piled his high, he might spill the food and disgrace himself, quite apart from looking gluttonous. Elizabeth, of course, would have taken what she wanted, gluttonous or no. Spurred by her example, he reached out for a couple of bridge rolls, topped them with a strawberry tartlet, a flapjack and a slice of ginger cake. There was still no sign of the tea. He was beginning to feel embarrassed, aware of people jostling behind him. They wouldn't understand about the teapot, and just assume he was holding up the queue.

'I'll have lemonade instead,' he said, but he was talking to empty air. One waiter had his back to him and the original one had vanished. To cover his confusion, he took another cake, only to wish he hadn't. Now he did look greedy. Could he put it back, surreptitiously? Just as he was doing so, the waiter reappeared.

'Your tea, sir. Please help yourself to milk and sugar.'

He sloshed milk into his cup, looked in vain for the sugar, then hastily stepped aside from the serving table, balancing cup and plate precariously as he wove his way through the crowds. There were no empty seats to be had. Every single chair was taken, and once again he envied the camaraderie – groups of chatting, laughing people, taking their tea together. They were obviously at home with each other, and at ease in this rarefied setting. Perhaps they'd been to the same schools – Winchester or Eton. There would be no one here from *his* school.

Extricating himself from the crush, he stood on his own, wondering how to eat and drink when he had only two hands, and both were occupied. If he put his plate down on the grass, it might be a breach of etiquette, and unwise, in any case. Muddy fingers wouldn't look too clever.

He transferred the cup and saucer to his left hand, just above the plate, which meant the saucer was squashing his cakes. But at least he had a hand free to pick up the cup and drink. He grimaced as the tea went down – sugarless and tepid. Next he manoeuvred the plate on top of the empty cup, and tried to shake his bridge roll free of its topping of jam and cream, which had adhered to it from the disintegrating tart. He took a cautious bite, tasting strawberry-flavoured smoked salmon. His flapjack had fared no better. A gloop of egg mayonnaise from the second bridge roll made a bilious yellow trellis across the nobbly brown square. Well, never mind, the food would be mixed up anyway, as soon as it reached his stomach.

Having eaten his fill, he retraced his steps to the lake, and hid the empty cup and plate behind a convenient tree. No one could see him here, thank God, except the coots and ducks. Even they were in pairs, he noticed – every Trevor with his Elizabeth – some of them positively devoted, following each other closely in the water, as if they couldn't bear to be parted for a second.

It was too cold to stand still for long, so he decided to explore the grounds, passing one of the military bands *en route*: a dozen or so brass players, garbed stylishly in red and black, and sheltered by a marquee. Their march was so lively and jubilant, it began to lift his mood. Elizabeth *might* come back, change her mind, admit she'd acted too hastily. There was still a chance – if he finished his current book, found a decent publisher, began to earn some royalties. . . .

He suddenly noticed a swarm of people milling from the tea-tables towards the central enclosure in front of the palace steps. The royal party must be due to arrive. He had lost all track of time, but he joined the crush of bodies and let himself be carried along. At that moment, the heavens opened again and everyone around him began putting up umbrellas. As he was poked in the eye and prodded in the ribs, he cursed his own stupidity in bringing neither coat nor brolly. But after Elizabeth's bombshell, he had been in such a state of shock, it was all he could do to button up his shirt.

Head bowed, he struggled along, rain seeping into his already damp suit and dripping down his neck. He finally came to a halt behind a barrier of people, at least a dozen rows deep. It was impossible to tell what was going on beyond. All he could see was the backs of innumerable heads and a phalanx of umbrellas.

All at once, the strains of the National Anthem filled the air. Despite the pouring rain, people visibly straightened, standing to attention.

'Sit on the ground in protest,' his father urged. 'Those royals are a bunch of free-loaders, living off the fat of the land.'

Ignoring Len, he consulted his sodden programme, to try to work out what was happening. According to the timetable, Gentlemen at Arms should be forming 'lanes' for members of the Royal Family to move through the tide of guests. Although he craned his neck to see, no Gentleman at Arms was visible. Indeed, had a troupe of lions and tigers arrived on the scene, or a bevy of topless showgirls, he would be none the wiser, since his view was totally blocked. Wasn't it absurd, he thought, that all these hordes of talented people should be peering and pushing and jostling, in a vain attempt to see an elderly woman, whom most of them had never met and probably wouldn't like?

He turned on his heel, and fought his way through the crowd that had formed behind him. He was leaving this party – *now* – going home for a restorative bath and a decent cup of tea.

He strode across the mushy grass, almost slipping in his haste. An abandoned shoe lay on the ground – a frail, strappy thing, hopelessly unsuited to the terrain. For some reason he couldn't fathom, he picked it up and put it in his pocket, then set off again, uncertain of his route. He had lost all sense of direction, and the driving rain restricted his field of vision, blurring any landmarks that might have been familiar. He remembered entering by the Grosvenor Place Gate and then following a circuitous path, bordered by trees and shrubs. But there was no sign of that path, and indeed he appeared to be plunging deeper into the gardens rather than heading for an exit. The grounds were far larger than he'd imagined – a veritable country estate in the centre of London, complete with shrubberies, ancient trees, extensive lawns and flowerbeds.

In fact, he was just passing the most impressive herbaceous border he had ever seen in his life – a good 200 yards in length, planted with traditional flowers, and not a weed or deadhead in sight. Opposite was an avenue of exotic-looking trees, curving into the distance and providing shelter from the rain.

Not that he had any wish to shelter – his only aim was to leave this place and nurse his grief at home, yet as he continued his haphazard route, he felt increasingly disoriented. He had now come upon a rose-garden, again grandiose in size – row after row of floribundas and hybrid teas, all meticulously pruned and staked. He blundered to a stop in front of a massive marble vase, ostentatiously mounted on a plinth, and worth a cool two million, by the looks of it. Yes, he thought, his father was right. The royals *were* parasites: rich layabouts sponging off the state. He'd like to know just what it cost to maintain these grounds in good repair. The army of gardeners and groundsmen would be paid from the public purse – along with the flunkeys in the palace: the butlers, footmen, ladies in waiting, parlour maids and page-boys. And then the hordes of royal hangers-on, leeching cash from hospitals and schools, while they idled their futile lives away, killing foxes and shooting pheasants.

'Dad,' he said, 'you were right, you know – right about a lot of things.'

All those years ago, Len had warned him not to throw in his lot with Elizabeth. 'That bitch will do you no good, son, mark my words. Once she's had enough of you, she'll chew you up and spit you out.'

Exactly what had happened. Elizabeth – royal in name, and in the way she carried on, had been born with a whole cutlery-drawer of silver spoons in her mouth, and assumed she was superior to ordinary folk just because of an accident of birth. She had mocked his father's accent, refused to invite him to the house because he was 'coarse' and 'unprepossessing'.

He broke into a run, slipping on the treacherous grass. Tomorrow, no doubt, a troupe of royal retainers would restore the grounds to their pristine state: remove every speck of litter, every trace of vulgar commoners. Elizabeth, too, had her flock of underlings – cleaners, masseurs, manicurists, beauticians – all paid for by her family's wealth; wealth she had never earned, but accepted as her inalienable right.

Exhausted, he stumbled to a halt, now completely lost. He had reached a far less formal part of the grounds, with long grass and spreading trees – perhaps a habitat for wildlife. Well, *he* was pretty wild: wild with rage, wild with grief.

A tree reared up in front of him – a Royal Oak, in full and venerable leaf, looking as ancient and entrenched as the monarchy itself, with its sturdy, wide-girthed trunk and spreading branches. Slowly and deliberately, he unzipped his flies and let a furious stream of piss assault its roots and bark.

'Damn you!' he said, in his father's coarse, unprepossessing voice. 'Damn you, both Elizabeths!'

11

WIDOWS

'And then,' said Anne, pausing to tear the head off a prawn, 'they lowered the coffin into the grave and one corner sort of stuck. We all stood there waiting, with our hearts in our mouths, but it simply wouldn't—'

'Oh, God, how ghastly!' Carla interrupted. 'With Edward, it was just the opposite. They made the hole so deep, I felt they were dropping him down a well-shaft.'

'You're numb, though, aren't you, on the day. Nothing seems to register.'

'Absolutely.' Carla spoke indistinctly, through a mouthful of prawn and rice. 'I was stuffed to the gills with Valium, and couldn't even cry.'

'Oh, it's not done to *cry*. They expect you to be brave. We plucky little widows, soldiering on.'

Speak for yourselves, Bernice didn't say, putting her fork down with deliberate force. They'd been here an hour and fifteen minutes, consumed pre-lunch sherry and poppadoms, followed by onion bhajis and samosas, and were now well into their grilled tiger prawns, and still the conversation hadn't moved from death. Neither Anne nor Carla had spared her the smallest detail as they steered their separate paths through the initial diagnoses, the chemo and radiotherapy, the loss of hair and appetite, the Macmillan nurses ('treasures'), the hospice (Anne) and hospital (Carla), the funeral directors, and now the burials. And since Anne was a committed Christian, the afterlife would no doubt follow soon.

'Well, they finally got it in, but it was a tight fit, I can tell you. I think they tend to economize these days. They're so short of space in cemeteries, they probably ration everyone.'

'And those grave-diggers . . .' Carla rolled her eyes dramatically. 'In the old days they were properly trained, but now they use any old bod – refugees, immigrants, you name it. I'm not racist, you know that, but you'd think they'd show a bit of respect.'

Anne dabbed her mouth with her napkin, leaving a puce-pink smear. 'It was such a shame you couldn't come, Bernice.'

Wouldn't come, Bernice corrected silently, feeling a sudden rush of shame. She had never liked Sebastian. All the same, she should have made the effort.

'But I brought you some photos of the grave.' Anne rummaged in her bag. 'Look, aren't the flowers magnificent?'

'Yes, gorgeous.' Bernice surveyed the stiff bouquets, which, she mused, weren't that different from the daughters' bridal flowers, a decade or so ago. Amanda had carried lilies; Trish white and red carnations. She continued leafing through the photographs, seeing bridal gowns instead of graves. Weddings were as much a burden as funerals, but you had to work at friendship. She totted up all the gifts she'd bought – for birthdays, weddings, christenings – all the school plays she'd attended, sons-in-law she'd entertained, grand-children she'd minded. Not that she resented either the time or the expense. It was the lack of reciprocity that hurt.

Carla squinted at a photo of an elaborate heart-shaped wreath. 'We had mainly roses for Edward.'

'Of course you did. I remember.'

'No, I was telling Bernice.'

Bernice flushed. She had in fact been ill for Edward's funeral. Genuine tonsillitis.

'I'll never forget the scent. It seemed all wrong for a death.' Carla drained her wine, then sat nursing the empty glass. 'Actually, I'm finding it quite a strain keeping up the garden. If Edward could see his roses now, he'd weep.'

'We can only do our best, Carla.' Anne leaned across and patted her friend's arm. 'It's the same with Sebastian's soldier collection. I can't hang on to it for ever.' She let out a deep sigh, then shrugged as if to cancel it. 'More rice?'

'No, thanks.'

'How about you, Bernice? You've hardly eaten a thing.'

Bernice took a teaspoonful. Odd, she thought, that *she* was the one who had lost her appetite, not these grieving widows. But there was less room in her stomach than in theirs. Over the years, both her body and her mind had become clogged with curdled lumps of fear and regret. There was also less room in her home. Her modest studio flat was hardly a match for Anne and Carla's houses: detached, substantial villas, with extensive gardens front and back. She just wouldn't have had the space for Sebastian's army of lead soldiers, or Edward's forty-three varieties of tea-rose. Right from their college days, Anne and Carla had effortlessly surpassed her – in money, men-friends, confidence. And of course marriage had brought them more, in every sense – more wealth, possessions, relatives. And a variety of new friends in quick succession: friends from mother-and-toddler groups, friends from the school run, friends from the PTA and, eventually, friends from their children's college days. And then sons-in-law and grandchildren – the circles ever widening.

'Bernice, aren't you going to eat that sauce?'

'No, do you want it?' She passed the dish across, watched Anne spoon the now congealing sauce onto a little mound of rice, then tuck into the soggy greyish sludge.

'I've been so *busy*,' Anne said, pausing with her fork poised. 'People have been marvellous, but it means I've hardly had a moment to myself. Friends keep popping in to see if I'm OK, or they bring meals they've cooked, then stay to help me eat them.'

Bernice took a sip of Perrier, its champagne bubbles mocking. Being a widow was a starring role. Unlike a retiree.

'I find it helps to eat. It seems to plug the deep hole inside me. And sometimes I feel as if I'm eating for Sebastian, as well. You know how he loved his food.'

Yes, thought Bernice – though *she* would have called it greed. Sebastian was the sort of man who helped himself to the choicest piece of chicken, the largest chop, the creamiest cream cake, before remembering to pass the plate to someone else.

'And I'm still cooking his favourite dishes – things I don't even like. Last night, I made sweetbreads, for example; forced the whole lot down, and was still famished, would you believe?'

Bernice picked at her mangled bread roll. Romance was a matter of luck. Anne had met Sebastian at work. Little chance of that in *her* job. Or her ex-job, as she'd have to learn to say.

'Well, you'd better have a pudding, then.' Carla beckoned to the waiter for the menu. 'And, Bernice, surely *you* can manage something? How about the lychees?'

'No, really . . .' Lychees felt like eyeballs in one's mouth: cold and pale and slimy.

'The toffee bananas for me,' said Anne. 'They're delicious here – all gooey.'

'Make that two,' said Carla.

Bernice pretended to study the menu. Two was the proper number for friends. She had always been odd man out – the baby-sitter, house-sitter, the one who'd drop everything at a moment's notice, while the others went to parties or on exotic holidays.

'And coffee,' said Anne. 'Or would you rather have tea, Bernice? They do a very nice scented jasmine.'

'Actually I'm afraid I have to go. I've got, er . . . someone coming.'

Anne's blue eyes and Carla's brown swivelled to her face. 'Someone?' Anne repeated.

'The, er, washing-machine repair man. He said between three and six. I'm really sorry, but it was the only day he could manage.' Bernice withdrew a couple of twenty-pound notes from her purse and laid them on the table. She had eaten about two pounds' worth, in fact, but it was safer to pay more than you owed. Friends were not that thick on the ground, so why risk offending them? 'Lovely to see you both. I'll be in touch.'

The waiter hardly noticed her leave. He was busy taking Anne and Carla's order. She closed the door quietly, shivering as she stepped from fug to sleet. The wind fought back obstreperously as she struggled with her umbrella, blowing it inside out. With difficulty, she righted it, only to find it had two broken spokes, and hung lopsidedly above her, letting in the rain.

When she reached the traffic lights, she let them change to green three times before she crossed the road. Somehow she couldn't face her flat, or her perfectly functioning washing-machine that had never held a man's shirt or baby's romper-suit. Still dithering, she turned left, down a side street, following the road past a small parade of shops. All at once it dawned on her that she was walking towards the cemetery, as if to compensate for missing both the funerals – not that either Edward or Sebastian was buried in this drab municipal wasteland.

She tossed the crippled umbrella into the litter-bin, and wandered up and down, reading the inscriptions on the graves. 'Arthur Henry, beloved husband and father . . .' 'Mary, beloved wife. . . .'

She sucked the word like a fruit-drop, wondering how many of the beloveds might be lies. Though even a fake beloved, she felt, was preferable to none.

Turning down a narrow path, she spotted a bouquet similar to those in one of Anne's photographs: Madonna lilies speckled cream and gold. They were still in their sheath of cellophane, which was glittering with raindrops, but protecting the flowers from harm. She squatted in front of the gravestone – a slab of granite etched in faux-Gothic script. 'Elizabeth Amy Foster. Always a smile.'

'For God's *sake*,' she muttered, screwing up her eyes against the salvo of the rain. 'Always a smile' was Anne – bravely smiling through the pain of childbirth, and through her parents' tragic car crash; the ever-courageous widow, still smiling through her husband's death.

She tried to wrench the smile from that plumply glowing face, but it bounced back like a boomerang and hit her. Tears sprang to her eyes. Didn't *she* deserve some sympathy, for a change – letters of condolence, specially cooked meals brought by kindly neighbours? She was as much a widow as Anne was; as much a widow as Carla; in fact mourning throughout her entire adult life for the husband she had never had, the babies she had never borne. It was only a matter of luck. If she had worked in a different field, lived in a different country. . . .

On impulse she snatched up the lilies, clasping them to her chest as she strode out of the cemetery. There was no one around to see her – only the dripping bushes, only the naked trees.

The gate clanged shut behind her – and suddenly the sun was shining, and she was walking down the flower-strewn path towards her local village church. The heavy doors stood open, the organ pealing triumphantly, as she continued up the aisle; Anne and Carla in solemn step behind her, holding up her train. As she reached the altar, she passed her bouquet to Carla, relishing their switch of roles. *They* were now her handmaidens, serving her obsequiously; she the bride, the star.

'Always a smile,' Anne prompted, as bride moved towards the groom – a shadowy figure, taller than Edward, more handsome than Sebastian.

And, with a smile, a radiant smile, she repeated the response, speaking loudly, clearly, above the truculence of the rain. 'I will.'

'I will.'

'I will.'

12

EXILE

'You're wasting your life – washing dishes, for heaven's sake, in some fleapit of a café.'

'I'm not washing dishes,' she retorted. 'I'm a proper waitress now.'

'And when I think of what I paid for all that fancy education.'

'That was *your* choice. You were trying to make me someone you approved of. I wasn't even consulted, just sent off to that ghastly school.'

'I'm not arguing, Sarah. I want you home immediately. If you're not back within the month, I intend to come out there and bring you back – by force.'

'Then I'll run away. You won't find me.'

She had already run away, but obviously not far enough. She ripped his letter into shreds and flung the pieces on the floor. Of course he wouldn't come. He was so set in his ways he'd never break his precious routine, and he hated travelling anyway. She glared at the small white envelope with its bold, black, rigid writing; the full stops so emphatic they resembled tiny bombs. She had got into the habit of answering the letters back, out loud, as if he were standing there in person, issuing his threats.

The process was exhausting, though, and invariably left her drained. And this morning there wasn't even time for a restorative cup of tea. She was late for work already and, anyway, she had run out of clean cups. She glanced guiltily at the rising tide of clutter on the floor – dirty crocks, unwashed clothes, empty beer-cans, chocolate wrappers – all guaranteed to appal her father, were he to suddenly turn up.

Leaving the room in its sordid state, she banged the door behind her, then hurried down the three flights of concrete stairs. Stale cooking smells lingered in the stairwell, along with the occasional reek of urine, where some tramp had pissed himself. It was a relief to escape into the fresh, damp morning air; to remember that the sky existed – not just windowless walls. She gazed up at the leaden clouds, squinting against the rain. She didn't mind the weather, or the perilous holes in the pavement, now filled with dirty rainwater. In fact, she felt a gleeful pleasure in splashing through the puddles like a rebellious child intent on flouting Father.

As she entered the restaurant, she was enveloped in friendly greetings and the whiff of braising meat. *Kis Kakas* had become her home now – far more so than the bedsit, where she always felt alone, despite the noise from other tenants vibrating through the walls. Here she was someone special: the only female in the place, and the only person of either sex with blue eyes and ash-blonde hair – the adventurer, the English girl, who had left her home and country.

Tibor poured her a coffee while she tied her long white apron over her skimpy top. He was her polar opposite in terms of looks and build, being dark, swarthy, stout and short. Yet without his help, she would still be stuck in the back kitchen, washing greasy dishes. They worked now as a team, he acting as translator, to prevent any risk of her muddling up the orders. If she had tried to get a job in some ritzy restaurant in a big bustling town, she'd have been shown the door forthwith. But here in the sticks, they were glad of any extra help, and didn't care about her lack of papers or non-existent language skills, so long as the customers were happy. Which they *were*, so Tibor claimed. 'They men. You pretty girl. They like young pretty girl.'

Pretty! At present she felt gross. An angry red spot had erupted on her chin, and her fringe was falling over her face because she was trying to save money from her wages and didn't want to waste it on a haircut.

Having gulped her coffee, she started laying tables, which was simplicity itself – no fancy cloths or linen napkins, just a knife, a fork, a spoon. The cutlery was often smeared, but no one seemed to object. Next she fetched the salt and pepper sets, refilled the mustard and paprika, then checked the chair-seats, wiping off any crumbs or grease.

127

She went into the kitchen to wash out her dirty cloth. Heat and smells assailed her – rabbit stew, frying onions, rancid cooking fat. István, the cook, gave her his usual grunt of acknowledgement. He was making dumplings, pausing every now and then to fondle the smelly, dribbling dog that always accompanied him to work. Hygiene wasn't a priority at *Kis Kakas* and it would never cross his mind to wash his hands between the two activities. Her father would go wild, summon the Health and Safety Inspectors, and insist they close the whole place down. Yet, paradoxically, the dark womb of the kitchen seemed to offer her protection. Slowly but assuredly, she was changing nationality, changing parentage, shrugging off the influence of her oppressive English home, as foreign smells and foreign sounds seeped into her pores.

István opened the fridge, took out a slab of cherry strudel and cut her a generous slice. His hand was covered with dog-slobber and flour, but the strudel was a gift, and thus treasured, germs or no. She remembered once, a month before her eleventh birthday, asking for a big chocolate cake instead of any presents. It had seemed terribly important and, as the days ticked by, she could taste it in her mouth: sweet, soft, squidgy, dark. But when her birthday dawned, at last, there was no cake of any kind, just a book on Shakespeare, with tiny print and no pictures.

'You like?' asked István, returning to his task of shaping dumpling dough into balls.

'I *love.*' In fact, the strudel tasted odd, as if it had been stored too near a whiffy cheese, but in her mind it had become the longed-for birthday cake, made by her dead mother, who had floated down from Heaven and brought eleven candles with her and a pink and silver cake-frill.

Tibor stepped into the kitchen and touched her on the shoulder. 'Quick!' he whispered. 'He here. Again.'

'Oh, *no!*'

'He come yesterday as well. I tell him it your day off, but he very sad and don't eat.'

She checked her watch: 11.40. 'It's terribly early for lunch.'

'He want see you all the time – lunch, breakfast, dinner. . . .'

'Can't *you* look after him?'

Laughing, Tibor kissed his fingers to his lips. 'No. Only you he want.'

Returning to the dining-room, she approached the corner table and greeted László nervously. In response, a tidal wave of words crashed and foamed around her head, not one of which she recognized. The language never seemed so foreign as when László spoke it – a barbarous tongue she sometimes feared she would never understand.

She kept resolutely smiling – her job depended on it. At least there was no problem with his order. He always had the same: cabbage soup, followed by beef stew. 'I'll bring your soup,' she said in English, desperate to escape.

Once in the kitchen, she ladled viscous brownish liquid into a chipped brown bowl, trying not to think of how the soup was made. Into the ever-bubbling stockpot went every sort of leftover – potato peelings, cabbage stalks, bacon rinds and onion skins, chicken bones that customers had sucked, and the various bits of fat and gristle discarded on their plates – plus a few pigs' feet and pigs' penises thrown in for good measure.

László gazed at her with adoring-spaniel eyes as she placed the soup in front of him, along with a plate of stalish bread. This time, he didn't speak, just fumbled for her hand and gently squeezed it in his own. His palm was hot and damp. Whatever the weather, he seemed to be permanently perspiring. His eyes were black, beneath untidy brows; his hair thick and strong but greying. She couldn't guess his age, except he was centuries older than she was, but a lot younger than her father. But then everyone was younger than her father. *He* was immortal – like God.

She tried to retrieve her hand from his intense and clammy grip. It was not that she objected to the man, or even to his familiarities; she simply felt embarrassed because, according to Tibor, he'd fallen hopelessly in love with her. Love had always been a problem in her life. Her mother loved her, people said, but what was *that* supposed to mean, when her mother was only a gravestone, a photo in a frame? As for her father, *he* could only love her if he turned her into someone else, someone he was proud of.

She stole a glance at László, who was still devouring her with his eyes. How could he love her if he didn't know a thing about her? No one knew her – not really – not even her friends back home, which meant she was foreign, in a sense, to them as well. 'Your soup's getting cold,' she observed, taking a cautious step back. She often spoke in English to the customers. It seemed friendlier than standing there in silence, or repeating *ad infinitum* the few basic phrases she'd learned. If there were a God, which she doubted, it seemed odd that He should have created so many different languages, which made for mystification, complication and constant barriers.

While he ate his soup, she served another customer – a shrivelled stick of a man, with a runny nose and watery eyes. Tibor wasn't around to help but, by pointing to the menu, the old chap made his requirements clear: a cup of coffee and a slice of poppyseed cake. She smiled at him in gratitude. Smiling was important here – it brought in the business, kept her job secure.

'Sarah! Sarah!'

László was summoning her. He had trouble pronouncing her name, just as she did with his. She went over, smile in place. He pointed to his empty bowl, then picked up his knife and fork and mimed a show of eating. Presumably he was in a hurry for his main course.

She was back with it in minutes – another brownish sludge served with small grey dumplings that looked worryingly undercooked. The food at *Kis Kakas* was heavy, stodgy and greasy – cheap fatty meats, mostly cooked in lard, and rarely leavened by a vegetable (other than the eternal cabbage) or by anything that wasn't grey or brown. Not that she was complaining. Once her shift was over, she happily shovelled in whatever food was left: scraps of *Bárány Pörkölt*, a congealing portion of *Paprikás Csirke*, the last dregs of *Székelygulyás*. It was as if the dishes, with their exotic names, were completing her transformation into a foreigner, an exile; reconstructing her body-mass, cell by alien cell.

The restaurant was beginning to fill up. She and Tibor bustled back and forth, he explaining customers' requests, or aiding her with translations. All the while she was aware of László's eyes, following her around the room, as he chomped stolidly through his plate of food. As she served two other regulars, one teasing her, one flattering, she could feel his jealous glances scorching her like fire. One day, she feared, she'd catch alight and burn away to ash.

'Sarah! Sarah!'

Over she went again. He stabbed a finger at his empty bread plate. 'More bread,' that meant, and more of *her*. Obediently she brought the bread and was repaid with another torrent of words.

Perhaps Tibor could give her proper language lessons, on Sundays, when the place was shut, or on her evenings off. For all she knew, László might be telling her he was a Nazi or a paedophile, yet, there she was, responding with friendly nods and smiles. 'Must go,' she said in English. 'Other people are waiting for their food.'

Minutes later, he, too, was demanding food again – dessert this time: the *túrós pite*. She took a slice from the chilled cabinet and set it down before him. He held on to her arm, perhaps to physically restrain her from serving anyone else. There was grease around his mouth and a gloop of sauce had dropped on to his shirt. She was tempted to take a flannel to him, and scour it across his face, as her father had done throughout her childhood – always for her own good, of course.

He let go her arm, but only so he could touch her hair. Running his fingers along a strand of it, he broke into an effusive speech, obviously commenting on its length and colour. Well, it made a change to have her hair admired. Since she left school a year ago, her father had wanted it cut short, telling her repeatedly that she was too old to wear it hanging loose and dishevelled down her back.

Still clutching the strand of hair, László summoned Tibor and whispered something in his ear. With a gesture of annoyance, Tibor translated angrily. 'Stupid guy want cut off tiny piece of hair, to keep for . . . for . . . what you say?'

'Memento?' she suggested, giggling to herself, though adding an emphatic '*No!*' If she started giving snippets of hair to every enamoured customer, she'd end up more or less scalped – which ought at least to please her father.

The two men were still arguing, so she took the chance to nip into the kitchen with a tray of dirty plates. When she returned, László had finished his dessert, thank God, and was getting out his wallet.

Having taken his money, and a ridiculously large tip, she saw him to the door with a sensation of relief. It made her self-conscious when he observed her every movement; his black-treacle eyes imploring: 'Come over here. I want you. Forget the other customers.' Even now, he was reluctant to leave, kissing her hand repeatedly and finally whispering something passionate as he tore himself away.

Tibor happened to be passing and rolled his eyes dramatically. 'He adore you, he say. He cannot live without you.

*

131

'*Fekete kavet, vagy tejszinnel?* It mean, "Would you like your coffee black, or with cream?" '

'*Fekete kavet, vagy tejszinnel?*' she repeated after Tibor, shamefully aware of her mispronunciation. This language was so *difficult*.

'*Tejszinnel,*' he corrected.

'*Tejszinnel.*' As she tried to copy his intonation, there was a sudden rap at the door. She looked up in surprise. The restaurant had closed an hour ago, and the other staff gone home.

Tibor shrugged. 'We not here,' he said, pointing to the grammar book, to indicate they should ignore the interruption and continue with the lesson.

A second louder rap made her jump. Perhaps there'd been an accident in the street outside and someone needed help. 'Shall I see who it is?' she asked.

'*I* go,' said Tibor, getting up. He approached the door with caution, opening it just a crack, as if fearing a tramp or mugger. She watched in trepidation, picking up on his mood. Suddenly he was all but pushed aside, and in strode László, hair slicked down, face flushed. After a passionate few words to her, he swivelled back to Tibor and started talking rapidly, his voice rising in indignation as Tibor kept repeating, '*Nem, nem, semmi áron nem.*'

She felt totally shut out by her own incomprehension. Watching each man's face in turn yielded little information, beyond the fact that they were engaged in a heated argument, neither giving way.

At length, she interrupted, tugging at Tibor's arm. 'What's going *on?*' she asked.

'He want marry you,' Tibor snorted, with a mixture of anger and contempt.

'*Marry* me? She stared at him, aghast. 'But he doesn't know me from Adam.'

'Adam?' queried Tibor, frowning in confusion.

'We strangers,' she explained, lapsing into the Pidgin English Tibor used himself.

'He say you his angel.'

Angel? How little he knew! In her father's eyes, she was the Devil incarnate – an ungrateful, dutiless daughter who had run away and left him.

'He love you more than any girl in world.'

'Well, he can't have met that many,' she said sharply.

'Excuse me?'

'I – can't – marry – anyone,' she said as slowly and distinctly as possible. 'I don't *want* marry. Ever.'

'I tell him that.' Tibor clenched his fists in frustration. 'I say "Go away. We busy". But he stay.'

László suddenly stepped forward, took a small padded box from his pocket, opened it with a flourish, and held it in front of her face, to show her what was inside. She gasped in astonishment – a diamond ring, so large and sparkly-bright it must be worth a whole year's wages. Where on earth had he got the money to buy a ring like that? Could it even be stolen?

Grasping her hand, he tried to force it on to her finger, but she squirmed away and took refuge behind Tibor's back. 'I *can't* take this. Please tell him, Tibi.'

Another violent argument ensued, the two men shouting and gesticulating. Once again she felt excluded, like a tiny child who had not yet learned to talk, faced with furious grown-ups exchanging unintelligible insults.

Tibor turned to her in increasing exasperation. 'He say if he don't marry you, he *die*.'

She sank into a chair. Her hands felt clammy and her heart began to race. Marriage was always linked to death. Hadn't her own mother proved it?

Hardly knowing what she was doing, she made a dash for the door, slipped through it, quick as an eel, and out into the dark and windswept night. She could hear running feet, raised voices – the two men were coming after her. She dived down a narrow alleyway, managing to elude them while they raced on down the street.

She crouched breathless on the pavement, waiting till their footsteps died away. Where could she go, to be safe? She couldn't think rationally at all. Her heart was pounding, her legs were as wobbly as István's jellied stock – and all because of her mother: married, pregnant, dead. If László forced her into marriage, she might repeat the loathsome cycle – land up in her coffin exactly nine months after the wedding.

She struggled to her feet, shivering in the dank night air. There was only one solution: she must pack her bags and leave, hitch a lift to the airport, and go back home – *tonight*.

*

Step by cautious step, she made her way up the path, hardly daring to breathe. The house was in darkness, save for the dim glow of the porch-lamp and a light on in the hall. Fumbling for her key, she had a sudden premonition that her father had changed the locks. Would she be forced to sit on the doorstep all night, or sleep on a park bench? No. As she inserted the key, the door opened with near-miraculous ease, and she was standing in the hall – back home.

Or *was* it home? She had forgotten how oppressively tidy the place was, how unwelcoming and bare. No shoes kicked off on the doormat, no coat draped over the banisters, no sign of any human being actually living here at all.

She crept into the kitchen, nervously switching on the light, and blinking in the harsh fluorescent glare. She was absolutely raven-ous, her stomach like a famished baby screaming for its feed. But it was a shock to open the fridge. No rabbit carcass or calf's head, no huge jug of gravy, or fish-heads for the fish stock, no slabs of cheese or hunks of liver sausage, no poppyseed cake or sour-cream pie, no cherry strudel or almond tart. The only things in *this* fridge were a carton of low-fat spread, half an apple browning on a plate, and the dregs of a bottle of milk.

Her father had never been one for excess, but this was quite ridiculous. Was he starving himself? Or could he be away? She dared not go and check. If she set foot upstairs, he might wake and, in her present weary state, she couldn't cope with recriminations or endless questioning.

She poured herself a glass of water in an attempt to fill the crater in her stomach, turning the tap on cautiously, so it wouldn't make a noise. Next she checked the cupboards, but all they yielded in the way of food was a packet of mushroom Cup-a-Soup and a tin of sardines in brine. Typical of her father to buy synthetic powdery soup, and fish in brine rather than in luscious glistening oil. There wasn't even any bread. The bread-bin was empty, and the fruit-bowl on the table held only a plastic lemon.

She sat with her glass of water, staring down at the spotless Formica table-top. The kitchen was so clinically clean, it reminded her of a morgue. And it was as cold as a morgue as well, nothing like the steamy fug in *Kis Kakas*. What in God's name was she *doing* here? She had come tearing back on impulse, allowing panic to

134

dictate to her. Stupid to be so terrified of marriage. These days, childbirth didn't kill you, and she needn't have children anyway. Besides, what was the alternative? If she stayed here with her father, she would die another sort of death, one of suffocation, entangled in his web. He would control her every movement, vet any man she dared bring home. It would be no worse to marry László than some ghastly creep her father liked. And no worse to learn a foreign tongue than have to speak his language of rules and prohibitions. If she became László's next of kin, she could escape her father's influence, legally, officially. She must catch the next flight back, sneak off before her father woke, pretend tonight had never happened – the whole thing a dream, a nightmare.

There was just one major problem: she hadn't got a penny to her name. The airfare and the taxi had completely cleaned her out. So how could she find money for a second lot of fares?

She tiptoed back to the hall. Her *father* had money – he always kept an emergency supply in his top left study drawer, hidden beneath a pile of papers. Wasn't *this* an emergency? And it wouldn't really be stealing. She could simply borrow it, then pay it back at a later date, when she wasn't so hard up. László might even help. He must have cash, to have bought that diamond ring. In fact, if they did get married, he might give her little treats: haircuts, flowers, cakes for all her birthdays.

Determined now, she slunk into the study. Her father's desk was as neat as always – not even the odd pen or pencil allowed to clutter up its surface – only the photo of her mother in its formal death-black frame.

She stared into the woman's eyes: *blue* eyes, like hers, so people said. She was sick of hearing tales about her mother – old family friends constantly singing her praises: how pretty she was, how vivacious; with such a gift for music, such a lovely figure. And those famous words she had spoken on her deathbed. Her father loved repeating the whole saga: how he'd sat there, holding her hand, weeping unashamedly as she whispered with her dying breath: 'Look after Sarah. Always.' Of course he'd welcomed that request. 'Look after' gave him power. 'Look after' meant constrain. Restrict. Repress. Bind hand and foot. Which is why she'd left in the first place. And why she was stark staring mad to be back.

With a guilty look behind her, she eased open the top left drawer, removed the pile of papers and saw with relief that the money was still there – the same stout brown envelope, marked 'Healthspan Vitamins', stuffed with twenty-pound notes. She'd take more than she needed – he could afford it, couldn't he? And, with any luck, she'd be back serving customers in *Kis Kakas* before he even discovered it was gone.

She was about to shut the drawer when she heard a sudden noise on the stairs, and stood paralysed with fear. He must have woken up and be coming down to confront her. Quickly she stuffed the money back and took a nervous step towards the door, only to freeze again in terror as she realized she was trapped. If she emerged from the study, she would walk right into him. Her stomach somersaulted, and words of apology began forming in her mouth. She'd said so many sorrys in her life, they would fill every drawer and cupboard here, if her father were to store them.

'I . . . I'm really sorry, Dad. I . . . came back unexpectedly. I can't stay. I . . .' The words shrivelled on her tongue as she stood staring at the figure in the doorway – so utterly different from the father she recalled: no longer strong and stern, but a gaunt shadow of a man, pathetic in his faded silk pyjamas, his once dark hair now frosted with grey. She leaned against the wall, bracing herself for a furious tirade.

But he said nothing at all, just returned her gaze in bewilderment, as if unsure if she were real or not.

'I'm sorry, Dad,' she said again. 'I didn't mean to wake you.'

'I wasn't asleep. I never sleep these days.'

Silence. She pinched herself. *Could* this be a dream; both of them hallucinating?

'You're . . . back,' he said, at last.

'Yes. No. I just needed a few things – winter clothes and stuff. I can't stay. I. . . .'

'Would you like a cup of tea?'

Tea? Could she be hearing right? Where were the accusations, the angry shouts and threats? 'Thank you. That would be nice.' She followed him into the kitchen. '*I'll* make it.'

'No. Let me. You sit down. You look tired.'

She sat, too shaken to argue. He was *waiting* on her, actually concerned about her welfare.

'I'm afraid there's not much milk. I didn't know you were coming.'

'Nor did I. It was . . . sudden. You see . . .' She *had* to explain; had to tell him she was off again – and soon.

'We could have tea with lemon, though.'

'Yes. Nice. Thanks.' Monosyllables were all that she could manage. She sat bolt upright, watching while he boiled the kettle and got out the flower-sprigged cups – the ones they used for special visitors. In the clotted silence, the clock's ticking sounded frantic, as if it were saying all the things she was failing to say herself. She made another attempt. 'Look, I've got to go. I'm only here for an hour or less.' Again she broke off, registering the hurt look on his face.

He came to sit beside her and, as if she were a child again, spooned sugar into her tea – not her usual ration of a few mingy, grudging grains, but three heaped generous spoonfuls. She took a sip of scalding tea, deliberately burning her mouth. It was imperative that things returned to normal. Anger she could deal with, but not being spoiled, indulged.

'Take your coat off,' he urged. 'Then it'll look as if you're staying.'

Deliberately she kept it on. She *wasn't* staying, and that was the end of it.

'How *are* you?' he persisted, mopping up a droplet of tea that had dared besmirch the pristine table. He hadn't changed in that respect – clearly as obsessional as ever. In fact, she half-expected him to snatch her cup, wash it up and replace it neatly in the cupboard before she'd had a chance to drink her tea. But he contented himself with moving the teapot a fraction, so it was exactly in line with the sugar-bowl.

'Are you all right?' he repeated. 'Not ill or. . . ?'

'No, fine,' she mumbled, catching his eye and immediately looking down. His own eyes seemed so sad.

Suddenly his thin gnarled hand reached out to touch her hair. The touch shocked her like a bolt of lightning, her scalp vibrating with the charge. Why wasn't he complaining that her hair was a *disgrace*? Dishevelled, tousled, ragged at the ends? But no, he was actually holding a strand of it and, even more amazing, slowly stroking it, which he had never done in his life before, not even when she was tiny.

'Your mother had hair like this,' he whispered, so softly she could barely hear. 'Hair like an angel.'

An *angel?* She was speechless

His hand moved to her cheek, the gentle pressure of his fingers pleading with her, wooing. 'Don't leave me, Sarah. Like she did.'

Hardly knowing what she was doing, she unbuttoned her coat and let it slip from her shoulders, hearing its sigh of soft submission as it fell helpless to the floor.

She was no longer cold, though.

Strangely.

13

THIRTY-NINE SHIRTS

Joyce sank down on to the pile of dirty washing, pressing her face into a pair of pink silk knickers – smelly knickers she had worn too long. She turned over on to her back and pulled Alec's dressing-gown right across her face, the towelling rough against her cheek, its stink of bacon fat and sweat rancid in her nostrils.

Light from the window lasered through her eyes. She wondered what the time was. Ten o'clock? Eleven? She had been awake so long last night, whole centuries had passed. But when dawn broke, at last, it was still Monday. Washday.

She made a feeble effort to get up; sagged down again into the dressing-gown's embrace. She was disobeying Malika, who had made her promise to stay vertical until after the late evening News. According to Malika, sleeping in the daytime was a symptom of depression – as were uncontrollable weeping, binge eating, *not* eating, panic, guilt, self-hate, self-harm, loss of purpose and loss of libido. Libido! She gave a sudden laugh, the sound skidding to a halt. Laughter felt peculiar, if not downright perilous.

'Malika,' she mouthed, the word awkward in her mouth. Did the stress come on the 'Mal', or on the 'ik'? Malika had told her, twice, but her brain was like the soft grey fluff clogging up the washing machine.

An *English* therapist would have been simpler altogether, instead of a Hindu from Calcutta – and a rather eccentric Hindu, who wore a sari one week, and a shabby tracksuit the next, and whose soft white snowflake voice didn't match her hard black eyes.

That snowflake voice was always giving orders. 'Never lie in bed.'

'Shower and dress as soon as you get up.' 'Eat regular meals.' 'Make a timetable.'

The timetable was pinned up on the wall. Monday: washday. Her order for today to wash one single shirt.

Well, that was pretty daft, using the machine for just one shirt. Perhaps they didn't have machines in Calcutta, and Malika had meant wash it by hand. But why keep a dog and bark yourself?

She sat up slowly and started counting shirts. By now she should have A-levels in counting, considering the amount of practice she got counting sheep at night: dirty, greasy, stinking sheep that kept jumping gates, jumping gates – a million, billion, trillion gates; their bars grinning in contempt. Odd, she mused, that sheep should rhyme with sleep. Deep-sleep sheep. Bo-Peep.

'Fifteen, sixteen, seventeen . . .' Alec was continually buying shirts now, in desperation at ever finding a clean one. And he wore them for a whole week, instead of just one day.

'Twenty-two, twenty-three, twenty-four . . .' Soon he'd have to buy more pyjamas – unless he gave up sleeping, like her.

The washing had long since overflowed the laundry basket and now formed a makeshift bed – a double bed of his and hers: pyjamas tangled with night-dresses, y-fronts caressing knickers, tights serpenting round socks, bras cosying up to longjohns.

'Thirty-eight, thirty-nine.' She clutched the fortieth shirt: white cotton with a faint grey stripe. OK – she'd wash it. Therapy cost money, so she ought to do her homework as a service to the National Health. But it could go in the machine. She simply didn't have the energy to find a bowl, run water.

She chose the hottest programme. That would give her longer to lie dozing on the floor, while the machine chuntered through its cycle: pre-wash, main wash, extra rinse, final spin. Easier to be a machine – pre-programmed, busy, purposeful – something that didn't agonize, or think. If only they'd invented a shopping-machine, one that checked supplies, made lists, got itself to Sainsbury's, even put the food away. She and Malika had once made a list together.

'Cornflakes,' Malika had prompted.

She'd tried to remember what they tasted like. It was years since she'd eaten breakfast, and Alec had taken to going out to Starbucks.

Malika's pen was poised. 'Toilet rolls? Detergent?'

'No!' she'd shouted, suddenly annoyed. How dare this woman

interfere! It would be floor polish next or Brillo pads.

'Caviar,' she whispered, imitating Malika's snowdrift voice. 'Mango sorbet, Turkish apricots stuffed with honeyed nuts.'

She and Alec had been to Turkey once. Long ago, when they still had holidays. She shut her eyes, breathing in the smells of the bazaar – ripe fruit, oregano, sizzling lamb kebabs – mixed strangely with the tang of Ishmet's hair-oil. She had met him on the second day, when Alec's upset stomach had confined him to their hotel room. Wandering out disconsolately into the clammy midday heat, she had found a modest café to eat her lunch-for-one, then over-tipped the waiter, as if to compensate for taking up a table. The waiter spoke good English, so she asked him the way to the harbour. It would be cooler there, less claustrophobic. A short, stocky man, sitting at the bar, got up and said he'd take her; told her he was going there himself.

They walked in silence for a while, she blinking in the glare. The sun was so bright, it made all the colours ache – the sky smarting blue, the trees stinging painful green. All at once he gripped her arm and steered her down an alleyway. As they moved from gold to black, he suddenly lunged towards her and kissed her on the lips. The kiss was powerful, brutish; his tongue subduing hers; his teeth dangerously sharp. She hadn't pulled away. She *liked* the wildness, liked his foreign taste of mint and cardamom, the hint of violence beneath the soft white shirt.

His hands were at her throat, forcing the top button of her blouse – small sallow hands, the backs dark with tangled hair. 'No', she pleaded, and 'More' – both words at once.

His mouth had found her breast. 'No,' she begged, the word coming out as 'Yes'.

She leapt to her feet, opened the door of the washing-machine, plunged her hands into the hot and steamy aperture, and drew out the still dripping shirt. Running into the garden with it, she paused, blinded by the heat – clammy Turkish heat. Smells assailed her nose again: burnt meat, oregano, that swooning whiff of hair-oil. Steadying herself on the post, she pegged the shirt up on the wash-ing line, and watched the wind surge into the fabric, bellying it out. The sleeves reached up to embrace her, but angrily she slapped them down, refusing to let herself submit this time.

Clenching her fist, she punched it into the soft, white, sagging stomach; felt the chest collapse. Then, stumbling back inside again, she collected up the other thirty-nine shirts, the creased pyjamas, dirty pants, soiled singlets, smelly socks. She left her own washing where it was. That she would deal with later – first she must pay her debt to Alec.

Once the machine was loaded with as much as it could take, she tossed the remainder into the sink, and ran the water scalding hot. She would wash all day, if necessary, wash till her hands were red and raw.

She showered detergent onto the shirts, thrust her arms into the Everest of bubbles and began pummelling stained collars, rubbing grimy cuffs. The exercise felt strange, as if her deadened body was slowly coming back to life; blood pumping round her veins once more, her lungs sighing with relief.

She turned on the radio, to drown the noise of the washing-machine, which was shuddering and gasping, as *she* had gasped and shuddered, lying under Ishmet.

She trounced another shirt. No – Ishmet was dead. She could see him through the window, hanging limp and lifeless.

Reaching out a soapy arm, she ripped the tattered timetable from the wall. It left a pleasing clean patch, a satisfying blank.

At last, the affair was over.

And she didn't need Malika any more.

14

BABY IN THE GYM

'Good, good. Well *done!*'

Jean stiffened. That cooing voice again, that syrupy sludge of praise poured out for some pathetic guy who had simply managed to walk a few slow paces on the treadmill. The treadmill beside him was empty. She sprang up onto it, as she had done yesterday, mumbled a hello. Neither of them responded; neither of them heard. Of course not. They were too bound up with one another. It was like a love affair – no, more akin to a *mother's* love: the mother doting on her baby, praising him, encouraging him.

'Try it just a fraction faster? Excellent! You're really making progress.'

Jean increased her own speed, broke into a run, as if trying to drown the pillow-soft voice with the pounding of her feet. Yet the couple's presence had somehow become essential to her. She *needed* them to spur her on, give purpose to her workout. She followed them around now, from treadmill to cycle to exercise mat, modelling her routine on theirs.

'Stand a little straighter, Bruce. And don't look down. That's much, much better. Brilliant!'

Brilliant just to stand up straight! Jean cast the man another glance, without slackening her own speed. He even *looked* like a baby, with his pale, plump limbs, bald head and baggy white nappy-shorts. For the last two weeks, he had showed up every morning, arriving on the dot of eight, as *she* did, to be instantly taken in hand by Mummy. The cost must be astronomical. Personal trainers didn't come cheap – if the woman *was* a trainer. Her willowy figure and long blonde hair suggested more a film star or a fashion model. She even wore full make-up – totally inappropriate for a gym – and a fine gold bracelet and neck-chain, presumably to match the ostentatious gold logo on her pink designer tracksuit. The male trainers were a different breed entirely – muscly guys, with short, no-nonsense haircuts, dressed sensibly in white singlets and black shorts. But Bruce didn't want a father – he wanted Mummy – Mummy every day, cosseting and coddling him.

'Now, I'm going to put the gradient up a fraction. D'you think you can manage that?'

As the woman adjusted the dial for him, Jean increased the gradient on her own machine, turning it as high as it would go. Already she could feel the ache in her legs, but pain was what it was all about, not empty praise and pampering.

Sweat was beading her forehead, seeping into the fabric of her T-shirt. She gloried in the sweat – the physical sign of her prowess. If the guy would only look in her direction, she could provide him with an exemplar of how a treadmill ought to be used. But despite their proximity – less than a yard away from each other – he was totally oblivious of anyone but Mummy.

She took a swig from her water-bottle, the rhythm of her exuberant feet echoing through the gym. Her heart was pumping wildly, her whole body galvinized, and partly because of the contrast with the neophyte beside her, still walking at a slow and cautious pace.

'That's enough now, Bruce. You've done marvels today, but we don't want to overdo it.' The woman leaned across and decreased the speed, gradually slowing the machine to a stop. Then she went over to the water-cooler and poured a drink for him, placing the cup carefully into his hands. Jean suppressed a smile. A wonder she didn't decant it into a feeding bottle and feed Baby on her lap.

'Now we'll do a stint on the exercise bike.'

We. That was rich. This trainer wouldn't do a thing, except stand there looking elegant and doling out encouragement. Jean gave them a few minutes' grace before joining them on the bikes. She'd return to the treadmill later, after Bruce had gone. It was important to stay close to them, in order to keep herself working at full tilt. The bike next to theirs was free, thank heavens, so she adjusted the seat and pedals, and selected the toughest programme on the dials.

Bruce was working at a much lower level, but received his usual adulation.

'Fantastic! You're doing really well. Try not to round your shoulders, though. Can you keep your back a little straighter?'

Of course she could. With a perfectly straight back, she began peddling even faster, achieving three or four rotations to each of Bruce's timid ones. It put considerable strain on her legs, but it was worth it for the approval.

'Terrific! Well *done!*'

She glowed. What she had lacked up to now was someone to take an interest, monitor her progress, make her efforts worthwhile.

'I'm really pleased. You've come on enormously in just the last few days. Now see if you can pedal a bit faster.'

It would require supreme exertion, but if it brought further praise, who cared about discomfort?

'Splendid! Keep going like that, and soon you'll be running the marathon!'

She could see herself breasting the tape, a thousand cameras flashing as the entire world's media recorded her achievement.

'OK, that's enough. We'll stop and do some floor-work. I don't want to overtire you.'

Certainly not. Jean followed the pair to the exercise mats and lay down on an adjoining one. She was annoyed to see the Scottish fellow, Alistair, doing press-ups on the third mat. The wretched man would want to talk, when she was intent on trying to focus on the training. There was enough distraction as it was – music from the radio, noise from the machines.

'Do you remember those abdominal crunches I showed you yesterday?'

Jean nodded. 'Yes.'

'Right, get into position – knees bent up and tummy pulled in tight. And don't forget, breathe out when you curl up, and in when you go down.'

Of course she wouldn't forget. It was second nature now.

'No, Bruce, you're doing it the wrong way round. Breathe *out* when you come up.'

Perhaps he had a memory problem – he must be in his sixties. She demonstrated a curl-up, breathing in an exaggerated fashion, to show him how it was done. But, as before, she was totally invisible.

Mummy and her baby comprised a universe in miniature, complete in and of themselves.

'We'll do another ten, Bruce. But can you take it a little slower? I'll count out loud, so you can keep in time. One . . . two. . . .'

Jean slowed her own pace, following the hypnotic voice – a soft, caressing voice that had no place in a gym. Yet the effect on her was energizing, driving her to feats of endurance. She was doing sit-up after sit-up, without the slightest strain.

'Nine . . . ten. Excellent! You're really coming on.'

She was indeed. Before this pair arrived, she had been working in a desultory way, with nothing to inspire her. But in the last two weeks, she had surpassed herself, achieving more than in the whole previous six months.

'We'll try some stretches now, to prevent your muscles stiffening up. Lie flat on your back and bend the left leg at the knee.' The woman leaned across and eased Bruce's body into the right position. 'Now hold the ankle with the opposite hand and gently pull it towards you.'

Jean copied him exactly.

'That's it. Perfect!'

Perfect. The word was like a unicorn: rare, precious, all but unbelievable. Radiant, she held the stretch for a full minute and a half, while Bruce collapsed after only fifteen seconds.

'Don't worry. You're doing well.'

Extremely well. She had not only increased her stamina, she was more flexible in every way.

'Now the other leg.'

That stretch, too, she held for ninety seconds, exulting in her prowess. Bruce was having difficulties just maintaining the basic position.

'You're quiet today, Jean,' Alistair remarked.

She grunted in reply, hoping to deter him by her terseness.

'Something on your mind?'

'I'm doing a new routine, OK? And I need to concentrate.' Already she had missed the instructions for the next abdominal stretch.

'Yes, both legs flat this time. That's good, except you're holding your breath. It's important to keep breathing, you know! And it makes the stretches easier.'

Jean inhaled slowly through her nose, letting the breath out to the count of four, while holding the new position.

'Great!'

'Great!' Jean whispered to herself, ignoring Alistair, who was now commenting on her leotard. She had bought it in the woman's honour and, since she had lost six pounds in the last two weeks, it showed off her figure well.

'Good. I think we'll call it a day now. But stay where you are and relax there for a little while. Make sure you take it easy. You need to rest after working out.'

Rest? No way. Jean sprang up from the mat, dashed over to the treadmill, turned the dials up high and began running at full pelt. Never before had she felt so alive, so happy with her body. If Mummy continued her encouragement, she would soon be the fittest person in the gym.

The next day, neither Bruce nor his trainer was there. Anxiously Jean scanned the clock. She was on the treadmill, as usual, but in danger of losing her balance, because every few seconds she kept glancing over her shoulder to check the time. Half-past eight and still no sign of them. Eventually she slowed to a stop and went out to the reception desk. Perhaps they were chatting with one of the staff, or having a drink in the café.

No. Neither.

Dispiritedly she returned to the gym for a session on the exercise bike, but her legs felt tired before she had even begun, and she pedalled in a half-hearted fashion, constantly looking around in the hope of seeing that distinctive designer pink.

'Hello,' a voice behind her said.

She jumped. Bruce? Aware of her, at last? She turned to see Martin, a guy she knew from work.

'It's a gorgeous day outside,' he said, plonking his bulky figure on to the cycle next to hers. 'Blue sky, bright sun.'

'Really?' She hadn't noticed. The only weather was in her head, and that was overcast.

'I'm off to Madrid tomorrow for a fortnight. It'll be scorching there, I bet.'

He continued to ramble on – Spanish food, Spanish art, what a bargain he'd got by booking on the Internet. Jean kept her eyes peeled, still watching for the pair. Perhaps they were coming at nine today, instead of their usual eight. She pedalled faster, spurred by hope, even responding to Martin's questions – no, she'd never been to Madrid; yes, she liked paella, though it wasn't exactly a staple of her diet. Her legs moved slower and slower as the clock-hands crept past nine: five past, ten past, quarter past. . . .

She dismounted sluggishly, mumbled goodbye to Martin, and walked on past the exercise mats. Somehow she couldn't be bothered with sit-ups or stretches. They'd have to wait till tomorrow.

Tomorrow, Mummy would be there.

She wasn't.

Jean waited till eleven, calling in sick at work, but saw only the usual crowd: Alistair and Martin, the Lithuanian girl whose name she couldn't pronounce, the man with the tattoos, the elderly couple who always did their workout together – but not the only two that mattered. Maybe Bruce was on holiday, away on business, visiting a friend. . . .

She gave them a week, returning to the gym at eight the following Monday. The place was crowded, as often on a Monday, but once she'd confirmed their absence, it felt as empty as a wilderness. Despondently, she went through her own routines, wondering why she bothered, then sloped off for a coffee.

Tuesday, she arrived at ten. Perhaps Bruce had changed his appointment time, preferring a later start. She hung around for a couple of hours, doing nothing very onerous, and finally ending up in the café again.

On Wednesday she came twice – morning and afternoon. On both occasions the gym was packed and now seemed less a wilderness than a raucous torture chamber. The glaring strip-lights hurt her eyes, and the grating sounds from the weights machines hammered at her skull, as if to crack it open. She skulked in a corner, observing every person who came in – shadowy figures made of mist, not the substantial, vibrant ones she yearned to see. At half past five, she abandoned her quest, trailed off home and put herself to bed. She *was* sick now – feverish, disoriented.

On Thursday she stayed in bed all day, continuously thinking about the couple and when they might return. Was Bruce retired, she wondered, or had he taken on a job with an earlier start, which meant he would have to move his sessions to the evening? She rushed to the gym to check, remained there till it closed, but this visit was as fruitless as the rest. She had stopped working out herself. All she did was exercise her eyes, as they swivelled from door to clock.

On Saturday morning, she approached the reception desk and asked to speak to Mac. An inveterate gossip, who had worked there twenty years, Mac knew the intimate details of most gym members' lives, as well as those of the staff.

'Hi, gorgeous, how's it going?'

'Fine.' She forced a smile. She and Mac were on friendly terms and often had a chat, but on this occasion she could barely speak at all. Her throat felt blocked, as if a large, rough-textured rock had been shoved right down inside it, and she had to clench her hands, to stop them trembling 'There's just something I need to know, Mac. That female trainer – the tall, slender one with long fair hair. . . .'

'You mean Annabel. She's not a trainer.'

'Oh?'

'Well, not *here* in any case. She works as a Body Consultant at the Oakwood Leisure Centre.'

'She *was* here, though, for several weeks. With her client, Bruce.'

'He's not her client – he's her uncle. Or *was*, I should say. He died two days ago.'

The blood drained from her face. *'Died?'*

'Yeah. It was very sudden. But he did have prostate cancer. In fact, he'd been ill for years, on and off. His niece was trying to save him, I reckon – working on his diet, drawing up a fitness programme, all that sort of thing. But' – he shrugged – 'I'm afraid she left it too late.'

'I see,' said Jean, looking down. The floor was badly scuffed, she noticed: tiny lines criss-crossing it – cracks opening up in her mind.

'Hey, are you *OK*? You sound a bit low.'

'I'm fine,' she repeated tonelessly, making her way to the gym. She lay down on the exercise mat where she had last seen Mummy, thirteen days ago. She shut her eyes, determined to block out every sound except that plush pink velvet voice.

'Brilliant,' it was saying. 'You're really making progress.'

She smiled. Mummy was encouraging her – the only thing that mattered.

'Now we'll do some floor-work. Remember those gluteal stretches

I showed you yesterday?'

Of course she did. Every word that Mummy spoke was etched into her mind.

'Right. Let's get into position, shall we?'

Mummy's hands were on her leg, easing it gently forward. How incredible it felt – that gossamer touch on her naked flesh. She held the stretch for a full ninety seconds, breathing deeply and rhythmically.

'Fantastic!' Mummy said. 'You've come on wonderfully well.'

Waves of pleasure rippled through her body. The voice was snowflakes falling on warm sand; icing sugar dusting fairy cakes; a soft spring breeze ruffling tender green leaves. 'We'll try some sit-ups next. Bend your knees up and pull your tummy in tight.'

As she came forward in the curl-up, the shining cloak of long blonde hair seemed to enfold her in an embrace. Now, at last, she was safe; Mummy's body shielding her from the sharp corners of the world.

'Can you take it a fraction slower? I'll count out loud, so you can keep in time. Ten . . . nine . . . eight. . . .'

Mummy was counting backwards, to a time before pain and loss, a time before Bruce displaced her – the hated brother, the cuckoo in the nest.

'Five . . . four. . . .'

Back further and further to a time before speech and consciousness, back even to the womb, when there was only her and Mummy – a whole universe in miniature, complete in and of themselves.

'Three . . . two . . . one.'

Mummy's face was blurring into a pink and golden haze – gentle colours, sugar-sweet: candyfloss and butterscotch. All boundaries were dissolving, and nothing else existed save sleep and milk, blissfulness and peace.

'Rest, my Baby, rest.'

She sank deeper into the mat. Yes, now she could rest for ever, with no rivals, no cruel brothers; Mummy's arms supporting her, holding her close and safe – the most beloved, perfect baby in the gym.

15

WEST END FINAL

'Is that the *West End Final?*' The man whipped a couple of coins from his pocket and slapped them on the pile of *Evening Standards*.

'No, I'm sorry. It's not here yet.'

'Well, it bloody well ought to be. I can't hang around all day.'

She ignored his whiplash tone. Some people were just naturally rude.

'When are you expecting it?' His hand danced an impatient jig on the counter. The fingers were stained with nicotine; the nails ragged, none too clean.

'Any second now.' Perhaps he wanted the runners for the Sandown Evening Card. An Irish guy last week had put ten grand on a horse – and won. Or so he said.

'OK, I'll give it five minutes.' Having retrieved his cash, he lounged against the kiosk, in the way of other customers. 'And I'll have a Coke while I'm waiting.'

Please, she corrected silently, handing him a can.

'It's not cold,' he complained. 'Can't I have one from the fridge?'

'I'm afraid the fridge is bust. The new one's coming Monday.'

'Bloody hell!'

There were worse things in life than having to drink warm Coke, but she kept her thoughts to herself. 'Fifty-five pence, please,' she said, holding out her hand, in case he imagined he could get away without paying.

The coins felt damp and sticky in her palm. She dropped them into the till, and turned to serve another customer. 'I'm sorry, we've run out of *Heat*. Would *Hello* be any use?'

The woman walked away without bothering to reply. Some of them saw her as a robot, not a human being – which was easier for them, of course. No need to be polite to a robot, or care about its feelings.

'The *Autotrader*, please, and a packet of chewing gum.'

She flashed the man a smile – a reward for the 'please'.

'You're new, aren't you?' he asked, pocketing his change. 'What's your name?'

'Irene,' she replied. It was as good a name as any, and she didn't want her real name to become public property, since this wasn't the real 'her'. Yes, she'd been pleased to get the job, but it was only temporary. She'd been born to do better things than sell papers in the Earls Court Road.

'Nice name.'

As his eyes strayed down her body, she stiffened in embarrassment. No man could ever fancy her, given her flat chest and skinny hips, not to mention the little matter of the birthmark. A port-wine stain, the doctors called it fancifully. *She* called it a hideous eyesore, purple, puffy, and covering half her cheek.

'So what happened to Jonah?' the man asked, offering her a piece of chewing gum.

'He left.' Her predecessor had been fired, in fact, after a stand-up row with the boss, or so she'd been informed. His loss was her gain, of course, though she'd been gobsmacked when they actually took her on. She'd been turned down for countless *other* jobs, in restaurants, shops and bars, and though no one actually mentioned her appearance, it was obvious, wasn't it? So she'd gone along for the interview with very little hope, not only on account of her face, but because they preferred men anyway, and tough, streetwise men at that. Well, she'd acted tough, and dressed tough – bought butch clothes in a charity shop (army fatigues and combat boots), and had her hair cropped close to her head.

'The *Final*'s coming now,' she told the waiting customer, who, with his lean build and pointy features, reminded her of a greyhound – a nervy creature, restless and on edge. She could see the *Evening Standard* van reflected in the glass of a shop-window just in front of the news-stand and, a couple of minutes later, Arnie wheeled his trolley up to unload the bales of papers. Greyhound barely gave her time to cut the strings before he grabbed a copy, tossing the money on to the counter and his empty can into the street. 'Don't you want the magazine?' she enquired of his departing back.

No answer.

The other bloke had also disappeared, but Arnie himself stopped to chat a moment, heaving the last two bundles from his trolley. 'How's it going, Iris?' he asked.

'Fine.' Iris was another of her alibis. She liked the name – liked most flower-names, actually, just because they didn't fit her image. On Wednesday, she'd been Poppy; Primrose yesterday. The regulars were catching on, of course. 'What's your real name?' two had asked already.

'Not telling!' It was Pat, in fact. Plain, boring, unisex. She'd been christened Patricia, but it had been used precisely twice: once on her birth certificate and once that day at the font – which, fortunately, she couldn't remember, since she must have looked a sight even in her christening gown.

'Oh, by the way, I may not see you Monday,' Arnie said, sucking on a Polo mint.

'Why? Are you having a day off?'

'No, I'm planning on winning the Lottery! It's a rollover – seventy-seven million this week. I should buy a ticket if I was you. I don't mind going halves, Iris. In fact, why don't I do the decent thing? *You* take thirty-nine million and I'll settle for thirty-eight.'

'Thanks,' she grinned. 'That's big of you!'

'Nah!' objected a dapper guy who'd breezed up to buy a paper. 'Don't mislead the girl. We need to make our *own* luck, not rely on lotteries.'

Pat was inclined to agree. She was reading a book called *Born To Win*, the true story of a thalidomide baby, born with stunted limbs, who had gone on to found a business empire at the age of twenty-eight. The book had made a deep impression on her, because it showed that even someone with a monstrous disability could succeed against overwhelming odds. And a birthmark was positively trivial compared with no proper arms or legs.

Once Arnie had trundled off, she reorganized the newly delivered papers. Half went on the counter, with a separate pile for the magazines, and the other half were stored underneath, as spares. In just two weeks, she had learned the ropes, thank God. The first day on the job, she'd been as nervous as a jellyfish, faced with all that money in the till, and scores of strangers looking at her. Now she realized they *didn't* look – or at least not the vast majority. Which was a great relief, of course. Even with her disfigurement, she was more or less invisible – just a mouth to tell them prices, and a hand to take the cash.

Yet *she* could watch the world, mercifully unwatched, and safe in her sturdy wooden box, which protected her from rain and sun alike. In fact, the news-stand was the perfect vantagepoint, situated as it was right opposite the entrance to the tube. However, most of the people coming up the steps seemed to look the picture of gloom: harassed mothers shrieking at their kids; young couples quar-relling; stressed city types snarling into their mobiles. And, in just ten days, she'd seen quite a slice of the darker side of life: male and female hookers waiting for their clients; a gang of stroppy black teenagers engaged in fisticuffs; cops with sniffer dogs, closing in on a drug-dealer, and a poor old crone, armed with an empty vodka bottle, collapsing in a heap.

'Do you stock *Vogue* or *Harpers*?' A woman in a petal-soft suede jacket had just glided up to the stand.

'Yes, both,' Pat said, taking them down from the rack.

'Thanks. I'll have *Vogue* – no, *Harpers*.'

The woman continued to dither, first flicking through *Vogue*, then slowly turning the pages of *Harpers*, lingering on the photographs, oblivious to the two customers who had just come up behind her.

'So which do you want?' Pat prompted. If she charged people for their reading time, she'd be a millionaire by now, instead of earning less than the minimum wage.

'I'm not . . . sure.'

Judging by her jacket and the snazzy bag slung across one shoul-der, she wasn't exactly short of a bob and could surely buy them both. 'Would you mind moving to the side?' Pat asked. 'You're welcome to browse, but if you stand there in the middle, no one else can see.' She expected a curt retort, but the woman appeared completely lost in the world of high-society gaddings.

As she served the other customers, a tourist approached, festooned with a camera and binoculars. 'Can you tell me the way to Notting Hill?'

She couldn't place his accent – an Aussie, perhaps, or a Kiwi. 'By foot or by tube?' she asked.

'Is it far to walk?' He grimaced at the rain. It had been falling most of July, in fact – a succession of endless drizzly days, grey and overcast.

'A couple of miles.'

'Christ! I couldn't walk a hundred yards, let alone two miles.'

'In that case, take the District Line. Down those steps, and it's just two stops from here.' On some occasions this week, she had felt like a one-man Tourist Office. Where were the Houses of Parliament? Did she know of a decent hotel in the area? Or some-where to cash travellers' cheques? And people always wanted toilets, of course, which were non-existent here, except in bars and cafés. It was quite a problem for *her*, and she'd already learned not to drink – no water, tea or coffee, however thirsty she might be – so she could last till the end of her shift. Although if she did get really desperate, she was allowed to ask Arnie to cover for her, or the Indian guy who worked on the tube but came up to the street for a smoke. And while they held the fort, she dashed off double-quick and used the loo in McDonald's. Another advantage of being male was that you could get away with peeing in a bottle, if you ducked down in the corner of the news-stand, out of sight of the customers, but she dared not risk it herself. Her boss might show up, to check on her, just as she was pulling down her knickers.

The woman had finally finished reading and closed both maga-zines with a deprecating shrug. 'I think I'll leave it, actually,' she drawled. 'There's nothing of interest in either of those.'

Well, you should know, Pat didn't say. She was involved with another customer, in any case – some poor old chap who looked at least a hundred, and was scrabbling in his purse to find a paltry 60p.

'My eyes are so bad,' he quavered, 'the coins all look the same.'

Pat leaned across to help, counting out the money for him from his well-worn plastic purse. Easy to assume that old folk were doolally, when they actually had a problem seeing and hearing. It was like people with unsightly faces, who were often regarded not just as ugly but as stupid, sly or shifty, whereas beautiful people were judged, more sympathetically, as intelligent and sociable. There was no proof of either, of course, yet one's looks determined one's future, without the *need* for proof.

'Take care,' she called to the old chap, who had been rudely pushed aside by a swarthy Mr Big, with black-treacle eyes and dirty-looking stubble. Thrusting a sheaf of £5 notes right in front of her nose, he mumbled something in an indecipherable accent.

'Pardon?' You needed language skills in this job – in fact, every tongue from Arabic to Bantu.

'Fifty,' he said – or she thought he said.

'Fifty *what?*' On Tuesday, a woman had wanted fifty bars of Toffee Crisp for her sister's fiftieth birthday. She'd been thinking about that sister off and on. Had she enjoyed her birthday – and the Toffee Crisps? Was it her favourite kind of chocolate bar, or would she have preferred a sweater? She'd never had a sister herself – no siblings at all, in fact. Perhaps just as well. *All* of them might have landed up with repulsive purple birthmarks.

'Fifty,' he repeated, thrusting the fives into her hand, then holding up a 50p piece. 'I want this' – he tapped the coin with his finger – 'plenty this. *You* take notes. *I* take coins.'

'Sorry, no can do. I need all the change I can get. I'm not a bank, you know.'

Irony was wasted on him. He not only failed to understand, he continued to implore. Amazing, she thought, the qualities this job required – not just a talent for languages, but patience and a sense of humour, a good grasp of the local geography, and degrees in both psychology and maths (not to mention sheer brute strength, to heave the bales of papers around). Eventually she got rid of him by dint of drawing him a sketch-map and marking Lloyds and Barclays on it, with a picture of some 50ps underneath.

Hardly had he gone, when another foreigner appeared – a young girl, this time, and Chinese by the looks of her. 'I want place to live,' she said.

Me, too, thought Pat. At present she was sharing what was optimistically called a studio flat (in fact, more an oversized cupboard), with a Ukrainian refugee who didn't wash.

'You have newspaper with place to live?'

'Yes, *Loot*'s the best.' She handed it over, pointing out the property section. After all, it cost nothing to be helpful. 'Do you want to rent, or buy, or share with other people?'

'I want buy.'

Another wealthy female. 'OK, you need to look here. And here.' Grabbing a biro, she marked the appropriate columns. 'And if you haven't found anything by Wednesday, I suggest you buy the *Standard*. The Wednesday edition has a special property section.' Only a few months ago, she had been searching it herself, feeling utterly alone and sick with apprehension.

'Thank you,' said the girl, extracting a £50 note from her expensive-looking calfskin purse and passing it to Pat. 'I don't know money. I just arrive – this morning. You take, please, what paper cost.'

Whole centuries seemed to pass while Pat stared at the £50 note. She had never seen one in her life before, but it seemed to symbolize the very thing she craved: financial ease and freedom. Once she had paid the basics – rent, food, fares, phone bill and electricity meter – there was nothing left from her wages. But if she only had some cash in hand, she could afford a drink in the pub, take herself to the cinema, buy some decent camouflage make-up that actually hid the birthmark, even splurge a tenner or so on something totally frivolous.

She reached out and took the note. For the last two weeks, she'd been absolutely scrupulous in giving the right change, down to the last penny piece. But this girl was clearly naïve, and almost asking to be cheated by announcing that she didn't know the money. If she were given change as from a £5-note instead of from a fifty, would she even notice?

Yes, of course she damn well would. Foreign or no, she couldn't be so stupid as not to understand the denominations of banknotes, however new she was to London and the currency. Even a total moron could tell the figure 5 from 50. Besides, it was morally wrong. In fact, she could hear her mother's voice shrill and shocked at the very thought of her daughter stealing. Yet who was her mother to tell her right from wrong? She wouldn't be in London at all if her mother hadn't walked out of her marriage. Her new bloke, Doug, a ghastly creep who must be pushing sixty, had broken up the family, and *she,* the superfluous daughter, had left home as a result.

Surreptitiously she rubbed the red triangle on the £50-note against a copy of the *Standard*. A smudge of the red came off, which meant it wasn't forged. So why was she standing motionless like a broken clockwork toy? It was worth a try, surely. If the girl objected, or looked puzzled, she could immediately pretend she'd made a mistake and hand over the rest of the change. And who would know?

Not a soul. No one was about – no one watching, no other customers waiting to be served. In fact, if she was going to do it, she'd better do it *quickly*, before someone did turn up.

With what she hoped was a disarming smile, she put the fifty in the till, just underneath her wage packet. Then she took out £3.50 in coins (mainly 10ps, so it would look more in bulk and volume), and passed them to the girl. Her stomach churned with fear as she waited for the outraged shout, the indignant foreign babble. But the girl simply put the coins in her purse, took the paper with a good-natured 'thank-you', and walked off down the street.

Pat stood stock still, the blood rushing to her face, waiting for someone to accost her, or the girl herself to come dashing back in fury and distress. She might even bring a friend with her, someone less wet behind the ears who could add up and subtract, and would *know* it was a scam. And, she, the culprit, would be instantly recognizable. 'Of course I remember who served me – a girl with a great big purple pockmark on her face.'

'*Standard*, please.'

Mechanically she took one from the pile, folded the magazine inside it and passed it across the counter. But her hands were trembling noticeably as she put the money in the till.

'A Twix bar, please, and a carton of Ribena. And have you got an *Independent* left?'

Nodding, she reached for all three items, doing the usual sums in her head. 'That's one pound fifty altogether – no, one pound fifty-eight. Sorry, wrong again – one pound fifty-five.' Her brain was barely working. She just had to get away from here, take a bus, take a tube, vanish into the stratosphere. She checked her watch: ten past four. Only twenty minutes left, thank God, until she handed over to Gareth. He was never late, but he liked her to stop for a chat. Well, she'd tell him she was in a rush – invent a dental appointment.

'Excuse me, please.'

A small, mousy couple had just come up, loaded with bags and cases, the man holding out a folder. 'Sorry to bother you, but we're looking for the Commodore Hotel. We were given this voucher by Apex Travel, but there doesn't seem to be an address on it.'

She peered closely at the paperwork. No address, no phone number, and she herself had never heard of a Commodore Hotel.

She had noticed from day one how many people appeared to be lost – wandering round in circles, sometimes close to tears, or totally confused because they didn't speak the language. This particular pair was English and she desperately wanted to help them, if only to make amends for the theft. But she had no idea what to do and, anyway, she must get rid of them, so she could take the £50-note from the till, before Gareth showed up. 'Look, I'm sorry I can't help, but there's a travel agent's a few doors down on the left. If you ask in there, someone's bound to know.'

The minute they'd gone, she extracted a fiver from her purse and put it into the till, to ensure the books would balance, then quickly grabbed her wage packet, together with the £50-note. Having stowed both safely in her bag, she looked up to see an old battleaxe demanding the *TV Times*, and another woman behind her, waving a clutch of postcards and a tenner.

Never had twenty minutes passed so slowly, despite the glut of customers. She seemed to be operating on autopilot, while her other self stood paralysed, appalled at what she'd done.

'Hi, Primrose! Or are you Poppy today?' Gareth bounced up to the news-stand with his usual cheery smile.

'No, I'm Marigold on Fridays.' In her present state of mind, the banter seemed inane. 'Sorry, Gareth, I've got to fly. I'm already late for the dentist. Everything's fine. There's plenty of change in the till and . . . No, the new fridge didn't come, but there hasn't been much call for drinks.'

Without waiting for another interruption, she bolted from the news-stand and down the steps to the tube, feeling slightly safer once she was swallowed up in the crowds. She stood waiting on the platform, wondering what to do next. Somehow she couldn't face going home to Acton. The small, claustrophobic flat *wasn't* home, in any case, and she balked at the thought of spending all evening with Svetlana, who'd keep prattling in her broken English and puffing on the foul fag-ends she picked up from the street.

While she was still dithering, a Wimbledon train came in. Well, why not go to Wimbledon? So long as she wasn't near the scene of the crime, she could breathe a little easier.

Yet on the train she felt that everyone was staring, not just at her birthmark, but at her bag as well, as if the £50-note was sparking like a firework, visible to all. Even if a seat were free, it would be impossible to read. She kept wondering if the Chinese girl was at this very moment marching up to Gareth, recounting what had happened. And Gareth would tell the boss and—

'Excuse me,' someone said.

She jumped almost out of her skin. They'd followed her, would take her in for questioning, lock her up, put her in a—

'I need to get out at the next station and you're standing on my bag.'

'Oh, shit! *Am* I? Sorry.' She disentangled her foot from the trailing strap of a backpack, which the woman standing next to her had put down on the floor.

Several other people got off, so she slumped down in a seat and sat with her eyes closed, pretending to doze, until they finally rattled in to Wimbledon. On emerging from the station, the first thing she heard was the wail of hysterical sirens, which immediately roused her fears again. They must be closing in on her.

Don't be stupid, she told herself. Sirens are just part of London life.

Coming from a sleepy town, she still wasn't used to the din, but she'd have to toughen up, and also change her attitude. Nicking fifty quid from a rich (and clueless) Chinese kid could be viewed as a brilliant stroke of luck, not a deadly crime.

Her throat was parched and her stomach rumbling audibly. She'd had nothing to drink since breakfast-time and nothing to eat save one small bar of Wholenut, gobbled between customers. She wasn't keen on pubs – still felt apprehensive about entering them alone – so she wove her way along the crowded street until she finally reached an anonymous-looking café. Having chosen a table in a dark corner at the back, she ordered a burger and chips and a Pepsi. Her drink was brought by a foreign waitress, with lank grey hair and a rash around her mouth. The poor woman seemed deadbeat. She'd probably been working since early morning and, as Pat knew from her own experience, standing on your feet for hours and constantly having to be polite (even to boorish customers) could leave you pretty knackered. And this woman wasn't young – in fact, seriously past her sell-by date, with swollen ankles and dodgy-looking feet, yet she was rushing back and forth with heavy trays. And she'd only be paid a pittance for her pains. Waitressing, like selling papers, never made anyone a millionaire.

She ought to exchange a friendly word with her, but she felt in no mood to talk, so she got out *Born To Win* and propped it against the ketchup bottle. Her Pepsi was ice-cold and served with a twist of lemon, and she sat sipping it appreciatively, relishing the unaccustomed treat. It was pointless feeling guilt. Now that she'd actually nicked the cash, she ought to try and enjoy it – enjoy being waited on in a café, instead of heating soup on a gas-ring, or sharing a tin of beans with Svetlana (who usually gobbled more than her half). And Wimbledon was bound to have a cinema, so she could take herself to see a film, and perhaps do a bit of shopping first – *not* in a charity shop. She had left most of her clothes up in Suffolk, and her father was so shattered at being on his own, she hadn't liked to ask him to pack them up and post them. If she'd been a decent sort, she'd have stayed on in the house with him, once her mother left, to provide a bit of company and help him cook and clean. But they had never been exactly close. Fathers wanted pretty daughters, not plain unfeminine freaks.

She bit into the burger, which was gratifyingly large, the meaty juices seeping into the soft whiteness of the bun. It came with a substantial salad and a pile of greasy chips. Salad was a luxury. A lettuce, for example, had too few calories to justify the 60p it cost. But here she had a wealth of stuff: frilly leaves and reddish ones, strips of yellow pepper, tomato halves, diced cucumber and slices of raw onion. She could almost feel the vitamins kicking up their little heels as they galloped round her bloodstream. The cost of the meal was probably more or less equivalent to two weeks' worth of electricity, but she didn't give a damn. She intended to relish every mouthful, not think about the bills.

She was definitely feeling better. Romantic music was playing in the background and, as the syrupy slush wafted over her, she pretended she was pretty, and dating some gorgeous hunk. Yes, they were sitting in the cinema, his arm around her waist, and he suddenly leaned across and kissed her in the velvety, exciting dark. And now they were in his flat, which had tiger-skin rugs and huge jungly tropical plants, and slowly, very slowly, he was coaxing her down on the bed, unfastening the fiddly buttons of her shirt and whispering—

'Can I get you anything else?'

Yes, please, she thought, a boyfriend made of flesh and blood, and a halfway decent face. Scanning the pudding menu, which the waitress had just brought, she ordered chocolate cheesecake with whipped cream. It only cost £3.50 – nothing when you had money in your purse.

A couple wandered in and sat down opposite, holding hands across the tabletop. People took so much for granted – having the cash to eat out, being able to look in the mirror without shuddering at themselves, even being part of a couple, for God's sake. At least her Dad had lived with her mother for close on thirty years, but perhaps that made things worse. He must be really lonely now, in contrast.

She booted him out of the café. This was her special evening, and she couldn't cope with another source of guilt. In fact, if she was planning to go shopping, she'd better eat up and get the bill, or the shops would all be closed. Having scraped the last vestige of cream from her plate, she called the waitress over and paid with money from her wage packet, rather than break in to the £50-note. That was sacrosanct, and before rushing ahead and spending it, she wanted some time on her own in the flat, just to gaze at her riches and gloat.

She sauntered out, arm in arm with her lover, and deliberately avoiding looking in shop windows, so the idyll wasn't spoilt by the sight of her actual face. At least it had stopped raining, and a few glints of golden light had forced themselves through the clouds, as if the sun had heaved itself out of bed, at last, and remembered it was summer.

'Stop! Stop! *Wait!*'

She froze. Footsteps were coming up behind her. The cops! They must have followed her on the tube, and finally decided to pounce.

She wheeled round at a touch on her arm, and saw not men in uniform but the waitress from the café holding out her book. 'You left this on the table,' she said in a breathless tone, still panting from her sprint.

'Oh, so I did. How stupid! Thanks ever so much for. . . .'

But the waitress was already out of earshot, racing back to the café – obviously she couldn't leave her customers. If fact, it had been decent of her to return the book at all, when she could have simply nicked it. That tired, plain, decrepit old soul, with her swollen ankles and bunioned feet, had actually taken the trouble to run after her.

She leaned against the wall, staring at the photo on the cover of the book: the author as a kid of five, with flippers in place of arms. For all she knew, that Chinese girl might also have some disability. Or have run away from home. Or be stuck with a father who was embarrassed by her looks. And there was no real proof she was rich. She might have earned the fifty pounds in some rotten low-paid job. Or invented the story about buying a flat, to make her feel less bleak. Didn't *she* indulge in fantasies, and for exactly the same reason? – the hunky lovers, top-notch jobs, business empires built from scratch.

Opening the book, she reread the blurb printed on the inside of the jacket. In taking this guy as a model, she had simply been deluding herself. When it came to fundamentals, there were no parallels between them. She lacked his basic skills and drive, not to mention his integrity. Honesty, he'd claimed in chapter one, has been his watchword and his guiding light.

Having removed the shoelace she'd been using as a bookmark, she placed the book on a window-ledge, in sight of passers-by. Perhaps someone would pick it up – a Chinese girl in trouble, a waitress with bad feet, an elderly couple, lost, with no address. Then she trudged back the way she'd come, forcing herself to face her cruel reflection in the windows: a thin, scraggy girl, badly dressed and disfigured by a birthmark – no, *worse* than that: a liar and a thief.

A few yards from the station was a news-stand very similar to the one she worked in herself. She stopped a minute to watch the bloke who manned it: a thin, round-shouldered guy, with a straggly grey moustache. He was good at his job – deft with the money, civil with the punters – though there was no spark of hope in his face, and his eyes looked sad and tired. Suddenly, on impulse, she got out her purse and extracted the £50-note. '*West End Final*, please,' she said, passing the note across. 'And keep the change.'

Before he could remonstrate, or indeed say a word at all, she dashed along to the station and down the steps to the tube. She had no more use for the money or the book. The money was a burden, the book irrelevant. It was time to face reality. She was going back home

– tomorrow – and if her father wasn't pleased to see her, well, she'd simply have to shove off somewhere else.

The fantasies were over. She *wasn't* born to win.

16

GRAPES OF WRATH

'Oh, Nurse, hello. It's me again. How *is* he?'

'We've moved him to a private room.'

'Why? Is he worse?' Eileen fought a flare of panic, mixed shamefully with hope.

'No. We just thought he'd be more comfortable.'

Hospital language required interpretation. How could her father be 'comfortable' with a tube in his nose, a drip in his arm, and when he was so skeletally thin he must feel every crease in the sheet? 'So where do I find him?'

'It's just past Florence Ward. I'll take you, shall I?'

They walked along the corridor together, Eileen struggling to keep up. She wondered how she appeared to this young nurse – an obese, arthritic Labrador trying to compete with a lean and eager greyhound? Neither of them spoke. There was nothing left to say.

The nurse tapped on Arthur's door and pushed it open. 'Your daughter's here to see you.'

The only reply was a grunt. Arthur wasn't one for greetings, let alone effusiveness.

'Well, I'll leave you to it,' the nurse said, turning on her heel. 'Ring the bell if you need me.'

Eileen leaned over the bed, looking down at her father's recumbent form. His skin was porridge-pale; his arms were two white sticks lying useless on the counterpane. She tried to manage a smile. 'How are you, Dad?'

'Awful! I don't know why they had to move me.'

'But isn't it nicer being on your own.'

165

'What, solitary confinement? I could die for all they'd know. No one's come near me since they brought the tea – and that was undrinkable.'

'Well, *I'm* here now.'

'Yes, and you took your time. I expected you hours ago.'

'I'm sorry.' She unbuttoned her coat and drew up a chair beside the bed. 'At least it's quieter here. You hated all that noise in the ward.'

'Yes, dreadful racket! Coughing all day, snoring all night.'

'So aren't you better out of it?' As she settled back in the chair, she suddenly caught sight of a luxurious bunch of purple grapes taking up most of the space on his locker. Where on earth could they have come from? *She* was his only visitor and had long ago stopped bringing him presents, since whatever she offered resulted in complaints. Flowers were a waste of money; chocolates a rip-off; fruit gave him indigestion, and, as for books, they were full of sex and violence, and anyway his eyes were too weak to read. 'Where did you get the grapes, Dad?'

'Don't *touch* them!'

'I'm not.'

'They're poisonous.'

'Poisonous?'

'Yes. They were stolen from another patient – one who died.'

'So how did they land up here?'

'The nurses brought them in. They want this bed for someone else, so they give me poisoned grapes.'

'Dad, that's silly, honestly. Grapes are very good for you. They're full of vitamins.'

'These ones aren't. They're tainted.'

'Why don't I give them a wash, then? I see you've got a basin over there.'

'Washing won't help. You can't scrub poison off. As soon as that useless cleaner shows up, I'll get her to put them in the dustbin.'

'But it's such a waste. *I'll* eat them.'

'No, my girl, you will *not*!'

She subsided in her chair. That tone of voice had to be respected. It had resounded through her childhood, so full of prohibitions, that even now, as a woman of fifty-five, she obeyed from sheer force of habit. 'Chewing gum is forbidden in this house.' 'You're never to

166

touch matches – you'll start a fire and burn us both to a cinder.' 'No, you can't have barley sugar. It'll only rot your teeth.' 'Take that dress off – *now!* I won't have any daughter of mine making herself look cheap.' 'I don't care *what* he's called. Boys have only one idea in their head. You'll land up like your mother, and you know what happened to *her*.' In fact, she didn't know. Her mother had disappeared long, long ago, in a vague and shadowy past, where memories were mere vapour-trails of mist. Often, she tried to imagine her, but all she could conjure up was a wraith – a wraith with neither breasts nor lap. She had been starving since her infancy. Deprived of mother's milk, she had been forced to feed on the world; biting into its tough volcanic crust, gagging on rocks and soil.

Abruptly she changed the subject. 'Did you see the doctor yesterday?'

'Yes. Silly ass! He doesn't know what he's talking about. I doubt he's even trained.'

'Staff Nurse Taylor told me yesterday he's one of the best in London.' Her eyes kept straying back to the grapes, the only splash of colour in the room. Everything else was white: white walls, white bed and bedding, scuffed white vinyl floor. Their deep exotic purple seemed to belong to another realm – a realm of sun and sweetness, far removed from this shabby, cash-starved hospital, full of decrepitude and pain.

She sat fidgeting in the chair. Most chairs, in her experience, were made ridiculously small, and this one in particular constrained her like a corset. But never mind her petty concerns – she was here for *him* and ought to be conversing. Which wasn't easy when there was no news to speak of, and he wouldn't want to hear about her day. She had always disappointed him: doing badly at school, failing to get to college, never learning to drive or travelling anywhere, remaining single and childless, and now stuck in a dead-end job until retirement. And then there was her weight, of course – the greatest crime of all.

In the silence, the beep of the drip and the hiss of the oxygen seemed more intrusive than usual, as if they were talking between themselves. She highjacked their conversation – she the hiss, her father the beep.

'Dad, I've just been promoted.' Hiss, hiss, hiss. 'That's why I was late. All the staff were toasting me as their new General Manager.'

'Wonderful!' Beep, beep, beep. 'I'm so proud.'

'And I've booked a cruise on the *Oriana*.' 'With my fiancé, Jonathan.' The one man in her life had been called Jonathan McGrath, but he had left her for a Scottish girl, thirty years ago.

'Fantastic!'

'And did I tell you about—?' She broke off as the nurse came in, to take her father's pulse and check the drip.

'Is it cold outside?' he asked her.

'I wouldn't know,' the nurse said, scribbling something on the chart. 'I haven't been out. Better ask your daughter.'

'Freezing,' Eileen replied. Though she might have well have said 'boiling.' Weather no longer existed for him. And nor did seasons or dates. 'You're better off here in the warm.'

The nurse was making for the door. Eileen longed to seize hold of her and implore her not to leave. With someone else in the room, she felt safer and more real. But, no, the door was already closing, and she and her father were trapped on their own once more. The silence swept back, dense and clammy like fog. She had never been good at small talk, and deep talk was too dangerous.

It was he who spoke, half sitting up and peering at her. 'You're looking tired. What's wrong with you?'

'Nothing,' she said, surprised that he had noticed her at all. Of *course* she was tired, flogging to the hospital every evening, on top of a hard day's work. And hungry, too, as usual – in fact, even more so tonight, having had to stay on, to type an urgent report. There hadn't been time to grab a sandwich, let alone sit down to a proper meal. She imagined reaching out for the grapes and eating the whole enormous bunch, cramming them into her mouth, crunching pips in her haste, delicious purple juices running down her chin. Or maybe better to spin them out – pop one in at a time and slowly savour its taste and texture. Yes, she could feel the silken flesh slipping between her lips, then exploding on her tongue in a spurt and rush of sweetness. . . .

'What are you smiling about?'

'Nothing,' she repeated. She must never mention food. Food for him was the enemy and, all his life, he had rationed it – half a slice of toast; butter *or* jam, not both; one teabag in the pot; cake only on their birthdays.

She broke off another grape and put it in her mouth. How

smoothly, moistly plump it felt, all but bursting from its skin – wonderfully consoling. Nothing was rationed here. A whole succession of grapes were plopping into her mouth, filling her empty stomach. Every one she swallowed magically replenished itself, so that the bunch remained in perfect shape.

'They've changed my pills, as well. The new ones make me dizzy. I just can't get on with them.'

'Have you told the nurse?'

'What's the use? They don't listen to a word I say.'

'I'm sorry, Dad.' She *was* sorry. His state was pitiable. 'I just wish I could do something to help.'

'You can!'

'What?' Her previous offers of help had met with dogged resistance. No, he didn't want her neighbour popping in. And as for being read to, he detested the idea. No, cassettes and headphones would get in the way of the tubes. And a back-rest was no use at all – the nurses would only remove it.

'Get me out of here.'

'Dad, I *can't*. You're ill.'

'Yes, and they're making me worse. They want this room for someone else. That's why they gave me the grapes.'

'Oh, come on, Dad, they aren't murderers! They're trying to make you . . . comfortable.'

'I'm coming home with you tonight.' It was a statement, not a request.

She tried to keep control of her voice. *His* had risen ominously. 'Dad, that isn't possible. Who'd look after you when I'm at work?'

'I don't need looking after. I'm not a child.'

He had never been a child, any more than she had. He, too, had lost his mother, and at an even earlier stage. When she'd died in childbirth, he'd been bundled off to an orphanage while still in swaddling clothes. That's why she didn't blame him – not for anything. Pain was genetic, like haemophilia or colour blindness. And pain could make you angry. As he *had* been, all his life.

Another cluster of grapes tiptoed into her mouth. *She* had avoided anger by building a protective gingerbread house around the starving hole inside. The walls were made of honeycomb, with barley-sugar windows. The tiles on the roof were brandysnaps, and the floor was solid marzipan. In the peaceful garden grew chocolate-flowers and lollipop-trees, and the pond was filled with soda-pop, with a bubbling Tizer fountain. And now she was constructing another wing – a luxurious purple sanctuary made of glistening grapes.

Her fingers were gloriously sticky as she continued glutting herself. The fruit was so ripe, it seemed to be fermenting in her mouth, turning to vintage wine. Yes, she was strolling through the vineyards of France, plucking bunch after bunch of the luscious purple globes. Green grapes weren't the same. Green was sour and restrictive and gave you bellyache, whereas purple was rich and regal; an intense and generous colour – the colour of excess.

Hot sun caressed her skin as she wandered the vine-clad slopes. Even the names of the grapes were poetry: Merlot, Shiraz, Cabernet Sauvignon – voluptuous names for the voluptuous liquid velvet in her mouth. She was stripping the vineyards bare, sating herself on purple. Never before had she felt so unafraid, so rapturously replete.

'Eileen . . .' said a voice; a feeble quavering voice, quite unlike her father's usual bark.

Startled, she opened her eyes, to see her father slumped sideways on the bed, his mouth drooling, his face a ghastly grey. She sprang to her feet to press the bell and summon help, then slowly sank back down again. At last, she understood. The grapes were his gift to her, his final parting gift, not poisoned, as he'd claimed, but sanctified and blessed. All his life he had rationed her, but now, at this solemn moment, he was making recompense, appeasing the famine, redeeming the starveling years. The grapes were her legacy, her sumptuous inheritance. He, who had restricted her, was now offering unstinted food; he who had banned indulgence, was telling her with his dying breath that she could – *must* – eat her fill.

She reached out for his hand. Never, in all their years together, had she ever held his hand, not even as a child. Touching was forbidden, along with all the other things. But as he faded, the prohibitions faded, and life began to open up and flower.

She let her fingers close round his. His hand felt small and bony like a fledgling bird. The flesh was unnaturally cold, so she cupped her other hand around it, to provide a cocoon of warmth. They sat together, peacefully, no sound except the whisper of the oxygen, the heartbeat of the drip. Then, suddenly, she felt the faintest flicker of his fingers answering the pressure of her own. He could no longer speak, but his hand was speaking for him, saying miraculously, triumphantly, and for the first time in his life, 'I love you, little daughter. I love you exactly as you are.'

17

NEW MAN

2 large pork chops
Juice of one large orange and juice of one small lemon
2 tablespoons of clear honey
1 large tablespoon of good quality marmalade. . . .

He scrutinized the jar of Cooper's Oxford marmalade, thick with chunky peel. That would surely count as 'good quality'. And he had managed to get hold of some very superior pork – Gloucester Old Spot, no less – grass-fed, free-range, and certified organic. If Lorraine could see him now, surrounded by recipe books and cooking utensils, she would regard it as a hallucination and pinch herself to wake up.

'So you thought I'd go to pieces,' he muttered to the second, disembodied Lorraine who held sway in his head, 'just because you walked out. Don't kid yourself. I've become a New Man – learned to cook, learned to shop. There's not a ready-meal or takeaway in sight. And I hope you bloody well feel sorry now. . . .'

He slapped the meat down on the chopping board and trimmed off the excess fat, imagining doing the same to her – hacking off great slices of her wobbly breasts and thighs – cutting her down to size, in every sense. The pink mottled pork did, indeed, remind him of her flesh: its waxy denseness, always slightly flushed. It maddened him the influence she had still: turning his dreams to nightmares, fouling up his brain with accusations, taunts.

Tossing the strips of fat in the waste-bin, he flung her remains on top, and closed the lid with a bang. Tonight of all nights, he had to bump her off; exterminate her finally.

He snatched up the recipe again, determined to focus on the job in hand. The chops needed seasoning, then searing in hot oil. First he sprinkled them with rock salt and best black pepper, ground coarsely from the mill, before heating the oil-and-butter mixture in the pan. As he watched it bubble up, he was aware of his own anger, frothing and sizzling underneath – an anger completely out of place in the romantic evening he was planning. God, the very thought of it made him come out in a sweat. He could hardly believe how nervous he was – a bloke of forty-two, for heaven's sake, twittering like an adolescent because he'd actually invited a woman to dinner the first time since the divorce.

He turned the gas to low and browned the chops for seven minutes each side, timing them to the second. Then he drained off the fat, saving just a tablespoonful, and added the finely chopped spring onions. One of the main attractions of cooking was its strict rules and accurate measurements – nothing left vague or imprecise. The spices, for example, were exactly specified: a level teaspoonful of ginger, half a teaspoon of turmeric and a quarter of a teaspoonful of nutmeg. As he measured them out, he already felt more in control. There was a definite satisfaction in following a recipe that was sure to turn out right, so long as he kept to the letter. What a contrast to normal life, with its uncertainty, its precariousness, its constant gambles and guesswork.

He transferred the contents of the pan into a casserole, then cut the lemon in half, pausing to observe its nobbly, pock-marked skin. One of the relaxation techniques they'd taught him at the clinic was to slow right down and really *look* at things – a grain of pepper, a crystal of salt, the green curly hair of a parsley sprig. Smells were important, too. He'd been told to be more aware of them – and of the outside world in general – and less preoccupied with his own disordered brain. He took a deep breath in – the sharp tang of citrus juices cutting across the waft of buttery pork, and all the other contrasting smells twitching in his nose: ginger, nutmeg, onion, garlic.

Next he mixed the honey with the marmalade, wishing he could make a marinade for Marie-Claire, spread the syrupy mixture on her as yet unseen naked body and slowly lick it off. Or hang a curl of marmalade peel over both her nipples and watch them grow eagerly erect. Ever since he'd met her, he'd been picturing her breasts – and, yes, now she was lying on the sofa of his mind, slowly peeling off her clothes. He could feel the velvety texture of her skin, taste her lemon-honey-ginger-flavoured kiss. . . .

Forcing himself back to the kitchen, he placed the dish in the oven. It needed a highish gas for the first fifteen minutes, then an hour and a half at mark three. Precise instructions again. If only there were similar precepts for love affairs and marriage.

Checking the recipe once more, he realized there was still the rice to cook – ideally twenty minutes before the pork was ready. And the apricots were meant to be poached just before the meal was served, and added to the sauce. Damn! Once Marie-Claire arrived, he wanted to devote his full, uninterrupted attention to her, not be fussing around with pots and pans. Surely best to finish the cooking now, then have a shower and change. He could always keep the rice warm on the electric tray he'd bought specially for tonight.

He left both rice and apricots simmering on the hob while he went to lay the table. He'd had to buy new china, as well as a complete new set of kitchenware. Lorraine had left him nothing but the oldest cups and plates, a few mingy knives and forks, and the oldest, battered saucepans. The cheek of it appalled him! She'd won hands down – kept the house and garden (while he'd been forced to move to a small and shabby flat), *and* been given custody of Ben and Alexander. They were meant to come and see him every alternate weekend, but half the time they didn't show up and, when they did, they fought. And, of course, if Marie Claire became a fixture, things could well be awkward with young kids underfoot. He'd hardly mentioned the boys to her, as yet. Best to take things slowly. . . .

Anxiously he scanned the table. Would it meet with her approval? He had bought a dark green cloth, to cover the stained pine, and matching linen napkins. But the room itself was crap – dark and mean and poky, with grubby walls and a cheap cord carpet in an unfortunate shade of grey that resembled cigarette ash. He could turn the lights right down, but she might regard that as overly seductive. He didn't want to scare her off before they'd even—

'You bloody cunt!'

He jumped. The bellowed curse was followed by a sudden crash and the sound of breaking china. The noise was coming through the wall – so sharp and clear there might as well not *be* a wall.

'God, you're a fucking cow! You spend all our money, then you break the place up and expect me to shell out more.'

The furious male voice vibrated through the thin partition, assaulting his ears, his living space. The adjoining flat had been empty up to now. A warring couple must have just moved in, or a gang of hooligans. He'd bloody well go round there and tell them to shut up. By the time he'd found his keys, however, the noise appeared to have stopped. He stood listening, ear to the wall. Silence – blessed silence. Maybe it had just been a temporary flare-up, or they'd moved to another room.

Tentatively he laid out the knives and forks, aware that his hands were trembling. He and Lorraine had engaged in shouting matches, and the mere memory of it made him sick.

'Go away,' he begged. 'I don't want you in my life now. I've met someone else, Lorraine. This is my new start.'

He put his whole attention on the table, folding the napkins into decorative shapes, laying out the serving spoons and cheese-knife. The cheese-board he was proud of. In Marie-Claire's honour, he'd selected all French cheeses – Camembert, Pont-L'Eveque, Bleu de Basillac – then added clusters of purple grapes and half a dozen fresh figs. Figs were aphrodisiacs, or so he'd read. If things went well, she might even stay all night with him and—

'You useless piece of shit, sitting on your arse all day and expecting me to wait on you hand and foot.'

He tightened his grip on the cheese-knife. This was truly awful. Supposing the row continued while Marie-Claire was here? He could hardly change the plans now and take her *out* to dine, when she had expressed such unabashed delight in the prospect of him cooking for her. Indeed, he had based the entire menu around her tastes. Pork was her favourite meat, she'd said, especially in a fruity sauce, and she adored anything with chocolate in – hence the chocolate mousse chilling in the fridge. And he'd made a chicken paté as the starter, because she'd mentioned her mother's *Terrine de Volaille* as being *'merveilleux'*. He couldn't waste all that elaborate food, chuck his time and money down the drain.

He broke off a grape, studying its purple bloom, in an effort to distract himself. He was over-reacting, imagining the worst. Marie-Claire wasn't even due here for another couple of hours, and the people next door would hardly go on quarrelling for *that* long. Even he and Lorraine at their worst had usually burned themselves out after half an hour of insults. He hadn't heard the woman's voice at all, as yet. Perhaps she was the passive type, just accepting the abuse. And *he* must do the same; simply ignore what was happening the other side of the wall.

'Get out, *now* – before you make me do something I regret.'

There was a sudden blood-curdling scream – female beyond question: high-pitched, anguished, terrified. There was no mistaking what was going on: the woman was being beaten up. He could hear the sound of heavy blows, accompanied by more desperate screams. He sprang towards the door. He must intervene, save her from assault. Then, all at once, things darkened, and *he* was the violent brute, laying into Lorraine, actually relishing her screams, enjoying the sensation of his fists against her yielding flesh as he punched her in the face.

He was so sickened by the memory, he rushed out of the flat and hurtled down to the basement, concealing himself in the grimy corner where people dumped their rubbish. Leaning against the wall, he glanced at the pile of lumpy dustbin bags, with their shiny, taut-black skins. How menacing they looked, as if they contained dismembered bodies, women's bruised and bloody parts.

No, he mustn't even think that way. He was New Man now and this was his new start. If he stayed down here and used his special breathing techniques, everything would gradually quieten down – his neighbours' quarrel, his beating heart, those memories he was frantic to forget. He squatted on his haunches beside an old cardboard box, full of magazines. What innocent, appealing names they had: *Ideal Home, Woman and Beauty, Good Housekeeping, Natural Health* – things he had never known in life, nor was ever likely to. He picked up *Country Living* and tried to lose himself in the glossy, stylish pages: a feature on equestrianship, an article on Blenheim, warming soups for chilly winter nights. . . .

God, the dinner! He had totally forgotten it. He dashed back to his flat, the smell of burning assailing him the minute he opened the front door. The rice had boiled dry; the apricots blackened to a gluey sludge. Turning the oven off, he rescued the pork – too late. The chops had shrivelled, the sauce was full of charred bits, sticking to the bottom of the blistered casserole.

With shaking hands, he scraped out both burnt saucepans and

tipped their contents into the bin. Next he binned the chops, and the ruined sauce. Then he went to the fridge, removed the chocolate mousse, and emptied the whole bowlful – cream and nuts and all – over the discarded meat and rice. Finally he threw away the paté, with its garnish of fancy lemon twists and cucumber curls. All so much empty show. How could he have ever thought to impress a girl like Marie-Claire, when he was rotten through and through?

Total silence from his neighbours now. For all he knew, the woman might be dead, or have been taken off to hospital fighting for her life. He hadn't lifted a finger in her defence. New Men were dangerous – too self-absorbed to intervene when someone was in peril; too busy making radish-flowers to spare time to help a victim of abuse.

Marie-Claire would be better off without him. When she rang the bell, he wouldn't be there – he had other plans for this evening. She'd worry, of course; might even fly into a rage and try to track him down. Not that she'd ever find him – not where he was going.

He knew the risks. New Men were self-aware. Better to disappoint her now than beat her up in a year or two; smash her fucking stupid face to pulp.

18

PAIR-BOND

'Oh, look, Claire, *look!* That heron's eating a crab.'

She stared down-river, in the direction of his gaze, but all she could see was an expanse of sludge-brown water beneath a slate-grey sky.

'He's tearing off the legs – he doesn't seem to like them.' Robert's voice was rising in excitement. 'And now he's gobbling the body, shell and all. You can see a great big bulge in his throat, and his head's jerking backwards and forwards in the effort to get it down.'

She continued to peer vainly towards the mud-bank, exposed by the low tide. If there *was* a heron sitting there, it was little more than a blur.

'Now he's having a go at the legs. I think they're too tough for him to swallow, though.'

She was excluded from this avian meal, but it would be unkind to ask to borrow the binoculars when Robert was deriving such elation from the spectacle.

'He's determined not to be beaten. He's picking bits of flesh off the legs and dunking them in the water.'

The details made her queasy. They were meant to be walking off their *own* lunch (not crab, but chicken casserole), but, so far, they'd proceeded a scant 200 yards. She had never imagined when they moved to London that her husband would become an avid bird-watcher. Back in Sussex, with wildlife all around them, he hardly knew a robin from a wren, and was invariably stuck indoors anyway, working on his book. But now he was out almost every day, prowling along this stretch of the embankment, observing gulls, grebe, geese, swans, whatever.

'Oh, blast! He's flown away.'

She blessed the departing heron. Now, perhaps, she could claim her husband's attention. She *had* to tell him – this afternoon. She had put it off and put it off, and Josh was getting tetchy, waiting for her decision. The stress of that decision had brought her out in a rash. And she'd developed stomach pains and headaches, crunching Anadin in the morning and swigging Gaviscon at night. 'Robert,' she began, her voice sounding unnaturally shrill, 'there's something I—'

'Oh, the cormorants are back! I hoped they'd come today, so you could see them, too.' He linked his arm through hers, patting her hand companionably. 'It's so nice to have you with me.'

'For a change,' he might have added – and with reason. Rarely did she join him on his walks.

'See, they're diving down to try to get a fish. It's incredible how long they can stay under. I timed one yesterday and it didn't reappear for a whole minute.'

'Gosh,' she murmured lamely. He was so keen to share his pleasure with her, he deserved some show of interest. Yet it wasn't easy to concentrate on cormorants, faced with the biggest crisis of her life.

'Let's time these two, shall we?'

She unlatched her arm with a sense of relief, to allow him to check his watch. It felt worse to talk betrayal when they were actually physically linked.

'Twenty seconds, thirty, forty, forty-five . . . Ah! One of them's back up, and, yes, with something in his beak.' He readjusted the binoculars, moving a step nearer to the bank. 'A small eel, by the looks of it. One gulp and it's gone! The other one's back up now, but she didn't get a thing.'

'How d'you know it's female?'

'I don't. I'm only guessing. Look – there she goes again!'

There was no chance of walking on until they'd observed this second diving-display (*and* a third and fourth), but finally Robert made a move. 'Darling . . .' she said tentatively, aware that his eyes were on the river still.

Her voice was drowned by a police launch speeding on its way upstream, churning the sullen water into a lively foaming wake. Those rolling waves reminded her of Josh – again: last night, sharing a bath, the water surging to and fro as he leaned forward to kiss her breasts. He had made her laugh, as always – asked why weren't nipples sold in shops, so women could ring the changes, mix and match long pink ones with stubby brown ones, keep a couple of spare pairs in a drawer? When she'd got home (late), Robert had cooked her supper; said she looked deadbeat, so she must let him wait on her. She had despised herself at that point, and detested Josh, as well. Things were never simple.

Robert stopped again, to scrutinize the strip of beach below. 'Want to borrow the binoculars?' he asked. 'There's a lot of activity going on down there.'

'Thanks.' She trained them on the water's edge, but the activity she witnessed had little to do with birds. She was back with Josh – in bed, he tying her hands to the headboard, telling her she was his submissive Egyptian slave, and that he, the ruthless slave-master, was about to ravish her.

'Anything interesting?' he asked.

'Er, just gulls, I think.'

'Yes. Great black-backed. They're my favourites. Can you make out what they're eating?'

'A plastic bag!'

'I'm not surprised. They're known to eat anything and everything – dead fish, live ducklings, old apple cores – you name it.'

'No, there's a sandwich in the bag, and they're trying to get it out, all fighting with each other and squawking in annoyance.'

Robert laughed. 'Let me see.'

He was lost to her again. Strange how she saw much less of him, now he had retired. It wasn't just the bird-watching, he had also developed a passion for the Thames, and spent hours in the public library, poring over histories of the Watermen and Lightermen, or working out the chronology of all the different bridges. And even when he *was* at home, he was often wired up to his headphones, listening to audiotapes of birdcalls, learning to tell a blackbird from a thrush. Yet how could she object, when what had first attracted her, twenty-seven years ago, was his passionate interest in anything and everything – stained glass, Norman churches, choral music, chess openings, Chinese calligraphy . . . It was *she* who had changed, not him.

'There's one really aggressive gull that's fighting off the rest, attacking all his rivals tooth and claw.'

Would Robert put up a fight, she wondered, attack Josh tooth and claw, once he knew about their liaison? Unlikely. He had always been a peaceable type, which made the whole thing harder. She couldn't bear to hurt him.

'He's won! He'd got the sandwich! And now he's practically choking himself to get the damned thing down.'

She laughed – an unconvincing sound. She was so tired from sleepless nights, laughter wasn't easy. Midnight to dawn was prison time, lying next to Robert, weighing all the pros and cons, wrestling with a crushing load of guilt; shamefully aware that she might feel differently about her lover if he didn't have his gorgeous house and garden. Could you run off with a man because you wanted a large kitchen again, and the sense of peace and space again, ached to grow roses again, and smell hay and honeysuckle? And if the answer were yes, then she was even more immoral than she felt. Yet she'd been completely unprepared for the sheer noise of the new flat: the roar of traffic on the bridge, the endless planes complaining overhead, the wail of sirens day and night, the racket from next door. Robert had talked her into Vauxhall Heights with his usual wild enthusiasm – the river view, the ten-minute-walk to the Tate, the ease of transport generally, the twenty-four-hour porterage. And she, too, had welcomed the prospect of an end to delays on South-West trains, and to dreary chores like mowing lawns or clearing out blocked drains. What she hadn't realized was that you could actually miss a lawn mower.

'You are *happy*, darling, aren't you?' he asked, as if tuning in to her thoughts.

'Well, yes, but. . . .'

There was a sudden flurry of wings, as all the gulls flew off. A tug was chugging downstream, towing two ancient barges, loaded with brilliant yellow crates. Robert was instantly curious. 'I wonder what's in there?' he mused.

'Search me.'

'I suppose it could be rubbish, on its way to the incinerator.'

Rubbish was how she felt herself, enmeshed as she was in deception, inventing evening classes or theatre trips with girlfriends, as alibis for her stolen time with Josh. She would slink back into the flat, feeling his fingerprints etched into her body, his smell reeking on her skin, his sperm leaking out between her legs. And instead of crying, 'I'm sorry, Robert, I *loathe* myself for this,' she'd trot out some harmless anecdote about the philosophy tutor's hayfever, or the promising young actor who'd received a standing ovation. If only she wasn't fifty-two, it wouldn't be so hard. But there'd never be another chance – she knew that. Either she stayed with Robert in the claustrophobic London flat, till decay set in, and death, or she got out *now* and began afresh, with a younger, wilder man.

Robert was still speculating, watching as the barges passed. 'That yellow makes the rubbish look so smart – if it *is* rubbish.'

Muck and dross concealed by elegant trappings. She had bought new clothes in Josh's honour, so he could have the pleasure of slowly peeling them off. If she were a black-backed gull or heron, Robert would admire her plumage, peer at it through binoculars, preserve it in colour photographs. As it was, he scarcely seemed to notice what she wore. But that was hardly grounds for divorce – most husbands were the same. No, she was locked in a deadly struggle between solid, married, rooted love and dizzy, dangerous, once-in-a-lifetime lust. 'Shall we go back?' she suggested. It was impossible to broach the subject, with so much competition from the river. She needed to sit him down in the flat, banish all distractions.

'So soon? We've only just set out. Unless you're tired, of course?'

'No,' she said quickly. Her tiredness seemed a double betrayal. 'Just feeling a bit . . . chilly.'

'Here, have my sweater.'

'But then *you'll* be cold.'

'No. I'm sweltering.'

'You *can't* be, Robert. I heard on Sky this morning that it's the coldest May since records began.'

'Oh, they're always saying that – the hottest summer, the wettest spring. It's just a ploy to give them something to talk about when there's not much on the News.' His voice was muffled as he removed his sweater, disentangling it from the camera and binoculars. Then he pulled it gently over her head and folded back the flapping sleeves. 'Better?' he asked.

She nodded, his tenderness redoubling the guilt. How could you compare an ardent lover stripping off your clothes with a devoted husband wrapping you up warm?

They strolled on, past a bench occupied by an elderly, unshaven tramp, sprawled along the length of it, clutching an empty cider bottle, and dressed in tattered trousers and a dirty shapeless jumper. By his feet were his few possessions: a pocket-knife, a tobacco tin, a rolled-up sleeping-bag. Whatever the horrors of his life, she envied the fact he owned so little, could move from place to place unburdened. If she did leave Robert, what would happen to their *stuff*? You couldn't divide a double bed in half, or a pinewood dresser and matching table, or a painting of Lake Windermere. In fairness, she should bequeath it all to him, but she had given birth to her children in that bed, entertained a wealth of friends at that battered pinewood table, collected pieces of china to display on that old dresser over a period of almost thirty years. And the painting had been a wedding gift from a friend they both adored.

'I wonder how they choose their benches,' Robert remarked, once the tramp was out of earshot. 'He's always there, every time I come – never on a *different* bench, by a *different* stretch of the river. I'd like to ask him, actually, but he's always dead to the world. Once, I thought he *was* dead, and was about to run for help, when suddenly his hand moved.'

Josh was equally immobile when he slept; lying as if anaes-thetized, barely seeming to breathe. No threshing about, no writhing in wild nightmares, not so much as a muffled grunt or groan. A total contrast to his lovemaking. Sometimes, perversely, she tired of all the panting and thrusting, all the dramatic sound effects, the bizarre positions and elaborate fantasies, and found herself missing Robert's set routine. Habit was a sort of aphrodisiac, contrary to what people said.

'I thought we'd walk on a bit further, darling – so long as you're not too cold.'

'No.' Boiling now, from Josh's embrace.

'I want you to see the greylag geese. Actually, I only realized they were greylags after a few sessions with my bird books. I'm quite confused, to tell the truth, by all the different kinds of goose – Brent goose, Canada goose, pink-footed, white-fronted, and even a *lesser* white-front, to make things still more muddling. The pair I'm going to show you produced a couple of youngsters about two weeks ago. When I first spotted them, they were little balls of fluff, but they've grown amazingly fast.'

Her mind slipped back to Josh once more. *He* had no offspring, and thus no complications – only a long-divorced ex-wife who, conveniently, lived miles away, in Melbourne. It was the twins who worried her. Although now grown up, with partners of their own, they'd be devastated by the very thought of her and Robert separating.

'Apparently greylag geese are famed for their devotion to each other. They mate for life, you see, and every year they cement their bond in a special sort of ceremony.'

She swallowed. So even geese could shame her.

'*We* should do that, darling, to celebrate our house-move. In birdy terms, we've acquired a new territory.'

'Yes,' she muttered tersely.

'Perhaps we could renew our marriage vows, like Paul and Jenny did last year. It would be nice to make it special.'

This was quite intolerable. She stared down at the ground: grubby, cracked, uneven – like her life since she'd met Josh. Sometimes she wished their dramatic meeting had never come about – though typical of his impetuous style to cannon into her while racing down the street, and leave her reeling, literally, then insist on making lavish amends with a bottle of Veuve Cliquot in a glitzy London bar.

'Birds often feel hostile to each other, so I read, even a male and female pairing up.'

'Really?'

'Yes. And frightened of each other, too. But their courtship displays overcome all that, and help them form a pair-bond.' He suddenly turned to face her, raised his arms and flapped them up and down like wings, making a jangling bird-cry.

Her face felt stiff as she smiled.

'And the male brings the female food. That strengthens the bond as well.' He rooted in his pocket, brought out half a tube of Rolos and shook a couple into her palm.

She transferred them to her mouth. The chocolate tasted stale and the toffee centres were sticking to her teeth; none the less, the bird-play was endearing. Josh would never adopt a bird role. Last week, he'd played Mark Antony, with her as sultry Cleopatra, naked on her burnished throne. Could she really love two such different men – Robert rooted in the real world, while Josh made constant forays to the realm of fantasy. And so different physically – Robert tall, angular, balding and blue-eyed; Josh short and solid, with luxuriantly thick black hair. Even their penises were totally dissimilar: the one long, thin and highly-strung; the other fat, squat, stubborn and opinionated. 'I think we ought to turn back,' she said. 'There's quite a wind getting up.'

'No, wait – the geese are just down there.' He pointed to a strip of stony beach on the opposite side of the river.

'Ah, yes, I see.' If only she could muster his enthusiasm for the two plumpish, dull-brown creatures standing side by side. 'If only' had been a constant refrain since Josh erupted into her life. If only decisions were less difficult. If only she could live with him, in his spacious, peaceful house, while staying married to Robert. Or spend alternate weeks with each of them. Or buy their Sussex home back, and. . . .

'These are *feral* greylags,' Robert was explaining, 'not the migratory ones that live up North. According to the Wildfowl Trust, they've been resident here in the South since the 1940s or 50s. A lot of them escaped from private collections and became naturalized over time.'

She gave a non-committal grunt. At this rate, they'd be out till nightfall. He'd spot feral dolphins next, or pelicans, or a pair of golden eagles.

'Oh, lord!' said Robert, frowning. 'There's no sign of the goslings. I hope to God they haven't been eaten by a fox.'

He refocused the binoculars, the silence increasingly fraught. If they're dead, she thought, he'll be devastated, and I can't upset him any further with a discussion about our future.

Then, all at once, he gave a cry of triumph and excitement. 'Wow! Look at that. It's amazing!'

'*What?*'

'Both the adults are lying with one wing raised. I thought they must be drying their feathers, but they're actually sheltering the babies from the cold. They've each got a youngster tucked beneath the wing. I saw the little heads pop up. Do look, Claire, it's enchanting.'

He passed her the binoculars and, all at once, her field of vision sharpened. She could see the markings on the feathers now, the two adult heads, with orange bills, the two barred wings sticking up. She zoomed right in with the glasses, until she could just make out two tiny fluffy goslings, each nestled under a wing – a picture of total parental devotion.

'Oh, heck – that dog – it's frightened them!' Robert winced, as a boisterous young Labrador plunged into the water, scattering the geese. Immediately the gander adopted a threatening pose, hissing frantically with neck and wings outstretched, while the female tried to soothe the startled youngsters.

The gander continued to hiss a warning until the dog eventually splashed out again and scrambled back up the bank. Once peace was restored, both parent geese started pecking around in the mud.

'Darling, pass me the binoculars. I want to see what they're eating. Their normal food is grass, but they're hardly going to find that in a river!'

'Hold on!' she said, intrigued despite herself. 'I can see green streaks on the mud. Maybe it's some sort of weed, or algae. Yes, the female's feeding one of the young, but I can't tell what's in her beak. Oh, and now the gander's found something and given it to the other one.'

Robert was standing behind her and put his arms round her waist. 'It reminds me of when the twins were born and, while you were feeding Adam, I'd be trying to pacify Amanda. We were quite a team, you know.'

Silently she nodded. Having two babies at once, both undersized, both colicky, had been an incredible strain, especially in mid-February, with sub-zero temperatures and the boiler on the blink. Strange how she'd forgotten, put that whole exhausting period completely out of her mind. Yet without Robert, she'd have fallen apart, adrift in dirty nappies and night feeds. Despite the pressure of his job, he had got up with her throughout the night, every couple of hours, brought her tea and buttered toast, or mugs of steaming soup, as she struggled to feed both famished, howling infants. Like the gander, he had protected her from every sort of danger, including bossy health visitors and interfering relatives – even including depression and self-doubt.

'Thank you,' she said suddenly, loosening her grip on the binoculars, and clutching both his hands instead.

'What – for showing you the geese?'

'No, for . . .' Her voice petered out. Some things you couldn't say; couldn't, mustn't do – not when you were indebted to someone,

someone who'd built the nest, driven away intruders, helped you rear the young, working tirelessly to find them food, taught them how to fly.

Turning round to face him, she raised her arms, as he had done, and, flapping them like wings, made a jangling bird-cry.

'Your mating-call?' he laughed.

'Sort of,' she replied. It was a cry of anguish, actually, addressed not to him but to Josh. 'It's *over*,' it said, in bird-speak, 'I hate to have to say it, Josh, and I'll miss you terribly. But I'd forgotten something crucial – Robert and I mated for life and I can't destroy the pair-bond.'

19

HOLY INNOCENTS

'Thank God,' he said aloud, as he stepped out of his house for the first time in four days. 'It's *over* and I've survived.'

He walked briskly along the street with a distinctly lighter step, peering in through the windows at other people's Christmas trees with a sense of almost triumph now, rather than his earlier dismay. The so-called festive season was nearly at an end – well, apart from New Year's Eve, when he always refrained from watching the television, to avoid the sight of revelling crowds popping corks, bursting balloons, or singing *Auld Lang Syne*. Christmas, though, was invariably more of a hurdle than New Year, if only on account of the fact that it started around mid-October and increased relentlessly in hysteria, until it built up to a surfeit of the things he most detested: Christmas carols, traffic jams, rich food and irritable crowds. And, more than once, it had ended for him personally with some domestic or medical crisis on Christmas Day itself – pneumonia last year; burst pipes the year before, and, the year before *that*, both Asian flu and a severely ailing boiler. This year, though, he'd been spared, enduring nothing worse than boredom and constant drizzly rain. And now, at last, things were back to normal: trains and buses running, supermarkets restocked, and – most cheering of all – the swimming baths open for business as usual.

Turning the corner, he jogged the last hundred yards towards the ugly red-brick building that housed the swimming pool.

Elsie greeted him effusively as he fumbled in his pocket for some change, receiving in return an entrance ticket, a locker-key and a thin grey towel that had stiffened after countless launderings. Who cared? The friction provided a stimulating body massage, completely free of charge.

'Nice Christmas?' she asked, resorting to her usual ruse of trying to detain him. He was here to exercise his heart and lungs, not his tongue and voice-box, but Elsie had a blind spot about people's predilection for mindless verbal intercourse.

'Not bad,' he muttered, shifting from foot to foot.

'Did you get away at all?'

'No,' he answered tersely, deliberately moving out of earshot, and then on to the men's changing-room. It was totally deserted, he was gratified to see, and all the lockers empty. With any luck, he'd have the pool to himself. Most of those who'd once frequented these old-fashioned municipal baths had been lured away by the new Oasis Leisure Centre, with its wave machine, its water chutes and its poolside café complete with tropical palms. He would gladly swap a fake palm tree or two for the pleasure of swimming in peace and, anyway, he much preferred this ancient institution, with its dingy tiles and bracing reek of chlorine, to the dubious delights of unisex Jacuzzis and Aqua Party Nights.

He whistled to himself as he stripped off his clothes and donned his swimming trunks. True, the changing-room was distinctly on the chilly side, but better that than an unhealthy fug. Neither he nor his parents had ever believed in mollycoddling. In fact, the tough regime of his youth (cold baths, unheated bedrooms, open-air gymnastics) probably accounted for his present blooming health. At seventy-five, he was fitter than most men half his age, though only because he worked at it, of course – eighty lengths a day; no cheating, no excuses.

Having left his clothes neatly folded in his locker, he walked towards the exit, pausing for a moment to douse his feet in the chlorinated foot-bath. It was these little touches he liked. There were no foot-baths in the Oasis, and dangerously few rules. Here, the list of prohibitions was posted on the wall and thus impossible to disregard. 'No running. No diving. No backward jumping. No spitting,' and a further series of equally essential 'No's'. Rules were indispensable in a swimming bath – indeed indispensable generally, to prevent chaos and disorder.

As he approached the pool, however, he was horrified to hear a rising tide of noise – whoops of excitement, gales of laughter, high-pitched squeals and shrieks. Emerging from the passageway, he stood transfixed by the sight that met his eyes. Instead of an expanse of peaceful blue, with the odd law-abiding swimmer gliding up and down, the entire pool was crammed with mothers and their children. Indeed, he could barely see the water at all for the profusion of floats and life-rafts bobbing on its surface, all in clashing colours: orange, yellow, turquoise, pink, disturbing the usual sober atmosphere. He edged a little closer, trying to digest the distasteful scene. One group was playing Ring-a-Ring o' Roses, ducking underwater as they chanted 'All fall down!' A few unruly youngsters were doing handstands in the shallow end, their undignified pink legs sticking up obscenely out of the water. What on earth was going on? Had they introduced some new-fangled Family Day and failed to inform him of the change – despite the fact he'd been coming here for close on thirty years? Elsie should have *warned* him, instead of asking intrusive questions.

Angrily he approached a woman standing at the side of the pool with a trio of small boys. 'Is this a mother-and-child session?' he asked, trying to make himself heard above the racket.

'Oh, no! Me and the kids normally go to the Oasis – and so do most of *this* crowd – but it's closed for the next few days.'

'*Closed?*'

'Yes, they had a break-in last night. Quite a lot of damage was done, so the police are still making enquiries.'

He backed away, uncertain what to do. Should he go back home, or sit around and wait for these interlopers to finish, or simply grit his teeth and join the fray? He decided on the last. He couldn't face another day caged immobile at home and, if he waited for the tribe to leave, another influx might well turn up to swell the ranks still further. Besides, if they had any shred of consideration, they would realize he was a serious swimmer and leave one lane free for him.

He entered the pool with difficulty, squeezing past several little ragamuffins who were using the steps as a perch. 'Excuse *me*,' he snapped, but the only response was a string of foul expletives. Disentangling himself from their naked limbs, he endeavoured to strike out in the breaststroke (the crawl was clearly impossible, given the restraints), but was immediately torpedoed by an obese young woman pushing her two babies on a float.

'Sorry!' she panted, trying to steer the float away, but only managing to obstruct him again a little further on.

'Can't you keep your distance,' he spluttered, choking on a mouthful of water he had inadvertently swallowed. She couldn't hear a word, though. The high-ceilinged baths formed a sort of echo chamber that roared and pulsed with sound. Every child without exception seemed to be yelling at the top of its vulgar little voice, with no regard for other people's eardrums. And the mothers were scarcely any better, bellowing at their children (and each other), or shrieking with uncouth mirth.

He veered swiftly to the right, to elude another female, her gigantic bosom inadequately restrained by a flimsy bikini-top, and her long black hair trailing in the water like a yard of slimy seaweed. In *his* day, women wore bathing caps and modest one-piece suits, and children were taught that the world was made pre-eminently for grown-ups, which meant that raw and callow juveniles must wait quietly on the sidelines until they, too, reached maturity. But things had changed beyond recognition.

Still forced to swim in fits and starts, it took him quite some time to complete even a single length and, instead of turning swiftly round at the far end of the pool and swimming back again, he found himself hemmed in by a trio of females, all with toddlers clinging round their necks, and all jabbering non-stop. Neither the mothers nor the children were making any attempt to swim, but were simply buoyed up by their water-wings, so that they were free to lark about. *He'd* been taught to swim by being thrown into a freezing lake and left to struggle on his own, and it had done him only good – toughened him up, taught him self-reliance. These pampered little princes and princesses would probably reach their teens still clinging to their mothers' apron strings, if aprons even *existed* now, which he doubted. Today's women didn't cook or clean – they were far too busy gossiping and giggling.

Having effected his escape, he steered a zigzag course to avoid a group of older children bearing down on him. 'Could you kindly keep in lane,' he gasped, swallowing another mouthful of water, which, he suspected from its taste, was strongly laced with urine.

'What you on about?' bawled the largest of the boys, showering him with water from his wildly kicking legs.

His reply was lost in a fit of coughing. Wasn't there anyone on duty who could control these hooligans? Raising his head, he peered around for the lifeguard, and eventually spotted him indulging in a tête-à-tête with a scantily clothed female. The irresponsible fellow was actually pawing the woman's flesh and thus unlikely to notice even if someone were to drown.

Shaking his head in disgust, he quickly changed direction to ward off an encounter with a baby on a large pink float, gibbering to itself like a manic chimpanzee. There were perils on all sides, however, and next he cannoned into a podgy child who'd been swimming underwater but suddenly erupted right beneath him, throwing him off-balance. This time he said nothing – no point wasting his breath. He'd simply have to regard today as an exercise in avoidance tactics and be thankful if he managed to keep afloat at all.

Screwing up his eyes, which were still stinging from the water, he wove his stop-start way back towards the shallow end. He needed not only goggles, but earplugs to deaden the noise. A large group of obvious ruffians was standing on the side, each endeavouring to out-shout the others. Normally, when he swam, he used the time to some purpose – working out mathematical teasers in his head, or compos-ing challenging crossword puzzles, but such mental gymnastics were totally impossible, given these conditions.

All at once, the whole group of boys jumped in at the same instant, throwing up a huge cascade of water and threatening to capsize him.

'Watch out!' he cautioned the little wretch who had surfaced near-est to him. 'You're not the only pebble on the beach.'

The child totally ignored him, screeching to a crony standing on the side to chuck him the 'bleedin' beach-ball'. The boy hurled it with such force, it sent up another shower of spray, dousing all in the vicinity. Then the entire anarchic cavalcade began to play a kind of water polo, with no regard for safety or decorum. He was compelled to retreat to the far side of the pool, using a series of ducking-and-dodging motions, to out-manoeuvre the many human obstacles. The effort was quite fruitless, though, since hardly had he shaken off the main group, when he was involved in yet another dangerous skir-mish. This time, a cluster of much smaller boys were using their plastic floats as assault weapons, banging them one against the other with a truly terrible din that reverberated around the roof and walls.

'Stop that!' he barked. 'Immediately!'

'Fuck off!' the ringleader yelled, spitting in his face.

Torn between outrage and humiliation, he hauled himself out of the water. Splashing and collisions he could cope with, just about, but not downright insolence. He stumped back to the changing-room, which, fortunately, he had almost to himself. Just one other man, a wizened little chap, was taking a pre-swim shower. Should he warn the fellow, he wondered, of the mayhem in the pool? No, best to hold his tongue – a rule he had learned long ago as a hated German (Catholic) child in very English (largely Protestant) Cheltenham.

Once dressed, he sat disconsolately on the dilapidated wooden bench. It was now five days since he'd swum and he was feeling stiff as well as out of sorts. The day stretched idly ahead, with no promise of diversion, no chance of useful work. Normally he stayed in the baths for the best part of the morning – an hour in the water, followed by a lengthy spell reading in the snack bar. There were no snacks on offer, in fact, and nothing to drink except over-brewed tea and coffee from the ancient drinks machine. But he had come to regard the small, dim room as almost his second home; somewhere quiet and civilized where he wouldn't be disturbed and where he could peruse his favourite German books in peace. Even fifty years after hostilities had ended, English people still distrusted Germans, so he had learned from early childhood to hide his disreputable origins and keep himself to himself. And it would certainly be wiser now to cut his losses and beat a quick retreat, than allow himself to be overrun by intruders from the Oasis.

However, when he peered in at the snack bar on his way to the main exit, he was pleasantly surprised to find it near-deserted; the only other occupants being a couple of elderly ladies and a small harmless-looking child. He chose the table furthest from them, opened his lunch-box and withdrew his little snack: a yoghurt with cherry topping, and a nut and raisin bar. He detested eating in public, but the women seemed oblivious of his presence, and the child was mercifully asleep. Blessed peace. At last. He might as well enjoy it until the tribe from the pool got wind of this small sanctuary and descended in their droves.

He prised the top off the yoghurt and, digging in his plastic spoon, watched the rich red topping seep into the creamy curd. In an instant, he was transported back to Weilburg and to the age of six or seven. He was sitting at an old pine table, eating his mother's *Bavarois*, which she made every year on this very day – 28 December, the Feast of the Holy Innocents. Like the yoghurt, the blancmange-like pudding was white, to represent the Innocents' fair young flesh, and the cherry sauce poured on top symbolized the shedding of their blood. Although he had long ago abandoned his religion, its rituals, prayers and Feastdays were etched deep into his mind. Hardly surprising, really, when his mother had devoted so much of her short, pious life to instructing him in matters of the Faith. He had noted as a child how she relished the barbarities, recounting stories of brave young virgin martyrs whose breasts had been sliced off, or who'd had their eyes or tongues gouged out with the aid of red-hot pokers. Thus the prospect of a thousand babies being slaughtered at a stroke appealed to her immensely and, as she beat the cream for her *Bavarois* and added eggs and sugar, she never failed to elaborate on all the gory details. The result, of course, was to induce in him such horror that, when he came to eat the pudding, it invariably made him sick, believing, as he did, that he was biting into infant flesh, and swallowing warm, sticky blood.

Pushing his pot of yoghurt away, he dropped his spoon in disgust. He could actually feel the wave of nausea rising in his stomach; feel the lash of his father's belt: his punishment for vomiting. His buttocks were marked with deep red weals – partly from the earlier whipping administered at dawn. It had been an old folk custom in certain parts of Germany to give children a good thrashing on the morning of the Feast, to remind them of King Herod's crime in slaughtering the Innocents.

'Then Herod was exceeding angry and killed all the men-children that were in Bethlehem, and in all the borders thereof, from two years old and under.'

He still remembered the Gospel from all those years ago, and remembered it in English, which he'd been forced to speak the minute they arrived – fleeing for their very lives – in this new confusing land. His parents had always been evasive about the reason for their flight, but they *had* made it unmistakably clear that he had to learn the language, so as to pretend to be an English boy. Not that anyone was fooled, in fact – least of all his contemptuous

English schoolmates, who bullied him unmercifully. Soon he became a sort of hybrid, no longer German, yet demonstrably not English, and hybrids, he discovered, were shunned as well as despised. Friends were now defunct, along with bananas and real eggs, and, with every passing month, even the ones he'd had in Germany seemed to fade and shrink like over-laundered clothes; cut off by half a continent and a wide stretch of alien sea.

'A voice in Rama was heard: lamentation and mourning; Rachel bewailing her children, and would not be comforted. . . .'

He was still kneeling in the cold stone church in Cheltenham, with its sickly mix of smells: incense and hot candle-wax and his mother's gardenia scent. The wooden floor pressed hard against his knees and he felt faint from lack of food. (It was forbidden to have breakfast before receiving Communion, in case God got jumbled up with tea and toast.) Aware that his father was watching, though, he joined his hands, closed his eyes, and tried to mumble the peculiar-sounding prayers. The Mass was dragging on interminably and he longed to make a dash for it – run away not just from church, but from Cheltenham and England, and keep on running, running, right across the sea and land, until he was back in his true home.

'Revenge, O Lord, the blood of thy saints, which hath been poured out upon the earth.'

The word 'revenge' was scary. Herod had killed his own son, along with all the other children, so he lived in constant terror that his father might do the same. Like Herod, he was always in a fury and always giving orders that had to be obeyed, so what was to stop him murdering one small and stupid son?

As he opened his eyes, the grey stone of the church dissolved into the brown walls of the snack bar. Slowly he rose to his feet, threw his untouched yoghurt into the litter-bin, and blundered along the passage to the exit.

'You off already?' Elsie asked.

'Er, yes,' he mumbled vaguely, unable to shift his mind from the fear-encrusted memories of the Feast. Shuddering, he glanced behind him, as if half expecting to see his father brandishing the whip; his mother ladling her pallid, corpse-like pudding into his waiting dish.

Elsie eyed him curiously. 'Are you OK? You've gone all pale and sweaty. And where's your swimming-bag? I've never seen you without it all the years you've been coming here.'

'Damn!' he muttered. 'I've left it in the . . .' He turned on his heel and stumbled back to the snack bar, stopping short to peer in through the viewing window that overlooked the pool. The children were still there – *boy* children, under-twos. And the women, too, were there, no longer clad in skimpy swimwear and jabbering away, but rending their long flowing garments, and weeping and lamenting. He watched in silence as Herod's vicious henchmen dragged babies from their life-rafts and began hacking at the helpless bodies; splitting tiny skulls apart by dashing them against the tiled surrounds. Whole groups of toddlers were savaged as they tried frantically to escape; their limbs dismembered, their budding brains bashed out. The soldiers showed no mercy. These children were potential rivals to mighty Herod's sway and, as such, must be destroyed – brutally, relentlessly, with no regard for pleas or tears.

Soon the pool was running red with blood, and scores of severed arms and legs floated pale and ghoulish amidst the brightly coloured inflatables. If he had thought the noise was loud before, now it reached a crescendo, as the shrieks of terrified victims cut across the barked orders of the assailants and the wild sobbing of the mothers. Some of the women flung themselves on the soldiers and attacked them with their bare hands, only to be cut down in their turn. Others retrieved the mangled bodies, cradling mutilated corpses in their arms; their screams echoing through the cavernous building in a hideous chorus of grief.

Suddenly he snapped his fingers, stepped forward, took control. 'Cease your grieving,' he ordered, repeating the words of the sermon that were now surging into his mind, as if he were back in church in Cheltenham on the occasion of the Feast. 'These children are not lost. In fact, their very death is their passport to eternal life. They'll be taken up to Heaven and given martyrs' palms – venerated as the first martyrs of the Church, doubly holy because they died in place of Christ. And you, too, will be honoured as Mothers of the Blest, celebrated every year with the Innocents themselves.'

The sobbing died away. What power a priest possessed – to

silence weeping women; transform vicious slaughter into celestial reward! Throughout his life, he had always lacked such power, living like a chrysalis that never dared hatch out, or emerge in its true colours, to soar up free and high.

He closed his eyes a moment, imagining whole congregations hanging on his words; massed ranks of soldiers marching to his diktat, obeying his commands. No longer a freakish foreigner with an unpronounceable name, cowering in subjection to a thousand childhood fears, he had come into his own, at last; enforcing strict obedience, ensuring iron control. His kingdom stretched for ever; his sway was absolute, and every subject in his lands must bow the head and bend the knee.

Raising his hand imperiously, he turned to face the pool again, and, at a stroke, order was restored. The soldiery disbanded, the women crept away, and a troupe of willing menials began swabbing down the tiled surrounds, scrubbing off the blood and gore. With gratifying speed, the water regained its former crystal clarity, stretching serenely and unsullied, with barely a ripple on its surface.

He smiled: a victor's smile. Now King Herod was free to swim his triumphant eighty lengths.

197

20

PARTY

'Come in. Lovely to see you.'

Why was everyone arriving at once? People pouring in – people she knew she knew, but couldn't place; their names vanishing in a thick curdled soup of terror and confusion. 'Oh, *Bob* – hello!' One face at least she recognized. 'Coats in here, on the bed. And Janice – you look gorgeous!' *Was* it Janice? Faces and bodies were blurring into each other; people she'd known for years changing their shape, their features.

'Gosh, thanks, what lovely flowers.' The fifth bunch she'd received, so far. She didn't have five vases, nor the time to arrange them. The poor things would die, as *she* was dying – dying slowly inside. She should never have thrown a party. It was a sort of madness, intended (madly) to cure her other madness.

'Bob, could you pour the drinks. Or get people to help themselves. All the stuff's on the sideboard.' She had bought three new corkscrews and tried them out in advance – that sense of startled relief as the cork shot out, free at last. 'Release *my* cork,' she'd prayed – the plug of fear stoppering her life.

The bell was ringing again. Another blurry couple, pressing a gift-wrapped package into her hands. Any decent hostess would make a note of who brought what, so she could write them thank-you letters in the morning. But if their names were all a jumble, how could she make the list? – or indeed hold a pen, when both her hands were occupied: a bunch of lilies in one, a box of chocolate truffles in the other.

'Andrew and Meg, this is Janice.' None of the three corrected her, thank God. She must be functioning on autopilot, although all else had slipped away: where they lived, what they did, whether they had children. She had invited all these people, sent out invitations, ticked their names off a list, yet half of them seemed total strangers, without histories or substance. How could nerves be so lethal, fur up one's brain like a kettle?

Someone was embracing her – a man who smelt of Polo mints. He seemed worryingly familiar. She closed her eyes, saw him naked on his back: hairy stomach, navel sticking out like a tiny hirsute knob. Yes, they had slept together long ago, but she couldn't remember what they'd done in bed, or even whether she'd enjoyed it.

'It's great to see you, Janey.'

She disentangled herself. No one called her Janey. 'Do go through and help yourself to a drink.'

It was unfair to rely on Bob to pour the wine. She should have hired a professional barman and, while she was about it, someone to answer the door. She was rushing from hall to sitting-room, and back again, and back again, trying to enact the role of hostess.

Oh, Lord! Simon was standing all alone, staring out of the window. He had just survived a divorce, and must be feeling desperate. If only Dr Brooks were here, to take care of him. *And* her. No, Dr Brooks was over, a remnant of her past. She was coping on her own now, without psychiatrists; proving she was normal, able to give parties, able to have *fun* – whatever fun was.

The doorbell again. She was tempted to ignore it. There was hardly room for any new arrivals. Already the walls were bulging out of shape; the floor buckling under people's weight. If any more turned up, she would have to ask them to lop off their arms and legs, to make more space. A flat full of amputees.

She ushered in Samantha – a name mercifully she recalled – squeezed her way back to the sitting-room, with Samantha and a few other guests in tow. 'Get them all drunk,' Bob had advised. 'That's the key to a good party.' She seized a bottle of white in one hand, a bottle of red in the other, and started sloshing wine into glasses. She longed for a drink herself – indeed could down a whole bottle straight off, except that alcohol and Valium didn't mix.

'Yes, I'm still at Saville and Forbes. Yes, enjoying it immensely.' The job was crap, and her boss kept her on only out of pity. But one of the skills of a hostess was learning how to lie. She shouldn't be

talking about herself, though – it was the guests who were important, and who needed introducing.

'Samantha, this is Juliet. We've been friends since primary
school.' Another lie. Friends were like God – an ideal that didn't
exist. One talked about friends, of course; as one talked about safety
and happiness, but all three were an illusion. Besides, no one would
want her as a friend once they saw beneath the façade.

She stepped on something crackly, and peered down at the floor.
A bowl of crisps had been spilt and trodden into the carpet. She
imagined someone stepping on *her* – crushing her beneath their
heel, scooping the debris into the bin. Nice to sit in a bin: safe and
dark and well-concealed, and to moulder slowly away until she
formed a vegetable compost, joined in death to tea-leaf friends,
cheese-rind friends, potato-peeling friends.

Frantically she poured more wine. Get drunk, she begged them
silently. Relax. Have fun. Show Dr Brooks I'm cured. He did nothing
for me anyway. Just took my cash and made me cry.

Most of the crisps and nuts had gone. People must be hungry. She
put the bottles down, grabbed a plate of quiche instead, and offered
it around. Shreds of cheese and pastry dropped on to the floor, as
guests bit into their slices and licked their greasy fingers. They
needed forks and plates and napkins, which she had laid out on the
table. But no one could get *near* the table. Every inch of her flat was
overrun – bodies blockading her bedroom and thronging the small
spare one, crowding her cluttered kitchen, and even jammed into
the bathroom; one couple perched precariously on the laundry
basket.

Bob was coming towards her – the only guest she was truly glad
to see. 'Could you pass the food round?' she asked. She had spent all
week preparing it, making salads and patés, worrying about
amounts. Supposing it ran out? And what about vegetarians and
people on special diets? Early this morning she'd panicked, rushed
out to the supermarket and bought a trolleyful of extra supplies,
including gluten-free and vegan, then worried even more because it
wasn't home-made like the rest.

'Food up!' Bob bellowed. 'Help yourselves.'

People began surging towards the table, jostling each other, causing blockages and bottlenecks. Someone's glass was knocked from
their hand and a pool of red wine began seeping into the carpet,

leaving a crimson stain. Blood, she thought – *my* blood.

'I'm terribly sorry, Jane. If you've got a cloth, I'll mop it up.'

'No, it doesn't matter, honestly.' It would seem rude to start cleaning carpets in public, and anyway how could she fetch a cloth when the hallway was totally blocked?

Bob was passing plates around and a platter of cold roast beef. They would need a knife *and* fork for that, *and* a chair to sit on, *and* somewhere to put their glass down while they ate. All of which were lacking. She should have made finger food – canapés, crostini; planned every smallest detail in advance. And all she'd done was think of Dr Brooks – how she hated him. And missed him.

Anton swooped towards her, cigarette in hand, a long worm of ash trembling on the end of it. 'Jane, do you have an ashtray, darling?'

'Use a plate,' she said, appropriating one from Bob. Ashtrays she had totally forgotten. Her party skills were nil. It was like a cripple trying to run the marathon, or a great, lumbering, mud-bound rhino imagining it could fly.

Andrew had come up to chat. 'Have you read the new Ian McEwan, Jane?'

'Er, no – not yet.' She didn't read at all these days. If she so much as opened a book, the print turned into accusing words, shouting at her, criticizing.

More questions fired in her direction – questions that were traps and didn't have an answer.

'Are you planning to go away this summer?'

'I'm not too sure.' She was *very* sure. Life was hard enough on home ground, so why risk holidays? So much of her had disappeared – her hobbies, interests, opinions, sex-life – most of which was due to Dr Brooks. He had stripped her bare, dismantled her defences, made her distrust everything: men, parents, pastimes, travel.

She pressed herself against the wall, needing its support: bricks and mortar behind her, concrete underneath. She tried to focus on the guests, to control her rising fear. Janice was biting into a Scotch egg – the hard rubbery yellow ball of the yolk eluding her mouth and plopping back on the plate. At least she *had* a plate. Simon was using his fingers, gnawing a greasy chicken bone, while Mark was tonguing up a little pile of paté from his palm. Everywhere around her, mouths were opening and shutting, teeth masticating, throats swallowing. All the food she'd cooked was now sliding down people's guts, churning in their gullets, turning to mush in their stomachs, to faeces in their colons – to be expelled tomorrow morning. Her party in the toilet-bowl, flushed away down fetid pipes, shunted in stinking clods towards the sewer.

'Aren't you eating, Jane?'

'Er, yes . . . In a sec.' Her stomach was full already – full of greasy grey stuff. And she felt sick from the smell of smoke. Two men were smoking cigars – an acrid smell, stinging in her nostrils. Ash was falling on the carpet, along with more bits of food. An oily lettuce leaf had found its way on to the sofa; a chunk of beetroot screamed a purple warning on the ivory-coloured chair. It was all her fault, for not providing ashtrays or a sufficient number of plates.

'Marvellous party!' someone said – a burly man with reddish hair. His name was on the tip of her tongue. Nicholas? No, Nigel. She had slept with him as well, before Dr Brooks had made her see that she didn't actually *like* sex and was only using men as father-substitutes. Nigel *had* been like her father – promising her the moon and stars, and providing only cosmic dust.

'We must get together again,' he said, winking in a suggestive way. '*A deux*.' He lowered his voice. 'I'll give you a ring tomorrow.'

Don't, she thought, trying to steer him off this perilous reef. It was hard to talk, in any case, against such a volume of noise. Dozens of different conversations had fused into a frightening roar, punctuated by howls and bleats. People were turning into animals, guzzling and swilling around her, shoving and pushing each other as they fought to reach the trough. She stood paralysed in her corner, watching cruel incisors tear through bloody meat; relentless talons ripping loaves to shreds. A tide of red wine was flowing over the carpet – a treacherous Red Sea, full of dangerous cross-currents. And someone had dropped a cigar butt, which had started a conflagration. Smoke was billowing through the room, flames licking at the walls, curling round the sofa, creeping towards her feet. Why had no one noticed the reek of charring flesh? Were they too intent on gorging, grunting, chomping, even to see they were in danger?

She herself was choking from the smoke; throat raw, eyes sore and streaming. She began pushing through the herd, avoiding fangs and claws; staggered on along the hall and flung open the front door. Taking the stairs two at a time, she hurtled down to ground level, then ran full pelt along the street. Behind her she could hear the flames, tearing through the apartment block, destroying the whole building. It came crashing to the ground, with an explosion like a shell-burst.

She kept on running, round the corner, past the church, across the main road and on again, finally panting to a stop in front of Dr Brooks's house. She collapsed on the path, her legs trembling underneath her. Only now did she realize what she'd done – left all her guests to burn to death, then coffined them in rubble.

She stumbled to the window and banged loudly on the glass. It was late on Saturday night. Dr Brooks was off duty, maybe even asleep. But she had to wake him, *had* to see him – only he could expiate her guilt. She hammered with her fists on the pane. 'Let me in,' she shouted. 'I'm a murderess, a murderess!'

21

ROSEMARY

'Rent payable, second quarter, due 24 June: £3,874. Monthly rates: £360. . . .'

'Damn!' Kenneth muttered, checking the figures against the new statement from the council. All the direct debits were now incorrect, and would have to be altered in line with the new demands. He could feel a headache coming on, and the printed lines on the computer screen was shrinking and fading, as if stricken with consumption and about to waste away. He probably needed new glasses, but since his mother had been diagnosed with macular degeneration, he preferred to avoid opticians. The condition was bound to be hereditary, like her bunions and high blood pressure, so better not to know.

'Coming for lunch?' asked Angie, pausing by his workstation. 'Me and Val thought we'd try that new Chinese place.'

'Sorry. I'm . . . er, going to the optician.' He watched the two women make their way to the door, his guilty gaze hovering at mid-thigh level. They wore their skirts so short, he sometimes found himself quite pink with thrilled embarrassment if one of them bent over to retrieve something from the floor. Their shoes were equally distracting: spindly heels, flimsy straps, red-varnished toenails on show. It never ceased to amaze him that women managed to walk at all, considering the extraordinary creations they wore.

'See you!' Val called, turning back to wave to him before vanishing with a sexy wiggle.

He checked his watch. 12.48. He never left the office before the dot of one, but today a seed of rebellion seemed to be sprouting somewhere deep down. Perhaps he'd throw over the traces and award himself twelve extra minutes of freedom.

Once outside, he stood perspiring in the heat, wondering where to go. It would be too stuffy in the pub, the pizza place was invariably crowded, and he loathed the rackety music in *Alberto's*. Maybe best to buy a sandwich and eat it in the riverside park. At least there'd be a breeze and a few friendly pigeons for company.

He joined the queue in the sandwich shop, where he dithered for some time, trying to choose between turkey breast and cranberry, and honey-roast ham and tomato, and finally opting for cheese and pickle. As he emerged with his package, he almost tripped over a small brown mongrel sitting outside on the pavement, panting in the heat. 'Good boy,' he murmured, sauntering on, only to realize to his consternation that the dog was trotting after him. It was a bitch, in fact, not a dog, and combined a poodle's curly coat with a spaniel's silky ears, plus a dash of terrier thrown in for good measure.

'Stay!' he ordered. '*Sit!*'

The dog obediently sat, but the minute he walked on, she got up again and continued to follow at his heels. He'd have to return her to the shop – she probably belonged to one of the customers. Dutifully he retraced his steps, the dog still shadowing him. 'Wait here,' he said, once they reached the green-striped awning. 'Your master or mistress won't be long.'

Again he strode off, this time at a faster pace, but the dog caught him up in seconds, eagerly wagging her tail.

'Look, you're very sweet, but you belong to someone else.' Back he went a second time, even overcoming his shyness to ask the people in the sandwich queue if any of them owned a small brown dog.

No. No one.

'There may be a name on the collar,' the man behind the counter suggested, as he slathered mayonnaise onto two brown baps.

'She's not wearing a collar,' Kenneth replied, aware of a nudge against his leg. The subject of their conversation had followed him inside.

'Probably a stray, then. You could take it to the police station, but they got better things to do, I'm sure, than track down missing dogs.'

'Thanks,' said Kenneth, and left the shop, the dog in close pursuit. Crouching down to pavement level, he tried to reason with her. 'Look, whoever you belong to will come looking for you *here*. They'll be frantic if you disappear with me.'

The dog fixed him with her Bournville-chocolate eyes – large trusting eyes gazing up at him with unalloyed devotion. '*Rosemary!*' he whispered, suddenly struck by the resemblance – the same big brown eyes, curly hair, optimistic nature. If his first and only girl-friend had possessed a short but emotive tail, she would have wagged it with the same eagerness as the dog was doing now. 'Rosemary,' he repeated, feeling a frisson of excitement, 'would you care to join me for lunch?'

The dog gave a joyous bark – the only noise she had made so far, and clearly an emphatic 'yes'.

They strolled along together, he smiling to himself at the bliss of being wanted again; no longer a shameful singleton. As they turned into the park, he looked out for an empty bench. He didn't want to share his girl, risk losing her a second time, suffer all that choking grief.

Unwrapping his sandwich, he gave her the first bite, glad she approved of his choice of filling. Cheese and pickle was clearly a winner, judging by the speed with which it vanished down her throat. Although tempted to eat the rest himself, the only decent thing to do was give it all to her, since she was demonstrably so ravenous. *He* could make do with the KitKat.

He broke the sandwich into manageable chunks, each despatched with the same lightning speed, and each acknowledged with a short grateful bark. Her eyes never wavered from his face, even after the last crumb was gone.

'I'm afraid that's it, Rosemary. If I'd known you were going to join me, I'd have bought half-a-dozen sandwiches, chicken legs, Scotch eggs, pork pies – you name it.' As he peeled the silver paper from the KitKat, the expression in her eyes changed from devotion to entreaty. Her need was greater than his. For all he knew, she could have been wandering the streets for months, scavenging in dust-bins, living on unhealthy scraps.

The chocolate provoked a rapturous reaction. She positively wrig-gled with joy, her pink tongue chasing the last delicious fragments from his palm. Then she sprang up on the bench beside him and licked his face, his nose. He closed his eyes, recalling Rosemary's kisses: the same exciting wetness, the same sense of a warm body pressed invitingly against his own.

He was roused from his reverie by a gentle nosing in the ribs. Obviously she wanted something else – a drink most likely, in this sultry weather. He opened his bottle of Evian, wishing a dog-bowl would appear, wafting magically down from the skies. Instead, he checked the litter-bin and found a Kentucky Fried Chicken carton, empty except for a wad of greasy paper. He removed the paper, filled the carton with water and set it down on the ground. Rosemary lapped appreciatively. She hasn't changed, he thought. Still the same love of food and drink; still the same enthusiasm for anything and everything. He was pretty parched himself, but he could always resort to the office water-cooler. *She* had no such amenities and must therefore finish the bottle.

'Walkies?' he suggested, once he had cleared away the litter. Her response was quite ecstatic – she began rushing to and fro, as if begging him to make a start and not delay a second longer. She was just his sort of girl, full of natural energy, yet content with simple pleasures.

There was a spring in his step as he turned towards the river and walked along the embankment, Rosemary delirious with glee as she ran in circles around him. She suddenly spotted a Border collie chasing after a ball, and dashed off to retrieve it herself, laying it proudly at his feet. The collie's owner stopped to chat, showering him with compliments. What a lovely dog he had – how intelligent, how lively! He swelled with pride, surprised to realize he was no longer feeling shy. It wasn't easy to be shy, in fact, when Rosemary kept making him new friends. Now she was scampering up to a Labrador, touching noses, exchanging intimate smells. And the Labrador's elderly owner was equally willing to communicate.

'How old is she?' he asked, stooping down to fondle Rosemary's ears.

'Er, three,' said Kenneth, reeling off a few more doggy details, some shamelessly invented – she had won top prize in the county show, as well as a gold cup for Obedience, and had been splashed across the local paper as 'Canine Wondergirl!'.

'Congratulations!' the old chap said, with genuine admiration. 'I'm afraid my poor pooch wouldn't win a prize for anything, except laziness and greed!'

They shared a chuckle, Kenneth surprising himself afresh by the very fact of laughing. It had been quite some years since he'd had anything to laugh about.

And now a young girl with a Doberman had joined them, the dog displaying a slavering interest in Rosemary's nether parts. More laughs, more mutual compliments. Kenneth could hardly believe he was the same dyspeptic, constipated grouch who had stumbled from his bed this morning, wishing it was Friday. His life had changed dramatically since then. He was no longer odd man out: the sole male in the office, the only one without a partner, and the only one who still lived at home (which, at his age, was pathetic and contemptible.)

'Well, I'd better get a move on,' the girl said with a friendly smile. 'Otherwise Rex will be complaining that he hasn't had a proper walk!'

'I know the feeling,' Kenneth said. 'They're bundles of sheer energy!'

As if to prove him right, Rosemary streaked ahead, bowling along the embankment with such vigour and vitality, he found it quite a struggle to keep up. Gradually the pavement petered out and became a grassy path, with easier access to the river. All at once, Rosemary plunged into the water and began swimming strongly upstream. Oh, God, he thought, she's leaving me! It's all happening again – the loneliness, the shock.

'Rosemary!' he yelled and, to his overwhelming relief, she immediately turned back, bounding up from the water's edge and shaking herself all over him. He barely noticed the muddy droplets bespattering his trousers. He was glorying in her loyalty, her astounding faithfulness.

He glanced upstream, in the direction she'd been heading. Perhaps she'd had an urge to reach the sea. The first Rosemary had always loved it – the salt tang in the air, the white lace frills of frolicking waves foaming against the rocks. If only they could go there now, gambol on the beach, run for miles and miles, with no fences, no constraints.

Rosemary gave a peremptory bark, as if reminding him of her presence. As if he could ever forget! He picked up a stick and threw it, enjoying the sight of her whirling off in a paroxysm of joy. She laid the stick at his feet, clearly entreating 'More!'

He threw it again – again – again – until finally she collapsed, exhausted, on the grassy bank, her pink tongue lolling, her eyes bright with love and gratitude.

'Let's rest a while,' he whispered, lying down and snuggling close beside her. Her coat was still thrillingly damp, cooling his flushed pink skin. He couldn't remember feeling so content, not in years and years. The only problem was the time – twenty to two already. He groaned to himself, dreading the long, hot afternoon, wrestling with stubborn figures. He had always hated the job – the 'good', 'safe' job his parents were so proud of, and had more or less dragooned him into, the minute he'd finished his studies. As a child, he had wanted to be a pirate, a magician and an astronaut, preferably all three at once. The reality was rather different. Instead of skulls and cross-bones, space stations and moon-landings, white rabbits and top hats, he was stuck in a windowless office with his tyrannical boss, Lavinia, and three brainless female clerks.

'Time to go back,' he said sadly, stroking Rosemary's neck.

She appeared to understand, since her tail immediately drooped. However, she followed him obediently as he swung away from the river and back across the park. He ought to call in at the police station before returning to work. It would make him late, of course, but he couldn't leave Rosemary at the mercy of perilous traffic, or faced with the risk of starvation. Besides, where else could he take her? Angie had an allergy to dog-hair and erupted in a prickly rash if a dog came within a mile of her. Anyway, Lavinia would probably sack him on the spot, were she to discover Rosemary sprawled on the office floor. She hated both animals and children, on the grounds that both were undisciplined, unpredictable and a bar to orderly work habits.

As they reached the park gate, Rosemary suddenly sat down on her haunches and refused to go a step further. 'Come on, darling,' he coaxed. 'We're late as it is.' He tried to push her to her feet, but she resisted with every fibre of her body. 'Rosemary,' he pleaded, 'I can't leave you here. It's dangerous. You need someone to look after you. I'd take you home, if it wasn't for my parents. But I'm afraid they've always forbidden pets.'

Rosemary remained unmoved – literally as well as metaphorically. It was as if she had bolted herself firmly to the ground with a series of strong steel rivets and, Lavinia or no, intended to stay where she was indefinitely. He tried to pick her up, but she actually bared her teeth – an appalling betrayal, he felt.

Desperately he checked his watch: almost five to two. Lavinia would go berserk. She had told him this morning that she needed those figures finalized and printed out by four o'clock at the latest. 'Rosemary, *please* come. I can't afford to get the sack. Mother would never forgive me – letting her down, shaming her in front of the neighbours. . . .'

Rosemary had turned away disdainfully and was no longer even listening. Pain pierced him like an arrow. It was all happening a second time – abandonment, rejection, the end of the affair.

'Don't let it be goodbye,' he begged. 'I'll do anything you like. Except I can't be late. You must understand that, surely? They'll fire me. I'll be on the dole – a reject.'

Rosemary shut her eyes, as if to block out his entreaties. Close to tears, he dragged himself away, through the gate, along the road, continually looking behind him, in the hope that she was following.

But there was not a sign of her. He was alone again, and headed for the office where he always felt more isolated still. He was a misfit there, lost amidst the general female banter, searching frantically for something to say, then saying it too late. And he never understood the women's jokes, or recognized the people they discussed: celebrities and pop stars, TV chat-show hosts – all unknown quantities. His parents didn't *own* a TV, and disapproved of any music save for hymns and Vera Lynn.

As he approached First Call Personnel, his steps began to falter. His watch said 2.14, and its ticking seemed to swell in volume as he imagined Lavinia's wrath. He forced himself to open the office door, flinching at the din: one phone shrilling, Val answering another in her silly twittering bleat, and Lavinia bawling Angie out for some petty misdemeanour. Quickly he shut the door again. How could he go in, switch instantly to office mode when his mind was back in the park, picturing his beloved girl still lying on the grass, prey to teenage bullies, or cruel, uncaring park-keepers? Why hadn't she come back with him when, up till then, she had barely left his side? Had he offended her, ignored her needs, thoughtlessly tired her out?

In a blinding flash the answer came – and it was nothing to do with offence. She *loved* him – that was clear – and had been trying to warn him, wordlessly, not to return to the office. Because she had his interests at heart, she understood, with faultless intuition, that the job was completely wrong for him, and would crush him to oblivion, were he to stay there any longer.

As if activated by a rocket-launcher, he turned tail down the stairs and stampeded back the way he'd come, past the sandwich shop, the greengrocer, the chemist, the launderette; still not slacking speed as he vaulted the park gate and dashed across the grass, where Rosemary was lying exactly as he'd left her.

His welcome was so jubilant, he stood grinning like an idiot, while Rosemary kissed him, licked him, capered wildly round him and, in a carillon of ecstatic barks, expressed her profound relief that he had understood her message. But they hadn't time to waste. He had vegetated long enough, lonely and imprisoned.

'Follow me!' she seemed to cry as she veered towards the river with almost supernormal speed. He dashed in pursuit, recognizing his guiding star, his luminary, his mentor. The pair of them careered along the embankment, faster and faster still, then along the grassy path, and further on, and further on, until they reached the bend in the river.

His heart was pounding with excitement, his triumphant feet thudding on the path, as Rosemary led him out of bondage. He knew where she was headed – towards the open sea, of course – towards liberty and freedom, glorious release.

22

MOVING

SOLD.

Elaine pushed open the kitchen window and stared up at the sign. The O became a howling mouth, shrieking out her grief. O for void, for loss. FOR SALE hurt so much less. FOR SALE meant time and hope – hope of a reprieve: a slump in the housing market, no buyers, no interest, Colin changing his mind, even.

'God! I'm so relieved,' he said, suddenly coming up behind her and putting his arm round her waist. 'Now I can sleep at nights.'

And I can't, she thought, banging the window shut. She detested the new place – its meanness, smallness, the vomit-coloured carpets, the roar of traffic from the road outside. The roar was swelling now in her head, even fifty miles away, threatening and discordant, and overlaid with the still insistent howls.

'OOOOOOOOOOOOOOOOOOOO. . . .'

'With any luck, we'll exchange contracts within a month. The Lloyds are as keen as we are to get cracking.'

As *you* are, she corrected silently. Not that he could hear. There was too much turmoil in the room.

'Well, I'd better make a start on clearing up the cellar.'

She had no intention of helping him with *that*. Even a glimpse of the cellar steps made her want to weep. She had fallen down them, thirty years ago, and not only broken her leg but lost her unborn twins. She had never managed to conceive again, despite endless tests and drugs. Since then, she kept her distance from the cellar, which had become Colin's territory, along with the loft and out-house.

'It'll take me ages to sort it out. It's stuffed to the gills with clutter.' He flexed his muscles, as if limbering up, before making for the door.

She tried to imagine the clutter – piles of junk, broken tools, old boxes, all festooned with spiders' webs, and the odd wasps' nest in a corner. And patches of grey-green mould on the walls, and a smell of damp and decay. 'While you're doing that, I'll go through all the china and glass and decide what to keep and what to chuck.' If only she could leave everything exactly as it was – all the cups on their cup-hooks on the dresser; all the tumblers safe in the cabinet; the three china teapots (one in the shape of a house) stacked neatly in the cupboard, along with the soup tureen, the carving platter and the cereal bowls with the cockerels round the rim. She longed to shrink them all to doll's-house size, so they would fit in the new flat; shrink the three-piece suite, the double bed, her generous desk with its six capacious drawers.

She fetched a pair of steps and started on the highest cupboard, first taking down the avocado dishes, with their matching green-bordered plates.

'Careful!' warned Colin, puffing back into the kitchen with a large cardboard box clutched against his chest. 'Those steps don't look too safe.'

'What's that?' she asked, peering down to look.

'My coin collection.'

'Coin collection?' Thirty-four years they'd been married, this November, and he had never, ever, mentioned collecting coins.

'D'you want to take a peek?'

She stepped gingerly off the ladder as he opened the flaps of the box. Inside were scores of smaller containers: tobacco tins, throat-lozenge tins, cigar boxes and jewel boxes, even several spectacle cases, all lined with cotton wool and filled with coins: worn Victorian pennies, dirty threepenny bits, commemorative coins from royal weddings and coronations, farthings, silver florins and a whole stack of coins that meant absolutely nothing to her: coins with holes in the middle, coins from unknown realms.

'That's a Roman semis,' he said, passing her a small brass coin.

'A what?'

'A semis. It's one thirty-second of a denarius. They're actually quite common, despite the fact they're nearly two thousand years old. Coins were made by hand then, and beautifully made, so they lasted.'

Why hadn't he told her all this *before*, shared his knowledge with her? And where and when had he got the coins? Surely he would have discussed it with her when he returned from an auction or a coin-shop?

'And this one's a beauty, isn't it? A George III "cartwheel" penny. See the date? – 1797. It's hardly worn or marked at all. We call that EF, which means extremely fine.'

That casual 'we' hurt. 'We' meant her and Colin – or had done till today.

'*Fleur de coin* is the ultimate. It's the term we use for flawless or unused.'

All these things he knew! She simply couldn't understand why he hadn't made her part of it. The ancient coins seemed strangers in her modern pine-clad kitchen, but for Colin they were intimate friends. No – more than friends: his precious little babies, wrapped in cotton-wool shawls. She watched the way he handled them, lovingly and lingeringly, cradling the weight of a heavy silver sovereign in his palm; holding a penny up to the light and admiring the inscription round the rim.

'I've been meaning to buy a proper mahogany cabinet, so I could display them properly.'

Display them for whom, she wondered? Would *she* ever have laid eyes on that 'proper mahogany cabinet'?

He began carefully packing them back, tucking his cosseted children into their tiny cots and cradles. Once they were safely stowed away, he took the box to the out-house, then went down again to the cellar. She remained sitting at the table, staring at a shred of cotton wool he'd overlooked. Somehow she had lost the will to continue with her own work. Colin's secret progeny were still whimpering in her mind – he their exclusive father, she barren and debarred.

She jumped as he banged back in, carrying another box, full of wine, this time – a good two dozen bottles, filmed with dust. As he placed it on the table, she did a quick check of the labels. Although they were badly stained and faded, she could make out the word *Château* on almost every one. Superior stuff, apparently.

'God knows what I'll do with this. It may be past drinking. Or on the other hand, it could be worth a fortune. I wouldn't know.'

No, he wouldn't. Colin was woefully ignorant about vintages or varieties of grape, and anyway preferred a pint of bitter to a glass of *premier cru*. 'Why did you buy it?' she asked.

'To drink, of course.'

'But we never drank it.'

'No. I was saving it for a special occasion.'

Like the twins' twenty-first birthday, she thought, picking up a bottle and tempted to open it there and then.

'I suppose we should have had it for our Silver Wedding but, to be honest with you, I clean forgot it was there.' Colin glanced at the clock 'God! Is that the time? I must get to the dump before dark.'

'The dump?' She shielded the bottle protectively. 'Don't tell me you're chucking *this* lot out?'

' 'Course not. It's the other stuff I've got to dump. Fishing tackle, diving gear. . . .'

She stared in disbelief. Colin had never learned to swim, and was less likely to go diving than to stand on his head in a peat bog. As for fishing, he had often told her he regarded it as cruel. 'I'm sorry, Colin, but I just don't understand what you're doing with either fishing tackle or diving gear.'

'It's not mine, it's Jasper's.'

'Who's Jasper?'

'A mate of mine at work.'

'You've never mentioned him.' A name like that would have hardly slipped her mind.

'Why should I? He's no one special.'

'Then why are you storing his stuff?'

'Because he asked me as a favour. His wife divorced him a couple of years ago, and *she* got the house and everything. He had to move to a bedsit, and there just wasn't room for all his gear.'

She glanced at Colin curiously, trying to fathom his expression. Although he was often busy in the daytime, they invariably spent their evenings together, chatting about this or that. Wouldn't he have *told* her about the divorce, asked if she minded housing Jasper's possessions? 'Surely you can't get rid of someone else's stuff without asking if they object?'

'I'm afraid the poor chap's dead. Heart attack. Last month.'

Even more extraordinary not to have said a single word about the sudden death of a colleague. He must be lying, covering something up.

215

He took the bottle from her and wiped it clean with a rag. 'Look, do you want to sample some of this, or shall I take it to an expert and see if it's worth a bob or two?'

She shrugged. 'Please yourself.'

'Well, I'll leave it here for the moment, until we've made our minds up. I must get the cellar completely cleared, so I can give it a damned good clean.'

Once he had gone, she sorted through the bottles, selecting a Cabernet Sauvignon 1999. She took a cautious sip, then swilled it round her mouth. It was good – remarkably good, full-bodied and fruity, with a hint of mingled blackcurrant and plum. But why hadn't her involved her in its purchase, knowing her love of wine?

He was back in a few minutes, loaded down with fishing rods, shrimping nets, a Neoprene wetsuit and pair of yellow flippers, and a large black cylinder flung across his shoulder. He took the load directly to the out-house, puffing from the weight of the cylinder. Had Jasper brought this stuff round, and, if so, where had *she* been? Why hadn't they been introduced, shared a drink, a chat?

She watched Colin cross the kitchen, empty-handed now, on his way back to the cellar. This was the person closest to her, her next of kin, her so-called nearest and dearest. Yet did she know him at all? – apart from obvious things like his voting habits or favourite foods? She shivered suddenly, keeping her hands cupped round the wine-glass, as if its vibrant red might warm her. If your husband was a stranger, then you were on your own, isolated, living behind a soundproof wall. If she didn't know Colin, then she didn't know anybody – there wasn't anyone else.

When he next appeared, he was holding a stuffed parrot in an elaborate gilded cage. 'Meet Polly,' he laughed, putting the cage down in front of her.

She shrank away from the creature. It seemed alive, its grey beak open, as if about to speak, its bold black gaze impertinent. 'What I'm wondering, Colin, is why I didn't meet Polly months ago, or years ago, or whenever it was you bought her?'

'Well, you never go near the cellar,' he said, wiping his hands on the dish-rag. 'Understandably,' he added quickly, seeing the look on her face.

'That's not the point. You could at least have *shown* me all this stuff, before you actually took it to the cellar.'

'I did – I'm sure I did.'

'I'm sorry, Colin, you did *not*.' She snapped her lips shut on the 'not', suppressing a sudden urge to slap him.

'Well, it's not important, is it?'

'Yes, I think it is. We're meant to be married, which means sharing everything.'

'Not everything.'

'Most things.'

'Elaine, I must get on. It's already half past four. Why don't you go upstairs and have a little lie-down. You look deadbeat.'

'I'm perfectly all right.' Clearly he wanted her out of the way. If she stayed here in the kitchen, he couldn't avoid her on his route from cellar to out-house, loaded with more of his booty. She took a sip of wine, but its rich bouquet seemed to have entirely disappeared. It tasted bitter and salty now, as if she were drinking tears.

'Gadzooks! On guard!' Colin burst into the room once more, waving a long, thin, rusting sword-like thing in circles round his head.

'For heaven's sake, be careful! You could *kill* someone with that.'

'You're telling me! It's lethal.' He gave a mock thrust and parry, battling an imaginary enemy with the vicious, stabbing blade.

'What is it?'

'A rapier. We got it for that fancy dress party.'

'I don't know what you're talking about.' As far as she could recall, they had never been to a fancy dress party all the years they'd been married.

'Ages ago. Up in Berwick-on-Tweed.'

On no account would they travel such a distance for a party. Unless – the thought appalled her, slashing into her consciousness with savage, sword-sharp force – she was losing her memory She'd read a terrifying statistic just a week ago: one in twenty people her age suffered from dementia.

'You must remember, surely? I went as a Cavalier – hired the whole costume from that theatrical place off Tottenham Court Road. And Douglas got me the rapier.'

Douglas she did remember – Colin's madcap cousin. But, Douglas or no, she would never have permitted Colin to handle such a dangerous weapon, or take it to a public place. Distraught, she drained her wine, seeing her face distorted in the glass. 'So what did

I go as at this party?'

'Florence Nightingale. You wore a sort of crinoline thing, with a white apron over it. And carried lots of bandages and medicines. How *can* you have forgotten?'

How indeed? Perhaps he was trying to frighten her. People did that sometimes – undermined you, sapped your confidence, suggested you were depressed, or living in the past. But that was different altogether from suffering from dementia. Anyway, how could she be gaga when she did the crossword every day, and read *The Times* from cover to cover? 'Look, Colin,' she said, adopting a brisk, businesslike tone, to counteract the image of the grim high-walled institution that had suddenly reared up between them. 'I don't know what you intend to do with that thing, but you can't just chuck it out. It could do serious damage, if someone were to stumble on it. It might even kill a child. I suggest you take it to the police station and ask them to dispose of it. And I suggest you go *now* – this minute.'

'No fear! I'm far too busy. They'll make me fill in all those stupid forms, which'll waste the rest of the day.'

Could he be scared of the police? He might have acquired the rapier not for a fancy dress party but to do away with someone. To do away with *her*. Most acts of violence took place in the home, or so she'd read in the paper. The bleak grey walls of the mental institution turned into a prison, with Colin handcuffed in a cell, begging for release. 'So what are you going to do with it?'

'I'll put it in the out-house for the moment. Then I'm off to the dump with Jasper's stuff.'

Once she heard the car door slam, she crept out to the cellar and stood at the door, paralysed with fear. She could see herself spread-eagled on the floor, one leg twisted grotesquely back on itself, the tiny unborn twins reeling with the shock of the fall. Although she hadn't actually miscarried until she reached the hospital, she always visualized their pathetic little bodies lying shattered on the cellar steps. Those babies already had names then: Anthony and Helen. Every July, she still remembered their birthday – what would have been their birthday – still filled imaginary stockings every Christmas Eve.

She forced herself to open the door, casting a panicked glance at the flight of steep stone steps, plunging down to peril and decay.

Already she was sweating with fear, wrinkling her nose against the smell of rotting remains. 'Don't be stupid,' she told herself, 'there's no smell whatsoever; no trace of blood on the steps.'

She took them one at a time, clinging to the banister rail, and ready to plunge back any moment to the safety of the kitchen. At last, she reached the bottom step and looked nervously around, astonished to see not piles of junk and swathes of dirt, but a clean and well-swept room – cluttered, yes, but cluttered with intriguing things. A model railway was laid out on a table, its metal tracks gleaming, the carriages liveried in smart maroon. On another table was a half-completed jigsaw puzzle of Van Gogh's Sunflowers, in radiant yellows and golds. And underneath the table was a row of Gro-bags, each boasting a crop of healthy-looking mushrooms.

The mushrooms she used for cooking were poor things in comparison – supermarket specimens: puny, plastic-packed. Yet here was Colin's own private home-grown supply, unrevealed, unshared. And she, too, loved jigsaw puzzles, especially challenging ones with a limited colour range. Couldn't they have done it together – upstairs? And there was room for the model railway upstairs – plenty of space in Colin's study, or even in the lounge.

She tiptoed over to inspect it, still feeling an intruder here, and thus trying to make her movements unobtrusive. Crouching down at eye level, she saw it was more than just a railway – a whole model village, in fact, with houses, shops, a church and pub and, in the centre, the railway station itself, complete with platform, level-crossing, goods yard and signal box. The detail was amazing. There were passengers on the station: perfectly proportioned little people, dressed in coats and hats, and holding miniature cases and umbrellas. Each railway carriage was meticulously constructed, even down to the interiors. One boasted a luxurious restaurant car, its tables laid with snowy white cloths and lit by tiny gold lamps. The others had plush upholstered seats, topped by minuscule luggage racks, and containing more small but lifelike passengers reading papers or smoking cigars.

What in heaven's name had all this cost? Not to mention the price of that *château*-bottled wine; those rare coins in mint condition. Was this the reason they'd been forced to sell their house? – not, as Colin claimed, because of the rising costs of running it, but because he had poured their money into this subterranean treasure-vault?

She sank into his easy chair. Even that was cosily set up, with cushions and a tartan rug. *One* easy chair, not two, though. Yes, that's what hurt, and much more than the cost – the way he had excluded her. Why should *he* mind losing their house when he had a village-full of houses here – a romantic little Happy Valley, entire in itself, and his alone?

And his empire spread well beyond the village. Wherever she looked were more of his possessions: a dartboard on the wall, flanked by two model ships, a pile of encyclopaedias, a brass telescope, an exercise bike. This was Colin's other life, which he had totally concealed from her. Oh, of course she knew that he was often in the cellar, but he always told her he was mending things: soldering an old radio, repairing a vacuum cleaner, stripping and varnishing a damaged grandfather clock. And when she queried the hours it seemed to take, he would go into laborious detail about *other* time-consuming projects – he was replastering the cellar walls, re-laying the concrete floor. Yet there was no sign or smell of fresh plaster, and the floor was neatly covered with off-cuts of their bedroom carpet. Yes, another bedroom, for his adulterous affair. This was worse than another woman – this was another universe.

'Elaine! Elaine! Where are you?'

She sprang to her feet. He was back, and looking for her. She darted behind an old workbench as she heard his feet tramping down the steps. Too late. He'd seen her, grabbed her arm.

'Darling, you mustn't come down here. You know how dangerous it is.'

She shook him off. Of course she knew – all the more so now.

He seized her by the shoulder, trying to usher her back upstairs. Wrenching free, she ran back up unaided. She *wanted* to escape, now that she had discovered his betrayal.

'Watch out! You'll trip.'

Who cared? If she fell again, there was nothing more to lose – no babies, and no husband. Both were lost already.

He pounded after her, letting out a flood of words, trying to excuse himself, trying to explain. He followed her into the kitchen and sat opposite, still jabbering away. She let the words wash over her, craning her neck to peer up at the SOLD sign through the window. The O was silent now – and rightly so. No point crying. No point speaking, either. She didn't intend discussing things with Colin. Nor did she intend moving into the flat with him.

This was not the man she had married.

23

MOTHER

Mother is frightened of everything, most especially her family. We children are volcanoes, waiting to explode. Father is a wild, flood-swollen river, about to burst its banks. Men in general are dangerous, constantly swelling up, erupting, and seeding more disruptive children – children Mother didn't want.

She fears us because she can't control us – not our thoughts or inner souls. But she spares no pains to control everything else about us: our clothes, bodies, movements, lives. We are forbidden to go out. Sun and rain are dangerous forces that may scorch or lash or drench. She keeps us in the sitting-room in a tight, unnatural circle, all our chairs facing in to hers.

The sitting-room is brown. The walls are brown, the chairs are brown, our clothes and shoes are brown. There are brown people in the brown photo-frames standing on the brown bureau – our brown grandmothers and grandfathers, brown uncles, cousins, aunts. They're made of wood, not flesh. Their wooden faces have dead brown eyes and unsmiling rigid lips.

Mother mistrusts all colours, especially red and green. Green is skittish and flamboyant; red passionate, extreme. Brown, at least, is sober and amenable. We sit in our brown circle, backs straight, feet together. No one moves or fidgets, no one laughs. Laughter is seismic – another perilous force.

The clock ticks on the mantelpiece, but the ticking is mere show. Mother has banished Time. Here, in her stifling brown cocoon, it is neither early nor late, neither light nor dark. The seasons are also banished because she is terrified of change. In Mother's world, buds don't open, leaves don't fall, birds neither mate nor warble, and rainbows, if they exist at all, lie flat and monochrome. Each season brings a different fear – the voluptuousness of spring, when sap relentlessly rises and raucous yellow daffodils are trumpeting their lust. The indolence of summer, with pollen-sated bees staggering from flower to flower, and young girls stripping off in public parks. And autumn's brilliance appals her; its bonfire-blaze, its power to fade and scar. And the finality of winter cements her fears of nakedness – naked trees, naked earth with an ice-chip at its core.

Although bees and birds are disallowed, we do meet other people – carefully selected ones, who come to see the family, praise our Mother's fortitude, eat her home-made cake. We children never eat. Mother cuts the cake and offers us a slice, but we've been trained to say, 'No, thank you.' Gluttony, like laughter, is the sister of excess. Once the visitors have left, the cake is put back in the freezer, double-wrapped in Clingfilm. (One cake lasts a year.) Mother would like to put us children in the freezer, dry up our dangerous juices, dampen down our heat. And Clingfilm would be useful, too, to gag our mouths, bind our budding breasts.

I eat only when I go to bed – great gulps and slurps of food. I fill the bed with apples, cooked buttery and soft, top them with a flaky-pastry duvet, and snuggle down into the warm embrace of custard, velvet-smooth as it seeps around my limbs. Or I float face-down on a vast rice-pudding lake, tonguing up its creamy, brown-skinned sweetness. Or plunge my face deep into a gâteau – strawberry glaze sticky on my cheeks, whorls of cream foaming through my hair. Mother doesn't know. At night, we leave the sitting-room and go up to our bedrooms. We all, including her, sleep alone in single beds. Mother hasn't got a vagina any more. She destroyed it several years ago, as a way of escaping Father, who doesn't sleep at all. Father is an engineer, who specializes in destruction rather than construction. At night, he rips up railway tracks, razes cities to the ground, breaks bridges into shards with his bare hands. When I hear the thuds and crashes, I take myself to Tuscany, where everything is calm. I feast on glorious pasta, spooning in great gloops of fettucine; cheesy silt glistening on my lips. Or dive naked into a steaming vat of spaghetti, wallowing in the rich, red, slippery sauce. Or wrap myself in sheets of hot lasagne and lie tingling in my mattress-baking-dish, while Italian chefs cover me with béchamel.

Unlike Mother, I do have a vagina, although I've never seen or touched it. The very word makes the brown walls blush. But one day, I know, I'll experience its shockwaves, bite into the apple, let the serpent jounce between my legs. My sisters never will. They sit here in the circle, rusting with disuse. I'm different – I'm the youngest and I plan to run away. Once I reach my eighteenth birthday, I'll creep out of bed at daybreak, and run and run till I'm a million miles away. Mother will be sixty then – she had me late, the last of six. And once I've cut the cord, I'll shout and sing and celebrate and stuff myself with food – real food that satisfies. 'Satisfy' is a word she can't abide: a full-bellied, fat-cat word that lies purring on its idle back. She has mutilated the dictionary, destroyed all my favourite words:

wallow
revel
frolic
junket
profligate
beguile.

I keep my plan a secret, although the castrated clock seems to understand. It, too, longs to rebel, to chime every tingling quarter-hour; to celebrate the whoop of noon with a crescendo of deep-throated peals. The people in the photographs are also counting the days, waiting for my birthday, when they can tear off their stiff collars, unlace their corsets, break out, go wild, unzip.

Meanwhile, I sit here, silent and straight-backed. I have no choice – I'm still in Mother's power. Her pursed lips clamp us to our chairs; her deep frown fences us in; her tight-coiled bun reproves our tousled curls. Mother cannot be defied. Or disobeyed.

Mother loves us.

And love is a corral.